Another blue door led into the vitamin processing room. Large funnel-shaped bags hung over narrow conveyer belts full of brown bottles that snaked through the area. A metal contraption that resembled a giant stamp hovered over the end of the conveyer. A large box of white safety caps sat on the floor next to a table with three chairs around it. Open boxes of surgical gloves were scattered throughout. This was obviously where vitamins were bottled and sealed.

Avanell was not in evidence, so Harriet crossed the room and exited through the door opposite the one she'd come in. She was in a short hallway. Restrooms were to the left. The first room to the right held printing and labeling equipment. The lights were off.

She chose the second door on the right. It opened into the large, high-ceilinged room that was the packing and shipping area as well as warehouse space.

"Avanell?" she called.

A single light fixture illuminated a corner at the back of the building. Harriet headed toward it. The warehouse had a concrete floor, and the heels of her shoes made a loud clacking noise that echoed off the rafters.

"Avanell," she called again.

She stopped. The silence was deafening. A compressor started. She resumed her path toward what she hoped was Avanell.

"Hello?" Harriet said in a louder voice. "Avanell?"

She arrived at the lighted corner. A large worktable was surrounded by stacks of boxes. A single chair was pushed back from the lone workstation. She came around the end of the table.

"Avanell!" she screamed.

Avanell Jalbert lay collapsed on the cold cement floor. It was as if an unseen puppet-master had abruptly cut her strings. Harriet dropped to her knees, avoiding the red stain that extended like a dark halo around Avanell's head.

Also by Arlene Sachitano

Chip and Die

QUILT AS DESIRED

A Harriet Truman/Loose Threads Mystery

BY

ARLENE SACHITANO

Arlene Sachitano

ZUMAYA ENIGMA   AUSTIN TX

2007

QUILT AS DESIRED
© 2007 by Arlene Sachitano

ISBN 13: 978-1-934135-25-9
ISBN 10: 1-934135-25-9

Cover art and design by April Martinez

Library of Congress Cataloging-in-Publication Data

Sachitano, Arlene, 1951-
  Quilt as desired : A Harriet Truman/loose threads mystery / by Arlene Sachitano.
     p. cm.
  ISBN-13: 978-1-934135-25-9
  ISBN-10: 1-934135-25-9
  1. Quiltmakers--Fiction. 2. Widows--Fiction. 3. Washington (State)--Fiction.
4. Murder--Investigation--Fiction. I. Title.
  PS3619.A277Q85 2007
  813'.6--dc22
                          2007015567

ACKNOWLEDGMENTS

This book could not have been completed without the love and support of my family and many friends. I'd like to thank my immediate family—Jack, Karen, Annie, David, Malakai and Alex—as well as my supportive in-laws Beth, Hank, Brenda and Bob and my nephews Brett, Nathan, Chad and Jason. In addition, I'd like to thank my friends Susan and Susan, who have listened to my story ideas without flinching more times than any human should have to, and have contributed their expertise in quilting and art as well as their knowledge of northwest Washington state.

My sister Donna deserves special recognition for being the one who first taught me to read and write. My critique group, Katy King and Luann Vaughn, provided input in their unique style that is at once insightful and kind. Special thanks to Vern and Betty Swearingen for sharing their knowledge of machine quilting and opening the doors of their quilt store, Storyquilts, to my prying eyes. As always, many thanks to Liz and Zumaya Publications for making all this possible.

Chapter One

Honey, you're going to be fine," Aunt Beth said and patted Harriet on her back. "I wouldn't be going on this cruise if I didn't think you were ready to take over the business."

The two women stood facing each other in the sunny yellow kitchen of Aunt Beth's Victorian house in the not-so-sunny town of Foggy Point, Washington.

"I've had not quite a month's practice, and you're not leaving town, you're leaving the country, for crying out loud. And all those people in your group have quilts they want stitched for a show that's three weeks from now." Harriet knew she was whining but she couldn't help it. "Let's not forget the part where you suddenly decided to retire and leave me with this mess until you find a buyer for the business, and I'm not sure exactly how that's supposed to happen when you're cruising your way through Europe."

"It's too late to worry about that now," Aunt Beth said, and handed her a ring of keys. "And if I'd given you time to think about it, you'd still be sitting alone in that house in Oakland, mourning for a man who isn't coming back. These open the door to your studio," she continued, ignoring the raw wound she'd opened in Harriet's heart.

Harriet wasn't mourning. Not by a long shot. She was angry. If Steve hadn't died, she'd have killed him herself—with her bare hands, too. And alone was just how she liked being. If you can't trust anyone then alone is the safest way to be.

"This one is for the outside door to your house, and this one your storage shed out back," Aunt Beth continued, pointing out individual keys. "You were one of the best young stitchers Foggy Point has ever produced. It's like riding a bike. It doesn't leave you, even if you do move away for ten years." She plopped a garish Hawaiian print hat she'd bought for her trip on her short

1

white hair. "Don't forget to water the pansies in the window box. They dry out pretty easily even this time of year. And try to visit Avanell. She says she's fine, but there's something going on. She looks worn down, and it's not from working. She's always worked a lot. No, something's bothering her. And all of a sudden she's doing all kinds of odd color combinations on her projects, too. A person doesn't change like that without some reason."

Avanell Jalbert was Aunt Beth's best friend in the world and had probably had a hand in Aunt Beth's plan to have Harriet run her business while she was gone.

"I've been gone fifteen years, not ten, and I will check on Avanell. But if you come back and I've lost all your customers for you, don't say I didn't warn you."

"You won't lose any of my customers," Aunt Beth said and pulled Harriet into a suffocating hug. "I love you, sweetie, and I have full confidence in you. And here," she said, and handed Harriet a lavender envelope. "Open this after I leave."

She pulled up the handle on her large rolling suitcase then tied a ribbon of purple fabric that coordinated with the purple nylon of her suitcase to the upright piece. She pushed the suitcase out onto the front porch and shouldered the matching carry-on bag.

"There's my taxi," she said and kissed Harriet's cheek. "Stop worrying. Everything's going to be just fine, you'll see."

With that, she whirled around, summoned the taxi driver onto the porch then followed him and her suitcase to the cab. Just like that, she was gone.

Harriet looked down at the envelope in her hand. She turned it over but found nothing but lavender paper and a sealed flap. No information popped to the surface to explain why Aunt Beth had given it to her. She tucked it into the pocket of her grey hooded sweatshirt and went back into the house.

One of the few possessions she had brought with her from Oakland was her cat Fred. Fred was big and grey and fuzzy—she wasn't sure from one moment to the next if she owned him or was just in his employ. She did know if she didn't get his milk bowl on the floor in the next sixty seconds there would be hell to pay.

"Here you go, Fred," she said and set his dish down on the blue fish-shaped placemat he'd brought with him from California. While he went to work on the milk, she poured a half-cup of his high-protein, low-residue, hairball-removing kibbles into his second ceramic dish.

When he was taken care of, she quickly ate a bowl of Kix and went upstairs to take a shower. In little more than an hour, her first customer would be knocking on the studio door.

She pondered as she washed what the first quilters might think if they saw how much the craft had changed since the first woman put needle to fabric in an effort to make a bed cover.

When people first came to the New World they had to bring cloth with them to make the garments and bedding they and their family would need, without knowing if they would ever be able to obtain more. Sewing small pieces together patchwork-style allowed them to use every scrap of fabric they had, re-using worn-out clothing and blankets as the filler. At first, all steps in the quilting process were done by hand with needle and thread. Then, as people settled in communities, they began to use large frames to hold the quilt while they attached the top, pieced layer to the filling layers. To avoid having the frame taking up their limited living space, pioneer women held bees where everyone would work on one quilt so it could be finished quickly and the frame put away.

Affordable bedding became available commercially, and electric sewing machines allowed those who wished to quilt to easily construct their project in their own home. Nothing changed until king- and queen-sized beds became the norm and *repetitive motion injury* became household words. Women who made more than one quilt a year were developing wrist and shoulder damage from holding and turning large heavy quilts as they guided them under the needle of their home sewing machine.

Enter the long-arm quilting machine.

Long-arm quilting machines are industrial-style machines manually guided over a fabric sandwich stretched onto rollers that feed the quilt top, stuffing or batting and backing fabric, allowing the operator to easily guide the stitching head around the surface in any pattern he or she desires. The machines are large, usually requiring their own bedroom or garage, and are also expensive. Most communities had one or more people like Aunt Beth who were skilled owner-operators, and who would quilt anyone's project for a nominal fee.

This was the job Harriet would be taking over while Aunt Beth was on vacation. It was well within the realm of possibility she could ruin dozens of quilts before her aunt returned, and the idea weighed heavy on her head.

She was in the kitchen again, wearing the fourth outfit she'd tried on after her shower, when she remembered the envelope. She retrieved it from her sweatshirt in the front coat closet and brought it back to the kitchen. She could count on one hand the times Aunt Beth had written anything longer than a shopping list. She had to admit she was curious.

There were several documents covered in fine print and signed and dated by Aunt Beth. Folded inside these was a single piece of lavender paper. Harriet took this out and started to read Aunt Beth's small, neat script.

"My Dearest Harriet," it began. It was ominously formal language.

> If I had tried to talk to you about what I'm going to say next, you would have argued and might not have agreed. I'm sorry to have made a unilateral decision, but I truly believe this is in your best interest.

She could feel the hair rising on her neck. She already didn't like whatever her aunt was about to tell her.

> I'm not selling my quilting business. I'm giving it to you.

Harriet felt her knees go weak. She grabbed for one of the kitchen chairs and barely landed on its edge.

> Consider it an early inheritance. Steve died five years ago, and you've been playing dead ever since. Take it from me, it won't bring him back. It's time to start living again.
>
> It's clear that won't happen while you're holed up in that shrine you've constructed in Oakland. I know he wasn't honest with you and I know you're hurt. I also know you sit there and go over the shoulda, coulda, woulda's and in the end nothing is changed. I'm sorry, but he lied, he's dead, you're alone and it's time to move on.
>
> Now we've come to the matter at hand. At my last physical, Dr. Boney said I need a change. I'm not sick. Don't get me wrong, I got a clean bill of health. But Dr. Boney said all the lifting and reaching I do operating the long-arm quilt machine is too hard on my right shoulder joint. He says if I don't slow down I'm going to have to have a shoulder replacement. I've

4

been careful with my money and your uncle Hank left me a little nest egg when he passed on, and it's done well in the market, so I began to think I don't really need to work, and, frankly, you do. I know you don't need the money, but, honey, you need to join the land of the living again, and I can't think of a better place for you to start over than Foggy Point.

Enclosed you will find the deed to my house, now your house. In addition, I've transferred the business into your name. Don't worry about what will happen when I get back. I'm not going to force myself on you as a tenant. I've purchased old Mrs. Morris's cottage out on the Strait. It's comfortable, and her daughter had the inside redone after Mrs. Morris passed last winter, so I'm sure it will be just the thing for me.

I hope you will not be angry with me and in time will come to see that this is for the best.

With all my love,

It was signed "Aunt Beth."

Harriet crumpled the paper and threw it across the kitchen. Then she checked the documents. Sure enough, there was her name on both deed and the doing-business-as form: Harriet Truman.

"What have you done?" she said aloud. "Fred? What has she done? Did you know about this? Can you even give somebody a house without them knowing about it?"

Fred jumped onto the table and gave her a head butt.

"When I'm done with my customers, I'm going to call Aunt Beth's attorney and see if this is for real, so don't you get too comfortable yet. Besides," she said and raked her fingers through Fred's fuzzy hair. "If she can give it, I can give it right back. Just you watch."

Chapter Two

Harriet paced the kitchen. How dare her aunt make a decision that affected her life? Granted, Aunt Beth had done a lot for her as a child, but she wasn't a child anymore. At thirty-eight, she could make her own decisions, even if that meant not deciding anything. And Aunt Beth completely missed the point where Steve was concerned. Yes, she felt a deep, aching void when she was able to get past her anger, but that didn't happen often. Steve had betrayed her on such a deep level, and his family and their friends had helped him. The relationships she'd had with those people were all based on a huge lie.

On her third pass across the kitchen she picked up her cereal bowl and Fred's milk dish, rinsed both and put them in the dishwasher. She contemplated changing her outfit again and wondered why. In Oakland her wardrobe had consisted of black and baggy; it was what she was comfortable in. She would have looked better in navy or brown, but she liked the harsh look black gave her. It suited her mood.

When she'd met Steve she'd fancied herself a fashionista, favoring asymmetrical lines and the color purple. After they were married, her tastes had become more sophisticated as she and her girlfriends ferreted out neighborhood boutiques and up-and-coming designers in both San Francisco and Oakland. It had all been a lie, though. If your friends couldn't tell you your husband had a life-threatening disease, how could you trust anything they said?

The morning after Harriet arrived Aunt Beth had driven her to the Wal-Mart in Port Angeles and purchased five T-shirts in primary colors, two white turtlenecks, a red flannel shirt and an off-white fisherman-style pullover. She had also put two pairs of jeans and one pair of khakis in the cart.

Aunt Beth wasn't willing to have the argument that would have ensued had she asked Harriet to participate in the selection.

"This will be a start," she'd said. "As grey as it is here, we can't have you skulking around in widow's weeds. You'll scare the customers away."

FINALLY, HARRIET PUT ON JEANS AND A WHITE T-SHIRT AND, IN LAST-MINUTE DEFIANCE, wrapped a long black chiffon scarf around her neck, tossing the tail over her shoulder.

She glanced at her watch; it was five minutes fast. She did a quick calculation and decided her first customer would be here in seven minutes.

The first customer of the day would be Aunt Beth's oldest friend, Avanell Jalbert. Avanell was a charter member of the group Aunt Beth belonged to; they called themselves The Loose Threads. Harriet used to go to meetings with Aunt Beth during the summers, when she was in junior high school; but according to Aunt Beth, only Avanell and longtime Foggy Point resident Mavis Willis remained from those days.

The group met every Tuesday morning in the classroom of Foggy Point's only quilt store, Pins and Needles.

She left the warm safety of the kitchen and entered the long-arm quilting studio. The studio had been a large parlor on the first floor of the three-story Victorian home. On the outside wall of the rectangular room, Aunt Beth had added a bow-windowed alcove and a door to the outside. The room was separated from the rest of the house by two locking doors—one leading to the kitchen, the other the dining room.

The alcove, which functioned as a reception area, held two chintz-covered easy chairs and a dark cherry piecrust table. Harriet crossed the room to the table and picked up the electric water pot. She went back to the kitchen, filled the pot and returned it to the table. Unmatched china cups, a basket of teabags and a full assortment of sweeteners crowded the tabletop. She arranged the cups and tea basket twice and, when she was satisfied the alcove looked sufficiently inviting to her customers, crossed the room to look for more of the decorated napkins she knew Aunt Beth had stashed somewhere.

She was bent over, opening lower cabinet doors in succession, searching, when the doorbell jingled and her first customer walked in.

"Hello," she said and banged her knee on the open cabinet door. She couldn't believe she had greeted her first-ever customer with a view of her rear end.

She grabbed her knee as she stood up and dropped the napkins in the process.

"I'm sorry," she said. "I'll be right with you."

"Take your time," Avanell said. "I'll just help myself to some tea, if that's okay."

"Oh, yes, please." Harriet picked up the napkins and brought them over to the table. Avanell had her tea steeping, had clipped the end of a honey straw and was stirring her tea with the open straw, dumping its contents into the hot liquid.

"You look just like you did when I left for college" Harriet asked.

"Aren't you sweet! I still had dark hair when you left, but it was from a bottle, even back then." She laughed. "I quit that nonsense a few years ago." She tucked an errant gray strand behind her ear. You look like you just got on the plane yesterday, and of course, your aunt has told me everything that's happened with you since the day you left."

"Only the good parts, I hope," she said, and wondered exactly how much Aunt Beth had told her friends in Foggy Point about her recent past. At the very least, the women would know she'd been widowed. Whether she'd filled them in on Steve's genetic illness that probably could have been treated, had he and his family not worked so hard to keep it a secret, would remain to be seen.

She poured her own cup of tea, sizing up Avanell in the process. She was a short stocky woman in her late fifties. She wore a tailored skirt in charcoal-grey wool flannel and a maroon paisley blouse with a cardigan sweater that looked like it had been hand-knit. Her grey hair was in a loose bun on the top of her head. She looked like the grandmother most children only dream of.

"Beth says you can run that long-arm machine even better than she does," Avanell said.

Harriet felt herself blushing. "I'm not sure I would go that far. My style is a little different from Aunt Beth's."

"Honey, no two quilters stitch exactly the same."

Harriet knew that was true, but she was also aware that most machine quilters had a signature pattern they used so often the judges at competitions could generally tell who had done the stitching on a piece without being told. She hoped to break that mold. She wanted her stitching to complement each individual project, not outshine it.

She pulled a stack of quilted squares from a shelf under the large layout table.

"Here are samples of the quilting patterns I do," she said. She had purposely used an array of fabrics in her samples—she had batiks, Civil War prints, thirties reproductions, brights, Asian prints and flannels. She hoped the woman would find something that matched her vision for her quilt.

"Let's spread the quilt out on the cutting table, and you can tell me what you have in mind."

HARRIET GASPED. AVANELL HAD HAND-DYED WHITE COTTON AND MADE A SERIES OF pieced blocks she then alternated with squares of off-white. She had used trapunto, a technique typically done on a neutral-colored background fabric, using dense stitching and extra batting or fill material to create raised areas, often in traditional wreath or flower designs. This design would only need machine stitching in the pieced areas.

The dyed-fabric colors were vibrant and had been pieced in intricate patterns. The points in the pieced areas were perfect and the color transitions seamless. It was utterly different from anything Harriet had ever seen. If this exemplified Avanell's stress level, she hoped it didn't go down anytime soon.

Avanell favored a wreath-like pattern from the samples that would give a circular impression to echo the curved lines of the trapunto. The border areas would be stitched with closely placed parallel lines that were set on a diagonal and would pull the eye inward toward the design. Harriet made careful notes regarding the lines and patterns.

"I'll put your quilt on the machine first thing," she said.

She gathered the sample squares up, carefully organizing them by stitch type. She fumbled and dropped the stack.

"Let me help you," Avanell said and smiled. "Are you nervous with your aunt being out of the country?"

"Does it show?" Harriet asked, knowing that it wasn't Aunt Beth's absence as much as her aunt's preemptive strike on her future that had her distracted. If she dropped anything else, Avanell was likely to gather her quilt up and run for the nearest exit.

"Only a little," Avanell replied. "Listen," she said "The Vitamin Factory is just down the hill. It wouldn't be out of my way to drop back by when I go to lunch to see how you're doing."

"That would be great," Harriet said. She couldn't believe she was acting like such a nervous fool. She was confident in her quilting ability; and when she'd moved to California, she'd made unique home furnishing accent pieces for an upscale furniture shop, so it wasn't like she hadn't ever had her work scrutinized by a paying customer.

Somehow, though, being in Foggy Point, where she would have to see those customers every time she went into the grocery store or picked up her mail at the post office was intimidating. And in spite of everything, she did want to do a good job, and Aunt Beth would be a hard act to follow.

It seemed like only moments had passed, but she had loaded the pieced top and its backing and batting onto the long-arm machine's frame and had stitched the first square area. She straightened and was rubbing the small of her back when the doorbell rang and signaled Avanell's return.

"I just finished the first part," Harriet said. "Come see."

Avanell didn't need an invitation; she came over and inspected the work. Harriet held her breath as Avanell rubbed her fingertips lightly over the closely spaced rows of parallel stitching.

"This is just what I'd imagined," she said and smiled.

Harriet took a breath of air. Maybe she would survive the next couple of weeks after all.

Chapter Three

I'M GOING TO RUN DOWN TO THE SANDWICH BOARD AND GET A BITE TO EAT," AVANELL said. "Would you like to join me? I thought I'd pop into Pins and Needles and look at the new Hoffman prints Marjory just got in on the way back."

Pins and Needles was the local quilt goods store, located in downtown Foggy Point and boasting seven thousand bolts of fabric as well as every tool and notion on the market—at least, it seemed that way to its devoted customers. Marjory Swain had purchased the store seven years before when the previous owner decided to trade the gray winters of Foggy Point for the sunny warmth of Mesa, Arizona.

In its past life the store had been oriented more toward the practical fabrics used in the construction of clothes—Marjory still kept a small room at the back of the shop devoted to dressmaking supplies—but Pins and Needles's main focus now was the making of quilts.

No matter how large or small, every reputable quilt shop can be counted on to carry the high-quality long-staple cotton that can be trusted not to shrink, twist, bleed or wear out before its time, as well as cotton thread imported from Germany and wound on slender spools in an array of neutral colors. They all carried several sizes and thicknesses of both cotton and wool batting, too.

Harriet made a point of checking out the quilt store in every city she visited. Foggy Point was no different. She'd badgered Aunt Beth into taking her to Pins and Needles the day she'd arrived.

Aunt Beth had opened the door to the shop, and a light floral scent had enveloped them. The main room was filled with bolts of colorful fabric. At the end of each row of shelves was a display of quilted samples artfully arranged around scented candles that she'd learned were made at a shop around the corner.

"Can I help you find anything?" Marjory had asked.

"I'm just getting my bearings," she'd replied.

"There's cookies in the kitchen there on your left, and if you need the bathroom it's behind the small classroom to the right."

Harriet found chocolate chip cookies on a hand-thrown pottery plate on the Formica-topped kitchen table. Two coffeepots and an electric hot water pot sat on a countertop beside the small sink at the back of the room. She'd grabbed two cookies and then strolled up and down the fabric aisles. Civil War prints, thirties reproductions, an ample selection of both pastel and bright children's fabric—Harriet ticked the selections off her mental list. This would do quite nicely.

Two large carved oak hutches stood along one wall and held the small tools and accessories that helped make any project go together smoothly. Harriet had noticed two Amish-style quilts her aunt had made hanging with several others on a cable that was strung from the rafters.

Marjory had followed Harriet's gaze to the display. "We try to change the quilts every month, but I'm a little late this time. Some months it's hard to think up an appropriate theme. When you get settled, you can join in if you want." She'd looked hopeful, but Harriet didn't plan on being here long enough to make a theme-quilt for a display. Even if she did think it was a clever way to keep people engaged.

"I'D LOVE TO COME TO LUNCH," HARRIET SAID TO AVANELL, TURNING HER THOUGHTS BACK to the present. "I haven't been to The Sandwich Board yet, either. Is it good?"

"They have a roast pork tenderloin on focaccia with fresh basil and homemade mozzarella that's to die for," Avanell told her.

"Let me get my purse." She went through the connecting door to the kitchen, grabbed her purse and denim jacket from the closet by the back door and left with her aunt's friend.

"How's it feel to be home?" Avanell asked as she put the car in reverse, maneuvered it into a tight circle and then turned it down the driveway.

Home? Harriet thought. This wasn't home. Not her home, anyway. She looked out the car window. The pastel-painted Victorian houses that lined Aunt Beth's street could just as easily have been in San Francisco, or even some parts of Oakland. As they dropped down the hill toward town the larger houses gave way to smaller bungalow cottages, tucked behind neatly planted juniper bushes and dogwood trees.

The car gave a sharp bounce, and Harriet jumped.

"Sorry," Avanell said. "Hot flash."

Her comment barely registered. The salt air rushed over Harriet. She held her breath but finally let it out with a gasp. She resisted with every fiber of her being, but it was no use—she *was* home. She could kid herself and try to pretend that her home was Oakland, but she'd felt it as soon as she'd driven into town, and waited while a doe and her twin fawns crossed Main Street unmolested and disappeared into a grove of pine trees. She'd been sure when she'd cruised past coffee shops with names like HUMAN BEANS and LUCY'S LATTES—not a franchise business as far as the eye could see.

She ran her fingers through her close-cropped hair.

"We gave the Vitamin Factory a face lift a few years ago," Avanell pointed out as the neighborhood gave way to a light industrial area. She slowed as she drove past her long, low building.

"I'm embarrassed to admit that I don't remember what it used to look like."

"No reason you should," Avanell smiled. "You were a teenager. You had much more on your mind than industrial buildings. Just for the record, we removed the fifties style brick facade from the office area and replaced all the old pink siding with dark green Hardy plank."

"It looks nice," Harriet offered.

Avanell laughed and turned the car left over the bridge that carried them across the Muckleshoot River and into the downtown area.

"Things look different here. What happened to the library?" Harriet asked.

"They built a new one two blocks over. Did a nice job, too. It looks Victorian, but without all the leaky pipes and crumbling plaster of the original.

Avanell guided her car to the curb in front of the restaurant and parked.

The food at the Sandwich Board was every bit as good as Avanell had promised. Harriet ordered the pork loin sandwich, while Avanell opted for egg salad on fresh-baked multi-grain bread with fresh basil and an aioli-style mayonnaise.

Harriet began to relax. They'd dispensed with the inevitable conversation about Steve, his untimely death and her resulting widowhood early in the conversation, with Avanell offering the usual condolences but not pushing for details.

Avanell then filled their lunch with stories of her own experiences with widowhood. She had raised three children who were now young adults. Her husband and brother had founded a vitamin distribution company at a time when America was just starting its love affair with supplements. Avanell's husband had died when her older children were in high school. With three sets of college tuition staring her in the face, she hadn't had a choice but to take his place in the company. She was self-effacing, but Harriet knew from her aunt that Avanell had turned the company from a modestly successful vendor of children's vitamins into a multi-million-dollar supplier of herbal supplements. Her natural cold remedy blend was taking the country by storm, and she was just introducing a line of herbal pet supplements.

Avanell was not only able to pay her children's college tuition, she also set up a scholarship fund that sent five deserving Foggy Point High School graduates each year to the college of their choice.

Harriet took advantage of Avanell's knowledge of the local residents and their buying practices. Avanell was more than willing to share what she knew about the other stitchers in the Loose Threads.

"Mavis Willis doesn't care a whit about competition. If she has a project that fits our theme for a particular show she enters it, but her main reason for quilting is to top the beds of her children and grandchildren with covers that suit their individual personalities," Avanell said. "And you can pretty well count on Sarah Ness to ask you to do her project about two days *after* whatever deadline you set."

"Aunt Beth warned me about her. She said Sarah makes a lot of quilts and is willing to pay a lot of money to have them stitched, so it's worth the aggravation."

"That's the truth," Avanell agreed. "She's on a mission to give everyone she's ever met a handcrafted quilt made with her own hands. She really cranks them out."

"Aunt Beth said something like that."

Avanell laughed. "I can imagine what Beth said. I'm sure the word *quality* was in there somewhere. Sarah's quite predictable, if you think about it. Your aunt Beth says that as soon as she hears Sarah's doing something for a show, she blocks out the last spot before the real deadline on her schedule and puts her name on it. Beth says she's never failed her yet."

Harriet laughed. The waiter brought the check, and Avanell had her wallet open and her card out before Harriet even had her purse open.

"Thank you," she said. "Next time I'll treat."

"When you have yourself established as the new It Girl of machine quilters you can pay. In the meantime, don't look a gift horse in the mouth." Avanell smiled.

She gave the waitress her card and was waiting to sign the receipt when a thin woman with long stringy hair and bad skin shuffled into the restaurant. The woman looked around and, when she spotted Avanell and Harriet, came over to the table.

"Can I talk to you?" she said to Avanell, and looked down. A line of sweat dampened her forehead.

Avanell's face lost its animation. "What's wrong now, Carla?"

Carla looked at Harriet and back to Avanell.

"It's all right, Carla. Tell me what's happening."

"Mr. Tony, he's got Misty in the office. He says she's been stealing vitamins and that's why we been missing inventory. He's called Sheriff Mason and says he's pressing charges."

"Is she stealing vitamins?" Avanell asked in a no-nonsense voice that was nothing like the friendly tone she'd used during lunch.

Carla looked at her feet. "Not exactly," she said.

"Don't keep me waiting, Carla," Avanell said. "Tell me the truth. All of it, now." She signed the Visa receipt and picked up her purse and sweater.

Carla hesitated, looked at Harriet again and finally spoke.

"Misty is pregnant. Maryanne and me have been saving the broken and chipped prenatal blends for her. We just throw them out after we count them anyways. The sheriff is on his way now," she finished.

"Go ahead and go," Harriet said. "I'll just take advantage of this nice spring day and walk home. It isn't that far."

It was clear Avanell was torn.

"Really, I'm fine. The exercise will do me good after this lunch."

"Thanks, I'll make it up to you," Avanell said and hurried after her employee, who was already shuffling out the door.

Harriet watched her leave. Aunt Beth was right; something was definitely wrong.

Chapter Four

HARRIET TURNED LEFT TOWARD POST OFFICE STREET. PINS AND NEEDLES WAS LOCATED around the corner and up the block. Aunt Beth had told her the previous store had been ten blocks down in a less prosperous part of downtown Foggy Point, but over the years had traded its way up as other, less enduring shops folded. Eventually, it moved into the coveted center-of-the-block location on Main Street that it currently occupied.

She looked at her watch. She still had an hour before her next customer was due to show up. She could spare fifteen minutes to see what was new.

"Hi, Harriet," Marjory called from the back of the store. "Make yourself at home. I'll be with you in a minute."

A slender woman who looked to be around Avanell's age was at the counter.

"I'm sorry, I sent Marjory to search her new shipment to see if she got a maroon fabric I need. How are you surviving with Beth gone?"

Harriet wasn't sure she'd ever get used to the way news traveled in this town. The Threads probably knew Aunt Beth had left before she had—and she'd watched the taxi drive away.

She'd been a child when she first lived here with Aunt Beth. Back then, Foggy Point had seemed a wondrous place, filled with beaches to walk on, woods to explore and friendly neighbors who always had a warm cookie and glass of milk for an intrepid explorer. She had been unaware then of how everyone knew everyone else's business, leaving little room for privacy.

"I'm Jenny Logan," the woman said when Harriet didn't offer any additional information. "I came late last week, so I didn't get to meet you. I'm bringing you my show quilt in…" She glanced at her watch.". . . not quite an hour."

"I'm on my way home now," Harriet said. She turned to go back out.

"There's no need to rush," Jenny said. "I'm going to look at the new fall fabrics Marjory got in. If I start now, I might get a Halloween wall hanging done this year."

"I'm on foot, though," Harriet explained.

"Why don't you let me give you a ride, then? If you would, you could give me some ideas for this crazy baby cover I have to make. My son Mark and his wife just had a baby boy. They're both in school at Texas A&M and want a maroon-and-white quilt with black-and-grey trim. I'm trying to figure out how to use those colors and have it still look like it's for a baby."

Harriet and Jenny spent the next fifteen minutes carrying bolts of fabric to a table in the smaller of the two classrooms that adjoined the retail area of the shop. They finally came up with a plan that used three-and-a-half-inch squares surrounded by two-and-a-half-inch strips. Scrap quilts are a popular style that use many small geometric shapes cut from a large number of different fabrics, in imitation of the quilts made by pioneer women. By going for a scrappy look, they were able to incorporate more grey tones and even some pink to soften the contrast, but still maintain the Aggies' color scheme.

They had just finished when Marjory returned from the staging area.

"Come here, child," she said, and held her arms out for a hug.

Harriet allowed herself to be pulled to Marjory's ample bosom. She could remember the first time her own mother had hugged her. A photographer had staged it for a magazine article. It was supposed to show the warm side of the world-renowned scientist. Harriet had been eighteen and had been summoned to her parent's home when *Time* magazine came calling. She'd always wondered if hugs would have felt more natural if she'd been exposed to them at a younger age.

She had seen Marjory several times since she'd returned, and the woman had employed the same bear hug on each occasion, oblivious to Harriet's discomfort.

"I'm so glad you've come back to Foggy Point," she said. "Your aunt Beth has been so worried about you."

Not so worried that she'd cancel her cruise to Europe, Harriet thought.

"I'm glad to be back, too," she said, not sure if she was telling the truth.

"You two just missed your opportunity to bask in the glow of Foggy Point's newest celebrity," Marjory said.

"Who would that be?" Jenny asked.

"Lauren Sawyer," Marjory replied. "She got some little company to publish her cat designs."

Jenny made a noise that was halfway between a snort and a laugh.

"You know she's counting on winning the overall competition at the Puget Sound Stitcher's Quilt Show," she said.

"She needs to," Marjory said, "She doesn't have the money to take out ads on her own. She's counting on a lot of free publicity when she does win."

"Are her designs that good?" Harriet asked, thinking of the intricate and unusual quilt Avanell had left with her that morning.

"You can judge for yourself," Jenny said. "I'm sure she'll be working on it tomorrow at our Loose Threads meeting. You are coming, aren't you?"

Aunt Beth had taken Harriet to the Loose Threads before she left for her cruise. People had been friendly enough, but she found it difficult not to feel like an outsider. Everyone talked about people and places that were foreign to her. And at the two meetings she'd attended with Aunt Beth, the group had treated her like she was made of spun sugar. As if one wrong word would cause her to dissolve.

"I guess so," she replied. "Sure."

Aunt Beth had reminded her that the Foggy Point quilting community was a small one, and she needed to keep herself visible if she expected to be the machine quilter of choice for the Loose Threads. She had also urged her to be the quilt depot for the upcoming Puget Sound Stitcher's show. Puget Sound was a regional show. Bigger ones were juried, which meant that competitors had to submit pictures and descriptions of their entries for screening before they were allowed to compete. For the Puget Sound show, anyone could display their quilt as long as they paid the fee and filled out a form. As the depot, Foggy Point quilters would drop off their submissions at Harriet's studio, and she would transport them to the staging area in Tacoma. After the show, she would bring the quilts back, and people would collect them from her.

This way, she would meet everyone in her area who was submitting, not just her customers. And, as Aunt Beth had pointed out, she could keep tabs on who else was long-arm quilting in the area.

She believed it was a smart business move, but she also knew Aunt Beth was worried about her and was trying to force her to get out and meet people. She didn't need to worry. Harriet didn't plan to be here long enough to need new customers, and she sure didn't need friends.

Marjory cut Jenny's fabrics, rang up the total and punched Jenny's Needle Points card. Jenny was one purchase away from filling her card, which would entitle her to twenty dollars in free fabric or notions. Harriet purchased two of the square-cut quarter-yard pieces known in the quilting world as fat quarters and received her first punch on her own card.

"I'm parked around the corner," Jenny said, and held the door for her.

Chapter Five

JENNY PARKED HER BMW SEDAN IN HARRIET'S CIRCULAR DRIVEWAY AND CARRIED HER quilt into the studio.

"This isn't as fancy as Avanell's," she said.

"It doesn't have to be fancy. I've seen a number of blue ribbon winners that were well executed traditional patterns. Workmanship and color choice make a big difference in a quilt."

"Avanell's are always well crafted *and* fancy," Jenny countered. "Who would have thought to combine trapunto with traditional pieced blocks and then hand-dye the fabric to boot?"

"It is a nice quilt," Harriet admitted.

"Lauren's nuts if she thinks anything she designed would outshine Avanell's work."

"I've never seen Lauren's."

"When you do, you'll see what I'm talking about. She has potential, but she just hurries too much, and she doesn't understand where the boundaries are between being inspired by someone's work and outright copying. Your aunt tried to explain to her that she couldn't trace pictures out of children's books and then sell them as her own patterns, but she doesn't understand."

"I hope she doesn't ask me to stitch anything like that," Harriet said.

"You won't have to worry—she does her own quilting on her home sewing machine. You're the quilt depot, aren't you?"

Harriet nodded.

"You'll get to see it then even if she doesn't come to Loose Threads. Check it out when you do—you'll see what I mean. Avanell would have to keel over dead for Lauren to have a chance, and even then it wouldn't be certain."

"Let's have a look at yours," Harriet said. She didn't want to be forced into taking sides before she'd even met Lauren.

Jenny's quilt was a simple double-four patch set on point. The basic form was four squares of fabric arranged to make a square. In a double-four patch, two diagonal squares were themselves made up of four smaller squares. She'd chosen a rich berry-toned floral as the focus fabric then combined it with pistachio and antique green batiks with a touch of dusty rose hand-dyed cotton. It was a queen-sized bed cover and was destined for the guestroom in Jenny's house after the show.

"This is very nice," Harriet said. "Have you thought about what style of stitching you want on it?"

"Well, I've toyed with the idea of putting smallish feather patterns continuously in the sashing and then just having parallel lines in the four patch blocks. I'm not sure, though. I would rather have the double four patch blocks as the focus."

On a quilt, sashing pieces were the rectangles of fabric used to frame the main blocks. Harriet had seen a lot of them where the designer had intended the sashing to enhance the pattern but in fact it had done just the opposite. In Jenny's quilt, though, it definitely added to the overall effect.

"What if we put a flower pattern on the double-four patch blocks with mirror images in the matching squares, and then did a simpler version of the flower in the sashing?" she suggested. "That way, the blocks will stand out, but the sashing will still seem like it's framing each block."

She showed Jenny a stack of flower sample blocks, and Jenny chose two she liked. She agreed that Harriet would do a flower that incorporated elements from both samples.

Satisfied that they had a plan, Jenny left the quilt on the table and took her leave. Harriet went back to work on Avanell's.

It took her about two to three hours to do an average job after it had been loaded onto the frame of the long arm machine. She had allotted twice that amount of time for the show quilts—she didn't want to risk a misplaced stitch.

Aunt Beth had suggested she limit the time she ran the machine to about twenty hours a week because of all the bending and reaching the operator had to do. That might be reasonable during normal times, but for the next two weeks, Harriet expected to be working eight or more hours a day, especially if she were going to be stitching who-knew-what at the last minute for Sarah Ness. Besides, she could always get a massage for her aching back after the rush.

She grasped the controls of her machine, pressed the blue go-button and began stitching.

Chapter Six

T HE FIRST WEEK OF BUSINESS FLEW BY. HARRIET FINISHED AVANELL'S AND JENNY'S quilts and stitched projects for Connie Escorcia and DeAnn DeGault. She had just finished loading Robin McLeod's yellow-and-blue log cabin quilt onto the machine frame when her phone rang.

She crossed the room and picked up the receiver. "Hello."

"You're coming to Loose Threads this morning, aren't you?" Avanell asked her.

"I think so." Harriet mentally ticked off the work on her schedule. She could probably afford to take a couple of hours off. "Yes, I'll come."

"I'll be coming from work, so how about if I drive to your place and leave my car and we can walk into town?"

Harriet decided a walk would be the perfect antidote to a week spent hunched over the long-arm machine. She agreed, and Avanell said she'd be there in a half-hour.

Foggy Point, Washington, sat on a rocky peninsula that protruded into the Strait of Juan de Fuca just east of Port Angeles. Harriet hadn't paid enough attention in geography class to know if the right-angle bend in the middle of the town's land mass disqualified it from the peninsula category or not. She thought it looked more like the head and claw of a Tyrannosaurus rex, with her own house sitting on a hill at the base of the claw. Rumor had it that the cove formed by the bend had been a favorite hiding spot for pirates back in early Victorian times, when Europeans first discovered Foggy Point's unique charms.

She heard Avanell coming up the drive. She gathered her purse and hand-stitching bag and Avanell's quilt and met the older woman at her car, putting the carefully wrapped quilt in the backseat.

"Are you all right?" she asked. "You look a little pale."

Wisps of grey hair trailed from Avanell's usually tidy bun. Lint clung to the lap area of her navy wool skirt. Dark circles smudged the area under her eyes.

"I'm fine," Avanell replied. "Things have just been a little hectic at work. One of our key employees left this week, and it's just getting harder and harder to find quality replacements. And...never mind, let's not drag this nice morning down talking about work problems," she said, trying but failing to lighten her tone. "Tell me how the quilts are looking."

"Yours is ready to bind, of course," Harriet said. "I'm done with all the show quilts that have been scheduled, and I still have a couple of days for Sarah Ness."

"Good for you," Avanell said and really did smile.

They discussed all the show entries they had seen as they walked. Each woman made her own predictions about who the winners would be for each category. Some would be judged by a panel of local quilting arts luminaries while others would be in categories that were voted on by the show attendees. They were still arguing the merits of Avanell's own quilt when they arrived at Pins and Needles.

"I don't care what you say, Avanell," Harriet said. "Your quilt is a shoo-in to win the overall prize."

"I agree with Harriet," said Marjory. "I don't care if Lauren Sawyer got her patterns published or not, Avanell, you still make a better quilt than she ever will."

"Thanks for the vote of confidence," Avanell said. "From your mouth to the judge's ear, I hope."

"You're the first ones here," Marjory said. "I put coffee on in the breakroom a couple of minutes ago, so it should be ready soon."

The Pacific Northwest is the birthplace of Starbucks and Seattle's Best, so people expect coffee to be exceptional even when it's served from a Mr. Coffee. Marjory's did not disappoint.

"I want to take one last look to see if I can find something better than what I have for the binding of my quilt," Avanell said. "What I've got cut just doesn't feel right."

Binding is the small but important finishing step in quilt-making. A narrow strip of fabric is folded into an even narrower strip and then sewn onto the edge of the quilt, encasing the raw edge of the top, the batting and the back. Judges expect the binding to be uniform, to have perfectly mitered corners and to be filled completely with quilt—that is, to not have any empty places or bulges in the edge. The color choice needed to be the finishing accent of the piece, not obvious but missed if absent, much like a frame on a picture.

"I just unpacked a box of new batiks," Marjory said. "I'm checking them in. You want to take a look?"

Avanell did, and followed her to a back room strewn with plastic-wrapped bolts of fabric. Batik originated in Indonesia and involves painting wax designs on fabric then dyeing the fabric, sometimes incorporating tie-dye techniques as well. The result usually has a background mottled with several coordinated colors and may or may not include the line-drawn images that are left when the wax is removed. Experienced quilters like the depth and movement batik fabric lends to their projects.

Harriet went into the larger of the two classrooms. Classes are an integral part of a successful craft store, and Marjory kept hers busy most afternoons and evenings with fabric-buying students and stitching groups with names like "Mumm Club" and "Peaceful Piecers."

"Hi, Jenny," Harriet greeted her friend as she came in and sat down. "How's your binding coming?"

They discussed the pros and cons of single layer versus double layer bindings until Mavis Willis arrived, followed by Connie Escorcia. At seventy, Mavis was the oldest member of The Loose Threads. She had tightly curled hair that in its prime had been copper-colored but had faded to a rusty grey. Mavis was a handpiecer—after cutting the fabric pieces that would make up her block, she did all her stitching by hand.

Her current project was an intricate series of triangles that formed a kaleidoscope pattern in shades of straw and khaki and putty, with connecting squares in a walnut color that stopped just short of orange. She was making it for her oldest son's birthday. Having raised five sons who had produced fourteen grandchildren, she was always working on something for a birthday or confirmation or some other occasion.

Harriet could hear Connie before she arrived in the room. Her laughter was infectious.

"Honey, I'm home," she called out as she entered the shop. "Where is everyone?"

"Back here," Harriet answered.

"What are you two doing sitting around?" she said and popped her head into the classroom. "There's new fabric out there. Come on, let's check it out."

Jenny and Harriet looked at each other, shrugged and got up to look at fabric. Hurricane Connie was a force to be reckoned with.

"Help me find a binding," Connie said. She held scraps from her quilt in her left hand and used her right one to drape cloth from the bolts over them.

Her offering would be in the art category. The upper right corner had irregularly shaped pieces stitched together in increasingly larger segments as they approached the center panel. The bottom left was a base of hand-dyed fabric with an abstract floral applique that flowed up toward the center and overlapped the pieced area. Connie's color palate was a warm one. This design had orange peel as the base color with pistachio, dusty mauve, peach and toffee shades as the accent. It would be a challenge to find a binding color that wouldn't distract the eye from the central pattern.

Sarah Ness arrived as they returned to the classroom; her cheap, designer knock-off perfume preceded her into the space. Mavis sneezed. Connie had decided to bind with a fabric that echoed the color in her hand-dye and gone to the cutting area with Marjory.

"Harriet," Sarah said. "I've been trying to call you."

"I haven't gotten any messages," Harriet said. "When did you call?"

"I've been calling all morning," she said.

It would be pointless to state the obvious, so Harriet moved on to what she was pretty sure was coming.

"What did you want?"

"I need my quilt stitched," she replied. "I have to have it bound and back to you by Thursday to take to the show, so I guess you'll have to do it this afternoon."

"Do you have it with you?" Harriet asked.

"I have the top in the car and I'm going to stitch the backing together while we're here."

"You're cutting it a little close, aren't you?" Mavis asked. "You know, Harriet might have someone else scheduled this afternoon."

"Well, do you?" Sarah demanded.

"This afternoon will be fine," Harriet assured her. "As long as I have it in my hands when I walk out of here."

Mavis shook her head and turned away to press a seam.

"I've been busy," Sarah said. "I've had meetings every night this week. And last weekend, I had a workshop in Seattle that started Friday afternoon and didn't end until noon Sunday. And I have to give a speech at the school board meeting next Monday night."

"I'm surprised she has time to grace us with her presence," Avanell muttered.

"What?" Sarah said and turned toward her.

"I was just saying I don't see how you get all your work done and still have time to quilt," Avanell said in a loud, slow voice.

Sarah's shoulders slumped a little in her crisp khaki blazer.

"It is hard," she said, "but I promised Marjory I would enter a project using her fabrics so it would help draw attention to Pins and Needles. I need to get some thread," she added and went out of the classroom and over to the notions hutch.

"I wonder if Marjory knows how dependent she is on Sarah's quilt," Jenny said with a smile.

Mavis pressed her lips together and studiously watched Harriet line up the two triangles she was about to stitch.

The group sat down around one of the larger tables and settled into their stitching routine. Lauren came a few minutes later and made a point of sitting at a smaller table by the window so she could talk but, at the same time, keep the work she was binding hidden below the tabletop.

The women spent a few minutes discussing their absent members. Robin McLeod had to take her daughter to the orthodontist. DeAnn Gault had a painter at her house and didn't feel comfortable leaving him there by himself. When they were satisfied they had accounted for everyone, they moved on to what everyone was doing this week. Harriet was not anxious to share her activities. How would she put it?

I'm going to see my aunt's attorney and undo the havoc she's wrought in my life.

Or maybe she'd just report on the stuff she was stitching then disappear quietly into the night as soon as Aunt Beth returned and leave them all guessing. That would keep them yakking for weeks, she thought and smiled to herself.

They had not yet asked Avanell what was happening in her life when the six-foot-three answer walked through the door.

Chapter Seven

H I, MOM," THE YOUNG MAN SAID, AND ABSENTLY FLICKED A STRAND OF HIS CHIN-
length black hair over his ear. Harriet could see the resemblance to
Avanell in his angular face, but his eyes were unlike any she had ever seen.

The color was a pale yellowish-blue that stopped just short of white. They
were large, and angled slightly, giving them a feline quality. His dark tan spoke
to time spent somewhere much farther south than Foggy Point.

He came around the table and kissed Avanell then held her at arms-length.
"You look really good."

"This hairy young man is my youngest son, Aiden," Avanell said, and
tucked another unruly lock of hair behind his other ear. A slight blush
darkened his cheeks. "He's been doing a research project in Uganda for the
last three years, where they apparently don't have barber shops."

"How very nice to meet you," Lauren said. "We've heard so much about
you."

"All good, I hope," he said, reminding Harriet of her own reaction to the
same pronouncement and making her wonder what *he* might have to hide. He
straightened up and turned toward the table full of women.

Avanell's oldest son was a few years younger than Harriet and had been a
pimple-faced teenager with a crush on her when she'd left for college. Her
daughter was a few years younger than that, and Aiden was the proverbial
afterthought. He must have been around when Harriet had lived with Aunt
Beth, but she was pretty sure she would have remembered those eerie eyes if
she'd seen them before. Then again, she had been pretty self-absorbed in
those days. Her anger at her parents for once again dumping her with Aunt
Beth while they partied their way across Europe under the guise of academic
research pretty well eclipsed anything that was happening in Foggy Point.

"My, how you've grown," Jenny said. "I can remember you eating Popsicles at my kitchen table with Mark. He's married and has a baby boy, but somehow it didn't occur to me that you'd be growing up, too." She smiled. "I guess when your mom said you were coming back to town, I expected to see that gangly boy with eyes too big for his face. Funny how your mind works when you get old and senile."

"You're not old," Aiden said. "And even though I've grown up, I really missed your Popsicles while I was in Africa. We had a small refrigerator run from a generator, but we had to stuff it full of animal medications."

"Aiden is a veterinarian," Avanell explained. "He just took a job at the clinic on Main Street."

"Welcome home, *mijo*," Connie said and stood up to give him a hug. Even when she stretched to her full height, Aiden had to bend down to receive her greeting.

Connie claimed she was five feet tall, but no one believed her. She had been the favorite first grade teacher of everyone who had passed through the doors of Joseph Meeker Elementary School in Foggy Point for the thirty years she'd taught there, including all three of Avanell's children.

"Will you be seeing cats?" Sarah asked. "My Rachel has been sneezing and I'm not sure if she has a cold or an allergy."

"I don't start for two more weeks, so I don't really know what I'll be doing. For all I know, I'll be scrubbing the kennels."

"Rachel can't wait that long," Sarah pressed. "Do you make housecalls?"

"I really can't see animals until I officially start at the clinic. I don't have access to medications until then. I'm still waiting for my stuff to arrive, too—I don't have my bag or anything," he said. "Sorry."

Harriet looked over at Avanell. Avanell rolled her eyes to the ceiling.

Sarah returned her attention to the seam she was sewing in her backing material.

Avanell was anxious to visit with Aiden, and no one could blame her.

"Go ahead and go with your son," Harriet said. "I've got to wait until Sarah finishes her backing, and I'm sure she won't mind driving me and her quilt back to my place."

Aiden gave her a curious look.

"I don't want to take my mom away from what she's doing," he said. "I know how important her quilting is."

"You always could charm the socks off a zebra," Mavis said. "But we all know your mom is going to win best in show even if she does take the afternoon to catch up with you, so you just go ahead. And we'll make sure Harriet gets home, don't you worry, Avanell."

It was a toss-up whether Sarah or Lauren had the nastiest glare for Avanell's retreating back. Harriet knew Sarah would have made an excuse to avoid driving her if it hadn't meant she would be walking home carrying the woman's quilt.

It only took Sarah an additional hour after the meeting broke up to finish her quilt back, and it became obvious to Harriet that if she sat in the same room with her, she would never finish. There seemed to be no end to the young woman's ego or her desire to talk about it, so she went to the kitchen and sat at the table with the latest copy of *Quilters World* until Sarah was done.

Chapter Eight

HARRIET DROPPED SARAH'S QUILT OFF IN THE STUDIO AND WENT INTO THE KITCHEN. Fred wove figure-eights between her legs, making forward progress nearly impossible.

She picked him up. "Well, Fred, we survived our first Loose Threads meeting on our own."

Fred meowed.

"And we discovered that Avanell has been holding out on us. She has a really hot-looking son we never knew about."

Fred jumped to the floor and fluffed his tail.

"Don't worry, Fred, you're the only man in my life and that's not changing." After what Steve and his family had done, she would never share her heart again. "Besides, Avanell's son is too young for us. He's probably younger than you are in cat years."

Fred flicked his tail and sauntered to the pantry where the kitty treats were stored. Harriet opened the door and gave him three fish-shaped kibbles from the foil pouch. She wondered what she'd do if she didn't have him to talk to. She'd like to think she wouldn't talk to herself, but you never knew.

Before Steve had died, she'd had girlfriends she could call anytime, even if she just had a random thought to share. She should have known. They had been Steve's friends. They knew the truth, and even after all the nights they'd stayed up laughing and crying when one of them had broken up with her boyfriend, and the days they'd spent bringing food and cleaning house for another one after she'd had a miscarriage—after all that, still, no one thought she was important enough to be let in on Steve's secret.

Harriet had spent the first year after Steve's death wallowing in self-pity. She rarely left their apartment, and spent her days going over their life together, trying to figure out if there had been clues she'd missed. She'd been sure it was her fault. If she'd just been less involved in her business, or spent less time with her faux friends, maybe she would have seen the signs of Steve's condition. And if she'd seen the signs, maybe she could have found some new treatment or therapy that would have saved him.

Eventually, she'd agreed to see a therapist; and now, most of the time, she believed what had happened was out of her control. Steve had suffered from Marfan's syndrome, an inheritable genetic disorder that was often fatal without aggressive medical intervention. Until as recently as 1977 there was little that could be done to reverse the damage to connective tissue it caused, particularly in the heart. Perhaps if his parents had sought medical intervention when he was younger things could have been different; but by the time she'd met him the die had already been cast.

She opened the refrigerator door and reviewed her options. Aunt Beth had disapproved of the pounds she had gained over the last five years. In spite of her own comfortable bulk, Aunt Beth had insisted Harriet was using her weight as a way to stay disconnected from the world. To this end, she had binge-proofed the house before she left on her cruise. There wasn't a chip, cookie or sweetened fat nodule of any kind. The refrigerator was filled with cleaned carrot sticks, pickled beets, tomatoes, cucumbers and precooked boneless, skinless chicken breast meat in several flavors.

Harriet pulled out a plastic bag and poured herself a bowl full of romaine lettuce pieces. She tore up two slices of chicken breast and added them to the lettuce. Her hand skimmed past the fat-free Italian salad dressing in the refrigerator door and settled on the bottle of creamy organic sesame, clearly an oversight on Aunt Beth's part. She promised herself a trip to the grocery store when she got all of the show quilts done.

She had a smaller project to finish this afternoon before she could start Sarah's—she had hoped to get Sarah's call last night. The deadline for receiving quilts to stitch had been yesterday morning, but Sarah was bold. When the call didn't come, Harriet had started a baby quilt one of Aunt Beth's regular customers had asked her to fit into her schedule.

Sarah was a good customer, but her lateness this time wouldn't allow Harriet to use the kind of care she had on the other show quilts. It couldn't be helped, and besides she was confident that if Sarah's didn't win a prize it wouldn't be because of her stitching.

She finished her salad under Fred's watchful eye and returned to her quilting machine.

IT HAD BEEN DARK FOR MORE THAN AN HOUR. HARRIET HAD FINISHED THE BABY QUILT and had about a foot left to stitch on Sarah's quilt when the brass bell tied to her studio doorknob jingled.

"Anyone home?" a male voice called. Aiden Jalbert stepped into the room. "Oh, good, you're still here," he said.

Harriet pushed the needle-down button and walked to the reception area, where he was pacing in great agitation.

"Of course, I'm here," she said. "I live here. Is there something I can help you with?"

She couldn't help but stare at those eyes. He was probably used to that.

"I'm sorry to bother you so late." He ran his fingers through his thick hair. "But I've got a bit of a problem, and I was hoping you could help me out."

Harriet took a good look at him. His white shirt was smeared with what looked like blood. His sleeves were rolled up to his elbows, and his left arm had a long scratch down its length.

"What happened?" she asked.

"I'm staying in a studio apartment over the vet clinic," he explained. "My mom was working late, so I took her Chinese food from that Rice Bowl place on Fourth Street, and since I was driving right past here on my way home, Mom asked if I would drop her quilt off. I guess she finished putting the trim on it at work this afternoon."

"Binding," Harriet corrected. "She finished binding it."

"Whatever," he said.

"If she finished binding it, where is it?"

"That would be the problem part," he said, shifting his weight from one foot to the other. "I was on my way here, and right at the bottom of your hill the car in front of me hit a dog. We both stopped, and the lady that was driving went to the two closest houses. No one knew who the dog belonged to, and it couldn't wait any longer."

"Please tell me you didn't wrap the dog in your mother's quilt," Harriet said.

The muscle in Aiden's jaw jumped.

"I couldn't let her lay there and bleed to death," he protested. "She's a big Lab, and I think she's pregnant. I didn't have anything else to use as a stretcher."

Harriet looked pointedly at his shirt.

He grabbed his shirttails in his hands. "My shirt wouldn't hold a dog that big. I know my mom will understand if it comes to that." The misery was clear in his voice.

Any kid who grew up to be a vet and then went to Africa to save wild animals had probably brought his share of damaged wildlife home to his mother. Avanell likely would understand.

"I can't promise anything, but go get it and let's see what we have."

His shoulders sagged in relief. He went out and gathered the quilt in his arms. Harriet watched him from the door and took it from him. She spread it out on the big cutting table then pulled up a tall stool for herself and another for Aiden.

"Here, sit."

"I can't until you say you can fix it."

"First aid for a quilt is all I can manage right now. If *you* keel over, I'm leaving you."

He looked at her and must have decided she was serious because he sat.

Harriet turned on the true-color ceiling lights over the cutting table then plugged in her freestanding Ott light and pulled it over to the table. In order to be sure the colors in a quilt truly complement each other, most quilters use lights that are made to match natural sunlight. Any stitcher worth her salt had both a floor version in her home and a portable unit for group gatherings.

Although it was possible to buy a true-color light that wasn't made by Ott, they so dominate the crafter's market that, like Kleenex being used to refer to all tissues or Scotch tape for all transparent cellophane tape, people called all true lights "Ott Lights."

She bent over the quilt, looking at the entire top surface, then flipped it over to look at the back side in two places. Aiden started tapping his fingers on the edge of the table. Harriet glared at him.

"You're killing me here," he said.

"Tapping your fingers isn't helping me do my job any faster."

She let him squirm for another two minutes. At last she stood up.

"You are one lucky dog savior," she said. "And it is especially fortunate that the blood didn't get on the cream-colored areas. Your mom used a hand-dyed fabric that has enough shading to it that I think after it's cleaned you won't be able to tell anything happened."

He shocked her by grabbing her in a bear hug and twirling her around in a circle.

"I knew you could fix it. Mom told me you're really talented. Thank you so much."

"Hold on here," she said, and pushed him away. "This isn't a done deal yet. It all depends on a few things working out just right."

"Anything," he said. "I'll do anything. Tell me. Just make my mom's quilt be okay. I'm begging you here."

"Calm down," Harriet said. She couldn't help smiling, though. "First, I need to fix this one place where the stitches are broken." She scooped it up off the table, grabbed her hand-sewing kit and headed for the chairs. Aiden sat on the ottoman.

"Can I do anything to help?" he asked.

"Here, hold this," she said. She handed him the half of the quilt she wasn't working on. She didn't really need anyone to hold it for her, but at least it would keep him from tapping his fingers.

"When I finish here, you still have to take it to the dry cleaners on Nisqually Street and get them to clean the spots and then get it back to me by Thursday morning. Can you do that?"

"I have to go to Seattle tomorrow, but I should be able to drop it off before I leave," Aiden said. "I just have to turn in my final research report, then I can drive back and pick it up."

"As long as you get it to me before ten on Thursday morning, it should be fine."

"I'll bring it to you Wednesday night as soon as I get back. I don't want to take any chances."

"Probably a good idea," Harriet said. "If tonight is any indication."

"This is probably a dumb question, but is there some reason we didn't just throw it in the washer?" he asked.

"It's not a dumb question, just don't ever do it. You never throw someone else's quilt in the washer. If they haven't pre-washed the fabric, it can pucker and bleed. And you pretty well never wash an art piece. They use techniques that aren't meant to stand up to water or agitation."

Aiden sighed. "I figured that would be too simple."

"You should tell your mom what happened," Harriet said.

"I know I should, but she seems really preoccupied and tired. I was hoping we could take care of this without her ever needing to know."

"It's your call," she said. "I'd tell her, if it was me, even if everything is fine."

"I'll tell her after it wins the blue ribbon. Then she'll think it's funny. And she'll be a lot less likely to kill me." He grinned. He'd probably kept Avanell on her toes when he was growing up.

Harriet tied a single knot in her thread, buried it in the batting and clipped the thread end.

"There you go," she said. She stood up and folded the quilt. "I'll call the cleaners in the morning, but you remind them, too, that it's hand-dyed cotton. And let them wash the pillow slip it was in, too. That way, you'll have something clean to put it in when you pick it up."

"Thank you so much," he repeated. "And I'm sorry I came barging in here in the middle of the night."

"Not a problem." She opened the door for him and watched as he carried the quilt to his car, gently setting it on the backseat. He was the one who looked tired, she thought.

Chapter Nine

HARRIET'S PHONE WAS RINGING AS SHE CAME DOWNSTAIRS AFTER HER SHOWER Wednesday morning. She dashed across the entrance, through the dining and living rooms and grabbed the phone just as the caller hung up. She didn't recognize the number the caller ID was showing her, but that wasn't unusual. She dialed.

"Oh, Harriet," Avanell said. "I'm glad you called back. I have a favor to ask."

"Sure, anything." Maybe Aiden had come clean.

"I need you to go to a Chamber of Commerce fundraiser with Harold."

"I don't date," Harriet said flatly. She could feel her face turning red.

"I'm not asking you to go on a date, honey. The company bought tickets to this thing a month ago. I was going to go, but we're shorthanded, and the end of the month shipping is piling up. We paid a hundred dollars a ticket, and I just hate to see it go to waste. Besides, Harold is a teddy bear. He's our finance guy. I can guarantee he'll be a perfect gentleman. And Delilah's Catering is providing the food, so you know it will be good."

Harriet didn't have experience with Delilah's Catering, but she knew her aunt used them whenever she was putting on an event. After days of lettuce and carrots, the thought of well-prepared food made her mouth water. For a hundred dollars a plate, they might get steak or prime rib, or even chicken with skin. She decided it wouldn't matter if Harold was a troll if she got hors d'oeuvres. She wondered what kind of rolls they would have.

"Okay," she said. "I'm there. When do I need to be ready?"

"Harold will pick you up at six. Dinner will be at seven."

"How fancy do I need to dress?"

"No blue jeans but leave the elbow-length gloves and tiara home," she said.

"Thanks, gotta go."

Harriet went upstairs and tried on the little black dress she'd brought with her from California. It was loose—days of lettuce and water did that to a person. She looked in Aunt Beth's closet. Her aunt was shorter and wider than she was, but a good scarf could make up for any bodily shortcoming. She knew Aunt Beth must have a stash of the things somewhere.

She opened the middle drawer of an oak chest and wasn't disappointed—it was crammed full of scarves of every size, texture and color. She picked a purple-and-blue bit of froth and tied it around the waist of her dress. You'd never see the look on the runways in Paris, but she had to admit it wasn't bad.

She changed back into her jeans and turtleneck and went back downstairs. She had a full day of stitching ahead of her—Aunt Beth booked long-arm stitching appointments months in advance. People often reserved spaces without even knowing which quilt they would bring when the time came. Harriet wasn't going to lack for work while she waited for her aunt to return.

SHE FINISHED HER LAST QUILT OF THE DAY AT FIVE-THIRTY. THAT ONLY GAVE HER A HALF-hour to get ready for her not-a-date, but that was more than enough. She dashed through the shower again, ran a comb through her short damp hair and got into her dress and scarf. She went down to the studio to wait. Since this wasn't a date, there was no reason to invite Harold—or anyone else, for that matter, into the private part of the house.

Aiden had said he would bring Avanell's quilt by this evening, and six o'clock could barely be considered that. But she had still hoped he would arrive before she left. Besides Sarah's, which she assumed she would get at ten tomorrow morning, Avanell's was the only one she didn't have. She had called the cleaners this morning as she'd promised, and they hadn't anticipated any problems cleaning it, but you never knew. She couldn't call Avanell, and Aiden had said he would be on the road most of the day.

In the end, she wrote a note and said she'd be back by nine. She admonished him to not leave the quilt on her doorstep, pinned the note to her door and hoped for the best. She really didn't want the quilt in his hands any longer than absolutely necessary, but it couldn't be helped.

Harold arrived, wearing sharply creased navy blue flannel pants with a crisp white shirt and red bow tie. Harriet gave him points for having his hair cut short enough he didn't have to deal with the possibility of a comb-over. His face was fleshy enough it was hard to determine his age.

He came to the front door in spite of her instructions to Avanell to the contrary. He took the purple pashmina shawl she had found in Aunt Beth's closet from her and draped it over her shoulders. It probably made her look old, but he didn't seem to notice. She glanced at his expectantly crooked elbow and brushed past him, leading the way down the steps to his car.

She nearly fainted at the door to the meeting hall as she inhaled deeply the rich aroma of food—really good, clog-your-arteries, high-calorie food. The scents of beef and garlic and roasted vegetables filled the air; tendrils of fragrance following her as she moved into the room. It was every bit as good as she had hoped. There were mushroom caps filled with a bread crumb-and-cheese mixture with toasted Parmesan on top, and crostini with pork liver pate with tart cornichons. There was a whole table of cheese that featured a wheel of baked Brie covered with dried cranberries, and an unusual goat's milk feta with herbs. And both bread and crackers.

And that was just the snacks. A succulent prime rib was the main course. It was served on warm plates with mashed garlic potatoes and a creamy horseradish sauce that was blended to perfection. The meal was topped off with a rich crème brûlée. It was a clever ploy—when the Chamber president asked for donations for the new playground equipment for North Park, donors were so satiated they opened their wallets wide in appreciation. Harold presented a check for a thousand dollars from the Vitamin Factory. For a non-date, it could have been a lot worse.

Harold pulled his black Cadillac El Dorado into her driveway at precisely nine p.m. She didn't want to make any snap judgments, but based on how quickly he had hustled her out to the car after the last speech was done he either had a hot date or a curfew. He drove just over the speed limit all the way home and had backed out of the driveway before she had her key in the door.

"Well, good night to you, too," she said out loud.

She had automatically gone to the studio entrance, since it was the nearest door to where he let her out on the circular driveway. She climbed the two steps to the small landing. She was still marveling about her evening as she reached for the doorknob with her key.

If she hadn't been distracted, she probably would have noticed sooner that her door wasn't locked. In fact, the door itself wasn't all the way shut.

She remembered locking it right after she turned the long-arm machine off.

She backed up slowly. She stepped down the two risers backward, reaching into her purse at the same time.

Damn, she thought. Aunt Beth had a collection of small decorative purses left over from an earlier attempt to combine her fiber arts projects with commerce. Harriet had helped herself to a purple-and-blue one. When she transferred the contents of her shapeless black everyday bag into it, her cell phone had made a bulge no matter how she positioned it. In the end she'd tossed the phone onto her dresser.

The crunch of tires on gravel shocked her out of her paralysis. She looked over her shoulder but couldn't see anything in the glare of the headlights coming slowly toward her from the downhill end of her driveway. The robber must have come back.

The small hairs rose on the back of her neck—she knew she couldn't run far in her black dress pumps.

She looked up the other side of the driveway. It was dark. If she could get around the curve, she just might be able to push through the hedge into Mrs. Morse's yard. She turned and started up the drive.

She heard a car door open then footsteps crunching in the gravel. The hedge was a few feet in front of her. The footsteps were getting closer. She reached the hedge and forced her way into the sharp branches. It was an old hedge; and once she was through, the leafless branches closed around her, giving the illusion of safety.

The footsteps stopped then started again. She couldn't see through the wall of leaves. She could envision the robber searching the driveway to see where she went. If he looked closely at the hedge, he would surely see the broken branches where she'd plunged inside.

He stopped again.

Harriet moved the branch in front of her face. She could see his form right in front of her hiding spot. She had to think. She felt around her for something she could use as a weapon—a large branch would have been handy. She carefully bent down and patted the ground by her feet. Her left hand closed over a cold metal pipe. She slowly lifted it. It wasn't a pipe at all. It was an oscillating sprinkler. Probably not the best weapon; but if she swung it with both hands, it should give her enough time to dash back to the house.

The man leaned toward Harriet's hiding place. He must be looking at her point of entrance. She raised the sprinkler as high as she could. Any minute now he would push the branches aside, and she'd have a clear shot.

A hand appeared on her side of the branches, quickly followed by a dark head. Harriet sprang. She hit the man hard.

"Ouch!" he yelled.

Harriet ran for it. She might have gotten away, but he reached up and grabbed her wrist with his free hand. His other was pressed to his forehead, where blood was beginning to seep through his fingers.

"Harriet, it's me—Aiden."

"Aiden?"

"Why did you hit me?"

"What are you doing here?"

"I brought my mother's quilt," he said. "Like I said I would. Wednesday night. I came earlier, but there was a note on your door that said to come back at nine."

"Aiden," Harriet said, "I'm so sorry."

"What were you doing running up the driveway like that and then jumping into the hedge? Did you forget to take your medication?"

"No, I did not forget my medication," she fairly shouted. "What am I saying—I don't have medication. And let go of me."

He dropped his hold on her wrist.

"Mom said you came here to recover," he said. "Then I see you staggering up the driveway and hopping into a hedge—in a dress. What was I supposed to think?"

"I wasn't staggering. You should try to walk in gravel with heels on. You'd stagger, too."

He moved his hand from his forehead, and blood started trickling down his forehead and onto his nose.

"Oh, my God," Harriet said. "I've hurt you. Let me look."

He took a step back, avoiding her touch.

"I'm not going to hurt you," she said.

"I think I'll take my chances and drive home."

"You can't go."

"Is that why you hit me? To make me stay?"

"Don't be ridiculous. I thought you were a robber."

"Of course, you did," he said, and turned to go.

"Can I at least use your cell phone before you go?"

"Are you serious? Use your own phone. I'm out of here."

She grabbed his arm. "Please," she begged.

"Fine," he said and pulled a flip phone from his pocket. He opened it and handed it to her.

She dialed 911.

"What are you doing?" he asked and grabbed for the phone. She turned away from him as she identified herself and described her problem.

"Yes, I came home from dinner a few minutes ago, and my door was open...Yes, I'm sure it was locked when I left for dinner...No, I didn't go inside. I wasn't sure if anyone was in there or not...Okay, I'll wait across the street. Thanks."

She flipped the phone shut and handed it back to Aiden.

"Someone broke into your house?" he asked.

"Yes, and I would have told you so if you hadn't been so busy accusing me of being mad."

"Sorry, I was a little distracted by being clubbed in the head with an oscillating sprinkler. Did they take anything?"

"How should I know? I found the lock had been forced and the door was slightly open. For all I know, the robber could still be in there."

"So, your door was ajar? That's your evidence of robbery? Maybe your aunt gave her house keys to one of her friends. That group does that, you know. Mavis scared me out of a year's growth when I was seventeen and thought I was home alone. I went downstairs after my shower to get a can of soda without bothering to get dressed, and...well, you can imagine. I haven't been able to find my mom tonight. Maybe she's in there using your aunt's big table or something."

My big table, Harriet thought, but didn't say anything. She could hear the siren drawing closer.

"Well, it's too late now," she said. "The police are almost here, and I said I'd wait across the street."

"Do you always do what you're told?"

Harriet was spared from having to answer by the arrival of the police.

Chapter Ten

I S ANYONE IN THERE?" THE POLICE OFFICER ASKED. HE WAS YOUNG AND ASIAN, AND wore a black plastic tag that said NGUYEN. Harriet took great comfort from the large gun strapped to his side.

"We don't know," she said. "This is my aunt's house. I live here now. But she's gone on a cruise. I got home and found the door unlocked and open."

Another patrol car pulled up; two officers got out. The driver was a skinny blonde woman with leathery skin, her partner a chunky, red-faced guy. The Asian officer explained the situation to the two newcomers, and they drew their guns and headed for the house.

"So, what did the guy look like?" the Asian police officer asked Harriet.

"What guy?"

"The one that popped *him*," he said, and hooked a thumb toward Aiden, who now had blood dripping off his chin. "Which way did he go?" He took a closer look at Aiden. "You want me to call an ambulance for you?"

Harriet and Aiden looked at each other.

"We haven't seen anyone," Aiden said. "And, ah, this is unrelated to the robbery. I got here just after Harriet discovered the door was open."

The officer took a long look at each of them. Harriet blushed but didn't say anything.

"You need to get that checked, it looks like you might need stitches," he said.

The three of them waited in silence until the other two came out of the house.

"There's no one in there," the woman said. Aiden gave Harriet an "I told you so" look.

The red-faced guy joined the group.

"Somebody's sure been here, though."

Harriet bolted for the door.

"Wait," Aiden said, but she was already out of reach.

She opened the door and stopped. Her mouth opened, but no words came out.

Aiden caught up to her. "Oh, my God," he said.

What was left of the quilts lay in pieces on every surface. Wisps of cotton batting hung in jagged ropes from torn edges. Thread spools were strewn over the floor and the cutting table top looked as if someone had picked up the thread rack and thrown it in anger. The piecrust table was on its side by the window, its tea cups in shattered pieces on the floor.

"Don't touch anything," the Asian officer said from behind them. "I've called the crime scene analysts. You'll need to stay out until they finish."

Harriet shivered.

"You can sit in the back of my car if you want. I can turn it on and run the heater."

"That won't be necessary," Aiden said. "If it's okay, we'll go back to my place so I can get a bandage on this cut. I'm living in the apartment over the Main Street Vet Clinic."

"Vet clinic?" Harriet said, and then screamed. "Fred!"

Aiden clamped his hands onto her shoulders. The policeman looked at him, but he had no clue as to who Fred was either.

"My cat," Harriet explained and started to cry.

"Your cat is fine," the female officer said as she walked over to the group. "He's a little freaked, but he's on the top shelf of the bookcase upstairs. He looked totally okay, and I don't think he's going anywhere. We'll make sure the crime scene people keep the doors shut."

The criminalists arrived and got out of their car. Harriet was relieved Darcy Lewis was one of them. Darcy was a drop-in member of Loose Threads, a petite, thirty-year-old single mother. Her brown hair was cut in a short shag style that made her look like Peter Pan.

"Aren't you the quilt depot for the Tacoma show?" she asked.

Harriet nodded silently, the misery apparent on her face.

"I'll start in your studio, and then we can let you in while we do the rest," Darcy said and joined her partner, an older man who carried two boxes of equipment into Harriet's workspace.

Foggy Point wasn't big enough to employ one criminalist full time, let alone the three they had, so they contracted their services to small communities all over western Washington. That meant Darcy got to do what she had always wanted to do without having to move to a big city, but in return she was on the road a lot. It was not unusual for her to get called out at night, which allowed her to use comp time and attend Loose Threads every now and then.

"You should be able to go into your studio in about an hour, give or take," she said. "Quilts can be repaired. Just be glad you weren't here when these clowns showed up."

HARRIET WALKED INTO THE STUDIO AND FLICKED THE OVERHEAD LIGHT ON. SHE AND AIDEN had gone to his apartment, where she'd helped him clean up the cut on his head and then applied butterfly strips. He assured her he was a quick healer and that in a few days no one would even know he'd been beaten with a sprinkler.

The workroom was a riot of color as they entered; but instead of a complementary arrangement of pattern and shape, the scene was harsh and discordant. Pastels fought with crayon colors and muddy browns and grays. Quilts were strewn everywhere, their bindings hanging like Spanish moss from the edges. The shelf cubicles were empty. The box of show quilts had been upended, and the remains were all over the floor. Carry bags of all types littered the space.

She went to the show quilts first. She picked up Connie's bright sherbet-colored one and held it up. It had picked up a few thread clippings from the floor, but it seemed otherwise intact. She folded it and laid it on the seat of the wing chair. Jenny's purple quilt just needed its binding reapplied on one side. It, too, got folded and placed on the chair.

DeAnn's hadn't fared as well. She had done a simple eight-pointed star block called *Peaceful Hours*. It had a second set of smaller points that surrounded a center octagon. Both sets of points were densely stitched, which allowed the octagon to puff up. Several of the octagons had been cut open. DeAnn could repair the tears and applique a motif in the octagons, but sewing small shaped fabric pieces over a background fabric with stitches that were essentially invisible was slow, painstaking work under ideal conditions. Performing the technique as a method of covering damaged fabric would be difficult, and it was unlikely it could be accomplished in time for the show.

Two seams had been split open on Robin McLeod's log cabin quilt, but again, it was damage that could be repaired.

There didn't seem to be a rhyme or reason to the carnage. Some quilts were shredded beyond recognition while others were barely touched, as if the attacker had tired of ripping them up partway through.

"I need to call the Loose Threads," she said with grim determination.

"You know it's almost eleven o'clock, right?" Aiden pointed out.

"Trust me, they won't care. I'm supposed to take their quilts to the show tomorrow. They're going to want all the time available to fix the damage, if that's even possible."

She looked around the floor, found the phone and then the phone book. She dialed Mavis Willis first. Mavis hadn't lost anything in the carnage, but besides Avanell she was the only group member Harriet had known for more than a couple of weeks. She was sure Mavis would know who should be called tonight and how to break the news of what had happened. Besides, with the contents of her desk in the mix on the floor, she'd need Mavis to fill in some last names and phone numbers.

"Honey, you just hang on while I throw on some clothes and grab my stitching bag. I'll be right over," Mavis said as soon as she heard the news.

"She's on her way," she told Aiden and hung up.

"I tried to call my mom again while you were on the phone," Aiden said and flipped his cell phone shut. "It's weird. She's not answering anywhere."

"Maybe she's working late," Harriet said. "The reason she didn't go to the Chamber dinner tonight was so she could work. Maybe she's still there."

"I guess. She must be out in the factory and can't hear the phone. It's just weird. Mom has to look behind the shower curtain to make sure no one is in the house after dark when she's home alone. It's hard to imagine her in the factory by herself. And it's not like her to be out of touch."

"Maybe she's not alone." Harriet didn't want to point out that his mother might have found a boyfriend in the three years he was out of the country.

Chapter Eleven

DARCY CAME THROUGH THE DOOR FROM THE KITCHEN TO THE STUDIO.
"We'll need to get fingerprint samples from you both for exclusionary purposes," she said. "It'd be good if we could get prints from your aunt, too."

"I think she had to be fingerprinted when she signed up to teach quilting at the middle school," Harriet said.

"I'll check when we get back to the lab, but that would help if she did."

"How does the rest of the house look?"

"Not too bad, actually. The studio was clearly the focus of the attack. A few drawers and closets were dumped, but it looks like they didn't do much more than pass through most of the rooms. I tried to wipe the print powder up as we went but watch for it. We don't need that on the quilts on top of everything else."

"Oh, my God," Mavis said from the outside door. She picked up the brass bells that lay silent on the floor and hung them in their customary place on the doorknob. She crossed the room and pulled Harriet into a warm hug. "Oh, honey, I'm so sorry."

Harriet felt stiff in her arms. She wondered what she was supposed to do—stand like a sack of flower and let the air be squeezed out of her? Or was she supposed to squeeze back? How did one accomplish that when their arms were being pinned to their sides?

Mavis released her. "Jenny should be here any minute. Connie is babysitting her granddaughter while her daughter works the night shift at the Best Western in Port Angeles. She'll come as soon as her daughter picks up the little one. I left a message for Robin, and talked to DeAnn, who will be along soon, also." She turned back to survey the room and seemed to notice Aiden for the first time. "What happened to you?" she asked.

Aiden had changed his bloody shirt and washed his face, but he still had an impressive-looking gash on his forehead.

"She hit me," he said, and pointed at Harriet.

"Well, you must have needed it," she said. She turned to survey the room again. She picked up a shoebox-sized plastic bin and handed it to him. "Here, pick up spools of thread and put them in this box." She moved to the cutting table. "Let's take a good look at each quilt and then sort them by what type of repair they need. We can separate the show quilts from the rest, too."

Jenny arrived and joined them. The women spoke only when they needed to discuss the disposition of an item. Aiden picked up all the thread then started on scissors, pins, cutters and other small tools. A sense of calm returned to the room.

"Anyone want coffee or tea?" he asked as he discovered the electric hot water pot. "The cups in here are toast, but I could go look in the kitchen."

"I think that's a splendid idea, honey," Mavis said. She looked at Harriet.

"Sure," she said. "Cups are to the right of the sink, or at least they used to be. I'll come with you." She folded Connie's quilt and set it on the pile that had come through the night's ordeal unscathed. She followed Aiden into the kitchen.

He had found the coffee mugs and was opening cabinets looking for coffee and tea when she came in.

"The coffee is in the refrigerator," she said. "And the tea is in the cabinet to the left." She pointed. "I'm going to look for a tray in the hall closet."

She stepped into the hall just as a streak of grey flashed down from the bookcase and raced up the stairs.

"Fred," she called. "Here, kitty." She headed for the stairs.

"He'll probably do better if you just leave him alone for a while," Aiden said from the kitchen doorway. "Cats don't usually like help with their problems."

Harriet resented the implication that an outsider might know more about Fred than she did. On the other hand, she had to admit that most of the emotional support in her relationship with Fred had been one-way. She turned back, got a tray from the closet and went back into the kitchen.

"He'll probably be fine tomorrow," Aiden offered.

"No, he won't," she said. "He will never be fine again. His sense of security, which wasn't very good after the move anyway, will be gone. And he'll blame me."

Aiden looked at her. He grabbed a handful of teabags and put them on the tray along with six mugs. "I have a headache where I got clubbed, thanks for asking," he said.

Harriet took the tray and headed for the studio. "You'll probably be fine tomorrow."

"Dios mio!" Connie said as Harriet walked over to the cutting table and set the tray down. "What happened?"

"A rival gang of quilters wanted to insure a win," Aiden said, and tipped the piecrust table back onto its feet. He put the electric kettle on it and plugged it in. "Tea anyone?"

Connie ignored him. "What do you think happened?" she asked Harriet.

"I wish I knew. I can't imagine my aunt having enemies, and I don't think enough people even know I'm here for me to be a target. So far, it doesn't look like anything big has been stolen. The sewing machines are here, the TV, VCR and computer are all here. It really does look like the quilts were the target."

Connie raised her eyebrows, "Maybe Lauren really does want to insure a win."

"Come on," Mavis said. "Let's not start any rumors."

"Okay, so what do we have here?" Connie asked.

"Harriet and I are sorting quilts," Mavis said. "I think we've found all the show entries. The two piles on the cutting table are the barely damaged and the really hurting. Jenny is dividing the damaged ones into categories according to type of repair. The ones in the chair seem to be okay. They need to be checked a second time and dusted off if they were on the floor."

"I'll work on reattaching binding. Those quilts have a chance of making it." With that, Connie grabbed a pastel floral-blended quilt and started pinning the binding back into place.

DeAnn arrived, and the women settled in to some serious stitching. Aiden stayed another hour picking up tools, spools and broken glass.

"Before I forget, I've got my mom's quilt in my car. Should I bring it in?" he asked.

Harriet nodded.

The dry cleaners had gotten most of the bloodstains out, and where they hadn't it looked like part of the dye pattern.

"At least one person in the group will have a repair-free entry," DeAnn said.

Aiden shot a panicked glance at Harriet, and then looked relieved when she kept silent.

"Is there anything else you ladies would like me to do before I go?"

"Unless you can sew binding with an invisible stitch, I guess not," Mavis said.

Harriet walked him to the door. "Thanks for your help tonight. And I am sorry about your head. I'll pay if you want to go to the doctor."

"I am the doctor. Besides, I've been in Africa, remember? This is just a scratch." He lowered his voice to a whisper and looked intently at her with those big pale eyes. "Thanks for your help with my mom's quilt." He held her gaze a moment longer then turned and walked out the door and got in his car.

Harriet took a deep breath and shut the door behind him. A slight flutter awakened in her stomach, but she pushed it down as quickly as it had appeared.

The women stitched for two more hours, fixing everything that could be salvaged without extensive reworking. DeAnn's quilt was a total loss, but she said she had one she'd made for her sister but had not yet mailed off she could substitute. Harriet agreed to pick it up on her way to Tacoma.

Mavis stood up and stretched. "I think we've done all we can here," she said. "Try to get some sleep before you leave."

"You want me to stay here with you?" Connie asked. "Give me a pillow and a quilt, and I'm good to go."

Harriet was touched.

"No, but thanks. The police are going to drive by every hour. And Darcy gave me a door alarm to hang on my bedroom doorknob. She uses it when she travels."

After crawling into bed late one night when she'd returned from girl's night at the movies and rubbing her foot up Steve's cold dead shin, she'd needed several years of therapy just to be able to sleep in a bed again. Several more years with the shrink, and she'd learned that sleep is a great way to escape anything and everything. Probably not Dr. Weber's idea of a successful outcome, but the net result was the same.

The women left, and Harriet turned off the lights in the studio and went upstairs. When she came out of the bathroom in her pajamas, Fred was lying on her pillow. She set her alarm and crawled into the flannel sheets. In spite of everything, she fell into a deep, dreamless sleep almost immediately.

Chapter Twelve

A FURRY HEAD BUTT WOKE HARRIET UP A HALF-HOUR BEFORE HER ALARM WOULD HAVE gone off at the ungodly hour of five-thirty a.m. Four hours of sleep had left her feeling as though wet sweatsocks had been stuffed into her head. Her eyes felt swollen, and her mouth was dry.

The night's excitement had apparently had the opposite affect on Fred. He was hungry and ready to start his day. She pushed him off the bed, but he jumped right back onto her chest and started licking her eyelids.

"Can't you be a normal cat and hole up somewhere for hours if not days to recover from your trauma?" she asked him. "Food is not the answer to everything." She wasn't sure how well she could sell that one, since she tended toward chocolate ice cream and M&M's in a crisis. "Come on, let's go see if we can find your food."

She pulled the plaid flannel robe Aunt Beth had loaned her on over the Oakland A's T-shirt that doubled as a nightshirt in her wardrobe. Fred wove in and out of her legs as she headed for the stairs.

He was in luck—the food cabinets in the kitchen were untouched. His bowl proved a little harder to find. There was a puddle on the placemat where his water dish had been.

She finally found the dishes under the dining room table. She could imagine her thief kicking them in frustration. Good, she thought. I hope he was real frustrated.

Now that she'd had a little rest, she was mad. The beautiful quilts her friends had made for the show had been vandalized for no apparent reason, and her aunt's studio—*her* studio—had been trashed. And she hadn't done anything to deserve it.

She fed Fred then called the police station. She was ready for some answers. Unfortunately, no one was ready to provide them. The desk sergeant assured her no one knew anything more than they had last night, and that they were doing everything that could be done to find out who was responsible. He also suggested she might want to call her insurance person.

Harriet made a mental note to call Bill Young when she got back. She didn't know what kind of coverage Aunt Beth had, but in Foggy Point, if you had insurance you bought it from Bill.

She ate a quick bowl of cereal then went into the studio to box up the show quilts. She grabbed a can of Dr. Pepper from the six-pack she'd kept hidden in her car until her aunt had departed. She hid them behind the orange juice in the refrigerator, just in case the diet police had the box bugged. She was trying to cut back on caffeine, but she'd earned this one.

The Loose Threads had gotten the quilts repaired and put back in their various carry bags, but she needed to find the show entry forms each person had filled out.

It was a shock all over again to walk into the studio. Aiden had picked everything up off the floor, but books, papers, batting and scraps of fabric were piled on every available flat surface, waiting for her to make some sense of them. She picked up a pile of papers and sat in the wing chair and started sorting.

It took most of an hour, but she found forms for all the entrants save one—Avanell's was missing. She thought back over the sequence of events the night before. Aiden had brought his mother's quilt into the studio just before he left for the night. She couldn't quite remember if she had seen a sheet of paper with it or not.

She was reluctant to call Aiden before seven in the morning after keeping him up so late. Besides, she was beginning to feel a little guilty about hitting him in the head with the sprinkler. In the end, she decided that, after a quick shower, she'd swing by the Vitamin Factory and have Avanell fill out a new entry. Avanell had told her at lunch she'd made a practice of arriving thirty minutes before her factory workers, no matter what. She claimed it had curbed an epidemic of tardiness a few years back, and she'd found the quiet time at the start of her day so useful, she'd just kept it up. Harriet hoped she wouldn't mind an intrusion.

With the quilts safely stowed on the backseat of her Honda and the paperwork on the passenger seat beside her purse, Harriet locked the house and studio and drove through the grey light of dawn to the Vitamin Factory.

There were two cars in the parking lot when she pulled into a visitor spot near the door marked OFFICE. She recognized Avanell's silver Mercedes. Harriet was surprised there weren't more cars. She certainly wasn't an expert on manufacturing, and she was probably being simplistic, but if Avanell was having trouble finding employees and the factory was falling behind schedule, shouldn't there be some people here working overtime? And shouldn't there be some underling sharing the burden? And what about her business-partner brother? If only Aunt Beth were here, Harriet thought. She probably would have some answers.

IT SHOULD ONLY TAKE A FEW MINUTES TO GET AVANELL'S SIGNATURE ON THE FORM, AND she could be on her way. She stepped through the door. A plain young woman with long sandy hair and freckles sat at a scarred wooden desk.

"Can I help you?" she said in a voice that made it clear she would rather do anything but. She chewed a tired wad of gum and slowly flipped the pages of a magazine.

"I need to speak to Avanell," Harriet said.

"I haven't seen her yet today."

"Isn't that her car in the parking lot?"

The woman kept her eyes on the magazine that was clearly more interesting than Harriet's questions. "Silver Mercedes? Yeah, that's hers. Maybe she's in the back. Sometimes she helps out in shipping this time of the month."

"Could you check for me?"

"They're too cheap to have an intercom here. You're welcome to go back and check yourself if you want. Just go through that door and follow the smell of vitamins." She pointed at a blue door marked "Employees Only."

"Thanks for your help," Harriet said and knew her sarcasm was lost on the girl.

"No problem," she said without looking up.

The door opened into a hallway. A large glass window on the right revealed an employee locker room; identical white smocks floated like ghosts on a garment rack. The shelf above it held what looked like fabric shower caps. On the opposite wall was a bank of grey gym-style lockers with combination locks hanging from their clasps. A wooden bench cut the room in half. Assorted pairs of white shoes were lined up underneath. She could almost imagine the workers who would inhabit the costumes within the hour.

She wondered if she would be contaminating their space if she walked out into the production area in her street clothes. She could have gone back and asked the receptionist but was pretty sure it would be a waste of time.

Another blue door led into the vitamin processing room. Large funnel-shaped bags hung over narrow conveyer belts full of brown bottles that snaked through the area. A metal contraption that resembled a giant stamp hovered over the end of the conveyer. A large box of white safety caps sat on the floor next to a table with three chairs around it. Open boxes of surgical gloves were scattered throughout. This was obviously where vitamins were bottled and sealed.

Avanell was not in evidence, so Harriet crossed the room and exited through the door opposite the one she'd come in. She was in a short hallway. Restrooms were to the left. The first room to the right held printing and labeling equipment. The lights were off.

She chose the second door on the right. It opened into the large, high-ceilinged room that was the packing and shipping area as well as warehouse space.

"Avanell?" she called.

A single light fixture illuminated a corner at the back of the building. Harriet headed toward it. The warehouse had a concrete floor, and the heels of her shoes made a loud clacking noise that echoed off the rafters.

"Avanell," she called again.

She stopped. The silence was deafening. A compressor started. She resumed her path toward what she hoped was Avanell.

"Hello?" she said in a louder voice. "Avanell?"

She arrived at the lighted corner. A large worktable was surrounded by stacks of boxes. A single chair was pushed back from the lone workstation. She came around the end of the table.

"Avanell!" she screamed.

Avanell Jalbert lay collapsed on the cold cement floor. It was as if an unseen puppet-master had abruptly cut her strings. Harriet dropped to her knees, avoiding the red stain that extended like a dark halo around Avanell's head

"Oh, Avanell," she whispered. "What happened to you?"

A thin thread of blood had trickled from the corner of her mouth and joined the congealed pool under her head. Harriet looked away and fumbled in her pocket for her cell phone. She dropped it, and when she picked it up again, her hand was shaking so hard she had to punch the numbers in three times before she connected to the 911 operator.

"You have to come to the Vitamin Factory now," she said. "Avanell Jalbert is dead…Of course, I'm sure." She reached toward Avanell; by sheer force of will, she touched the outstretched hand. She recoiled. It was cold, the fingers unbending. She fought to calm her lurching stomach. Avanell was definitely dead.

She told the operator to send the paramedics to the back of the factory and then hung up to wait. She stood and moved a few steps away. A horrible feeling of déjà vu washed over her. She wished she was a strong enough person to hold Avanell's cold hand until someone arrived, but all the therapy in the world wouldn't have made that possible.

It was while she was avoiding looking at Avanell that Harriet noticed her friend's purse lying on the floor. It was upside down, its contents in a pile on the floor. She looked back at Avanell, and saw the rayon lining of her left skirt pocket sticking out. Someone had searched her after they killed her.

For the second time in twenty-four hours, Harriet heard the sound of Foggy Point's police sirens approaching. The factory was soon engulfed by a rush of firemen, paramedics and police. Avanell was quickly pronounced dead and the warehouse declared a crime scene. Harriet was hustled back to the front office. She'd given a brief statement to the uniformed officer who had arrived first and been asked to wait for the major crimes detectives.

She was sitting on one of the three cracked vinyl chairs in what passed for a waiting room when a squat man in an expensive suit and fake tan arrived. The family resemblance was unmistakable. This had to be Avanell's business-partner brother, Bertrand de LaFontaine.

"What's going on here?" he demanded. His left forefinger nervously spun a heavy gold band on his ring finger. His graying hair was thin and styled in a comb-over. It was damp, as if he'd just gotten out of the shower. "Clarice said there was a problem and I should come right away."

Clarice must have been the helpful young woman Harriet had met on her way in. She was nowhere to be found now.

Bertrand de LaFontaine looked at her. She gestured at the employee door; and he went through it, opening it so fast it banged against the wall as he did.

She was still waiting for the major crimes detectives when Darcy Lewis arrived.

"Boy, you're keeping me busy tonight," she said without humor. "Is it true that Avanell is the victim?"

A nod was all Harriet could manage. Tears filled her eyes.

"I'm sorry," Darcy said. "It's just this job. Avanell was my friend, too. Did you find her?"

Harriet nodded again.

"That must have been awful for you, especially after last night. Do you want me to call anyone for you?"

"No, that's okay. Besides, Aunt Beth is still on her cruise. Do you have any idea how long I have to wait?"

"Are you waiting for the major crimes guys?" She looked at her watch. "They were just going out on a call when I got in last night. That's why I'm here this morning. There was a big drug bust over in Port Angeles that was some kind of interagency thing, so a bunch of our people are over there. I'll bet you can go. Just give your phone number to Briggs before you leave. I'll send him up here. He has to clear the area so we can get started anyway."

Darcy opened the employee door, and Harriet was alone again. She stood up and paced the length of the small waiting area. She searched her pockets for a tissue. She looked on Clarice's desk, but if the woman used tissues, she didn't share them.

Behind the reception desk, she could see two open office doors. She turned away and completed another circuit of the waiting area. On her next pass, she circled the desk and peered into the right-hand open door. A brass nameplate on the dark cherry desk read "Bertrand de LaFontaine."

A brown print box on the matching credenza behind his desk showed promise. Harriet stepped in. The box was empty.

Bertrand, she decided, must be one of those executives who didn't leave work until every piece of paper had been dealt with—all the polished wood surfaces were bare. If he had a wife or kids, they weren't represented here by photos.

A small occasional table sat between two upholstered chairs. It held a two-month-old travel magazine and the previous day's *New York Times*. She turned to the back wall. A small framed oil painting leaned neatly on the floor. Above it, a slightly smaller metal door hung open. She looked inside, being careful not to touch the door. The chamber was empty. If there had been anything in the safe, it was gone now.

She crossed the room, backed out of the office and pulled the door partially closed with her toe.

The left-hand door out of the reception area had to be Avanell's office. Harriet looked around one more time then stepped in. Avanell's desk had stacks of papers lined up along the front edge. Gold frames holding an assortment of photos of three children in various stages of growth were scattered over the bookcases, desktop and hung on the wall. There were wedding pictures and baby pictures featuring the older two children, and one of Aiden standing in front of a small cement building, surrounded by smiling black children. Harriet picked it up. It must have been taken where he worked in Uganda. She held it closer. His eyes were different. She couldn't be sure, but in the picture they looked brown.

At the back of the office another door stood open. She could see her elusive target sitting on a vanity table in what must be an executive restroom. She helped herself to a tissue from a shell-covered box.

The bathroom was larger than the one in Aunt Beth's master suite. In addition to the vanity, Avanell had a tub, shower and commode, a clothes closet and all the supplies a person could ever need to freshen up. A loveseat-sized sofa in soft peach velvet sat in a niche between the closet and the shower wall. A hand mirror lay broken on the surface of the vanity. A pink plastic hairbrush lay beside it, crumbs of glass imbedded in its rubber coated handle.

Harriet stepped to the toilet to flush her tissue. The bottom of the bowl held an assortment of pills. She recognized the characteristic rusty brown of ibuprofen tablets. Small white pills that might have been aspirin were dissolving into the water. She looked in the waste basket beside the toilet. Several empty bottles were inside. She took a second, more critical look around the room. Nothing major was out of place, but clearly someone had rifled through Avanell's things.

On the floor, a pincushion shaped like a woman's summer hat held glass-headed pins and several pre-threaded needles. Harriet picked it up and set it on the table next to a ceramic mug that advertised a Las Vegas casino she'd never heard of.

Scraps of red backing fabric and a piece of print binding were scattered on the floor—Avanell had probably sat in here to finish stitching it on her quilt.

The quilts! she screamed in her head. She had until two this afternoon to deliver them. She instantly felt guilty for thinking of the show when Avanell lay dead in the warehouse. She had to think.

She heard the muffled sound of a door.

Harriet had just returned to her plastic chair when the patrolman returned to the reception area.

"Darcy said I should get your name and number so you can leave."

"Yes, I'd appreciate being able to wait somewhere other than here."

He handed her a pad to write her name and number on.

"So, what's happening in the back?" she asked.

"Nothing, really. Darcy and Ed will be taking pictures for a while. They'll gather all the evidence they need before the body is moved. Then the paramedics will move the body to the medical examiner's office. Until they finish, we all just wait."

"Who's notifying her family?"

"Well, Bertie's in the back. He's her brother. He's been in the next room on his cell phone. I assume he's calling everyone who needs to be notified."

Harriet turned to leave but was blocked by the bulky form of Mavis Willis.

"Come here, honey," she said and pulled Harriet into another of her bear hugs. "Darcy called and told me what happened. You want to sit down? You look a little pale."

"I'm fine," she said, but knew she'd never be fine again. "I need to get the show quilts to Tacoma."

"I figured as much. That's really why I came. You shouldn't be driving alone after a shock like this. I'll come with you."

"Thank you," she said, grateful for the unexpected company.

They left the building; Mavis got her purse from her car and climbed into the passenger seat of Harriet's. She picked up the stack of entry forms.

"Oh, no!" Harriet said as she got in. "What do we do about Avanell's entry?"

"What's to do?" Mavis said. "She entered it in the show. In her mind, her quilt was there as soon as she handed it off. She deserves one last win."

"There's one tiny problem," Harriet said. "Aiden brought the quilt, but he didn't give me the form."

"Well, we'll just have to go get it."

"But his mother just died."

"That boy knows how important his mama's quilting was to her. He's going to want her to have this win. You just drive over there."

Harriet didn't have the energy to argue. She drove to his apartment over the vet clinic. Mavis pounded on the door until a sleepy Aiden appeared. It was clear from his demeanor his uncle hadn't called him yet.

Mavis spoke for a minute and then followed him to his car. He leaned into the backseat and rummaged around, waving a sheet of paper when he stood back up.

"Here it is," he said.

He came to Harriet's car and handed it to her through her open window. "I guess I forgot this last night," he said. He gazed intently into her eyes. "What's wrong?" he asked and put his hand on her shoulder. She could feel it burn through the fabric of her T-shirt. She fought the tears that were building.

Breathe, she told herself.

"We better get going," Mavis said as she clicked her seatbelt into place.

Harriet backed out of the driveway onto Main Street and pointed her car toward the highway.

"I feel terrible just leaving him like that."

"It isn't your place to tell him about his mom. Bertrand will call Michelle, Aiden's sister, and she'll come take care of Aiden. She lives in Seattle. The news will keep until then."

"Why won't Bertrand tell him?"

"Bertrand and Aiden don't really get on well. Avanell tried, but Aiden resented anyone trying to take his father's place. Michelle and Marcel were older when their dad died. I wouldn't say it was easier on them, but they were old enough to be naturally separating from their parents. Besides, George had been so thrilled when Aiden was born. It was like a second chance for him. He'd been so busy building the business when the other two were born he made it all up with Aiden. He didn't miss a minute of that boy's childhood."

"I just feel so bad for him."

"Yeah, but what can you do? His mama's dead and you can't bring her back. Waiting a few more hours to hear the news isn't going to change anything."

Chapter Thirteen

H ARRIET FELL SILENT. MAVIS PULLED OUT A SMALL BAG OF HAND-STITCHING FROM THE pocket of her coat and busied herself sewing small pre-cut pink squares to green fabric triangles.

She broke the silence when she finished the block. "Did you have a chance to look at the other entries?"

"No, I didn't. By the time we got everything repaired and cleaned up, there wasn't time to do anything but put them in their carry bags and pack them in boxes."

"Your aunt and I usually hang the Loose Thread quilts once they check them in. They have people available, but they don't mind having the help. One year your aunt's quilt was hung upside down, and Betty Swearingen's ended up with a permanent hole in the corner another time. We just took to hanging them ourselves. We should be in the back by the concession stand this year. This show has a popular vote award along with the judged categories, so, to be fair, they try to rotate who gets the front spot among the group entries."

Quilt shows could vary quite a bit. Some were held in actual exhibit halls that had some level of accommodation for the display of goods. Others were held in churches, libraries, granges and other less than ideal locales. Bigger shows had business entities that managed all aspects of the event, from judging to food service. The Tacoma show, like most regional shows, was run by the local guild, which meant the administration and the judging panel varied from year to year, making it a much debated event both before and after the ribbons were awarded.

Harriet followed the hand-drawn map Aunt Beth had left her to the X that marked the exhibit hall. It was a large cement block building painted pale green. She pulled into a spot by a side door marked "deliveries only."

Mavis pulled a collapsed wire cart from the back of the car and popped its sides into the open and locked position. Harriet loaded the first group of quilts and wheeled them into the exhibit hall. Mavis brought the paperwork.

A tall blond woman in a blue denim jumper over a pale yellow T-shirt greeted them. An embroidered name patch claimed her name was Jeri, and Harriet had no reason to doubt it.

Jeri looked at the entry forms Mavis handed her.

"Okay, let me see." She ran her finger down a list of names on the clipboard she was holding. "You have eight entries in The Loose Threads group exhibit and four in the individual category."

"Wait a minute," Harriet said. "That should be nine in the group and three individual entries."

"No, one of your group called this morning and asked to have her quilt hung at the front of the hall. I told her we couldn't shuffle the group entry positions. She told me her entry was going to be a contender for best of show and asked what she had to do to get it hung at the front entrance, and I told her that if she entered it in the individual category she could have the spot at the side of the front entry. She asked to have that change made." She shrugged. "She seemed pretty determined."

"Let me guess who," Harriet said.

"Lauren Sawyer?" Mavis suggested.

"I believe that's right," Jeri said, and found the name on her list. "Yes, Lauren Sawyer." She handed Mavis a printed list with the locations for each of the individual entries and the area for the group exhibit.

"Let's put the group quilts up first. Then we can deal with the award winner," Mavis said.

Harriet agreed, and they spent the next two hours arranging the Loose Threads exhibit so that each person's work complemented the one next to it. Avanell's distinctive piece was at the center of the display.

"Why don't we put up these last four and then come back to the group display and see if we still like it?" Harriet said.

"Good idea." Mavis picked up two of the bagged quilts and handed her the other two. "Let's do Lauren's last."

The first three displays were straightforward, and finally, they had only Lauren's left. Mavis pulled it out of its pillowcase and handed two corners to Harriet. She took the other two corners, and they opened the quilt.

"Oh, my gosh," Harriet said. "Is she delusional?"

The quilt top featured cats in various poses. The problem was, other than color, they bore the distinctive look of Kathy the Kurious Kitty. Kathy was the signature character in a children's book series by Su Kim.

"Does she really think changing the color makes the design hers?"

"Apparently," Mavis said. "We tried to tell her, but all she did was change the eye shape slightly. I'm surprised her publisher is willing to print them."

"Kathy the Kurious Kitty isn't as well known as Mickey Mouse or Snoopy, but jeez, she's in, like, fourteen books. That's got to count for something."

"Even if the cats *were* her original design, I have a hard time believing the judges would choose this quilt for best in show or, for that matter, would make it a winner in any category. It's sort of like how the Oscars never go to a comedy or children's movie." Mavis shook her head. "She just doesn't get it. Are you up for some lunch before we go back?"

"That sounds good," Harriet said. "I heard two women from the Seattle Stitchers talking about a place called The Tea Leaf. They seemed to think it has the best Chinese food in Tacoma."

"Well, let's go find it."

IT WAS AFTER THREE WHEN HARRIET PULLED INTO THE PARKING LOT OF THE VITAMIN Factory. Yellow crime scene tape flapped in the late-afternoon breeze. A lone Foggy Point police car sat in the visitor's parking lot.

"You go home, curl up with a good book and a cup of tea," Mavis said. "And try not to think about this."

Harriet waited until Mavis was in her own car and had started it before pulling out of the parking lot.

Fred was waiting in the kitchen when she came into the house and put her keys and purse on the counter.

"Anyone call while I was gone?" she asked him.

He walked to his dish and sat. She picked up the phone and dialed in the retrieval code then cradled the handset between her ear and shoulder so she could fill his food dish as she listened.

There were two messages that began, "This is not a solicitation." Anything that began with that disclaimer was sure to be a sales call. Harriet double-clicked the three button to skip to the end then erased them, unheard.

The third message was Aunt Beth.

"Just wanted to let you know I made it to England and spent two glorious days with your cousin Heather, and now she is about to drive me to the ship to begin the cruise. I know things are going well for you. I'll call again when we are under way. Love you, baby."

Why did Aunt Beth have to be so far away? Harriet wanted to scream into the phone. Things weren't going well at all. She'd let someone break into the studio, and then found Aunt Beth's best friend dead.

She was still thinking about Aunt Beth and was halfway through a message from Marjory Swain before she realized it. She replayed the message. According to Marjory, a group of women met at Pins and Needles once a month to stitch quilts for charity. Fabric suppliers donated bolts of fabric for local women to make into baby quilts that were then distributed to several agencies that worked with teen mothers. Over time, the project had evolved into a quilting group for unwed mothers. Apparently, Aunt Beth did the machine stitching for the young women and, in fact, had a collection of their work that was supposed to have been delivered to Marjory for tonight's meeting.

"I know you've had a rough time, what with the break-in and Avanell and all," she said, "but these girls are coming tonight to bind their baby blankets, and they are all so fragile. I hate to postpone it."

Harriet groaned. Last night everyone was concentrating on getting the show pieces ready for delivery. No attempt was made to sort out the rest.

"Come on, Fred," she said. "We've got work to do."

Chapter Fourteen

Aₗₗₗₗₗ...

A LITTLE OVER AN HOUR LATER HARRIET HAD FOUND NINE BABY QUILTS. SHE CALLED Marjory and agreed to bring the blankets to the store at seven. That gave her just enough time to eat. After the delicious Chinese lunch she'd had, she probably should march into the kitchen and make a big bowl of lettuce, but she didn't really feel like preparing food in there until she'd had a chance to scrub it from top to bottom, purging all signs of the break-in.

Aunt Beth had several large fabric tote bags that were perfect to carry the baby quilts in. Harriet bagged them and stashed them in the backseat of the Honda. She pulled on the fisherman knit sweater Aunt Beth had bought her and grabbed her purse and drove through a sputtering rain down the hill and onto Main Street. She parked in front of Pins and Needles.

The Sandwich Board didn't serve dinner, so she would have to explore downtown to find another option. When she'd lived with Aunt Beth as a child, she'd begged to eat at the Dairy Queen and McDonald's out on the highway. In those days, the ethnic food options in Foggy Point were limited to Chin's Chinese Food. She was glad to see things had changed. She passed a Thai restaurant and a sushi place but rejected them as being too similar to lunch. She was walking on tiptoe, leaning toward the street trying to see what was in the next block, when she hit a brick wall. Her purse fell to the sidewalk, spilling her cell phone and car keys in the process.

Warm hands grasped her by the shoulders.

"I'm sorry," she said. "I was trying to look up the block and didn't see you."

She looked up into the pale eyes of Aiden Jalbert. Dark smudges now underscored them. She felt her face turned pink as she took in the dark purple bump on his forehead.

"Here." He bent down and picked up her keys and handed them to her. "What were you looking for?" he asked, his voice flat.

"I was trying to find someplace to eat." She looked at the sidewalk. "I'm sorry about your mom."

"Yeah," he said. "I heard you were the one who found her. Thanks for telling me."

"That's not fair."

"I'm sorry," he said. "You're right. I don't even know you."

"I wanted to tell you," she said, feeling like a child telling tales. "Mavis said it wasn't my place."

"Right."

"I'm sorry."

Aiden sighed. "No, I'm sorry—really. Mavis is right. Finding my mom was bad enough for you. You didn't owe me anything."

Harriet didn't know what to say. When Steve died, she'd lashed out at everyone, and nothing anyone said helped.

"Look," he said, "I was just on my way to Tico's Tacos. You want to eat there?"

"Are you sure?"

"Yeah." He turned and stepped into the crosswalk. "It's right up there, around the corner." He pointed at a small storefront that sported the flag of Mexico. She had to hustle to catch up to his long stride.

The restaurant had three booths and a similar number of tables surrounded with chairs. Aiden led her to the center booth. Harriet closed her eyes and breathed. Her senses were bathed in the scent of baked chilies and marinated beef. Her tensed muscles relaxed.

Aiden nudged her shoulder, breaking her reverie. "Where'd you go?" he asked.

She was spared having to answer when a cook in the back nodded at Aiden and appeared moments later with a stone bowl that overflowed with chunky guacamole.

"Grácias," Aiden said.

"De nada," the man replied.

"I take it they know you here?" Harriet said.

"I went to school with Jorge's son. We hung out here and did our homework and ate guacamole and chips."

"Does he still live around here?"

"No, Julio's an environmental lawyer in Seattle."

Jorge took their orders and refilled their basket of chips. They picked at them in silence until he came back with their dinners.

Harriet's enchiladas were perfect. The green tomatillo sauce was spicy but not hot, and the tortillas were handmade. Aiden's chile relleno was encrusted in a batter that was light and crisp. A clump of whole green beans had been batter-fried and shared a flat bowl that was lined with a cooked tomato sauce.

They ate in silence, a faded pink-and-green donkey piñata hanging from the ceiling, its crepe paper-fringed foot inches from Aiden's head. The music of Banda el Recodo played softly in the background. Harriet snuck a glance at Aiden. His face had aged in the three days she'd known him. New lines creased its tan surface. He absently pushed a stray lock of dark hair out of his face.

"Thank you for steering me to this place," she said when she'd finished her meal. "I have to say, I'm a little surprised you aren't at your mom's. I would have thought the Loose Threads would be smothering you in hot dishes and sympathy."

"That would be the problem. That, and my family. My sister is there with her two kids. They're ten and twelve and spend most of their time fighting. Michelle actually tries to sort out what they're fighting about and ends up arguing with them both. Uncle Bertie is there greeting visitors like some kind of host with the most, and my brother Marcel is supposed to be arriving any time. I couldn't hack it."

"When my husband Steve died, I was so angry at his family I couldn't stand to be in the same room with them."

"I'm not angry. It's just weird. Five days ago I was in a cement hut with no running water and surrounded by poisonous snakes and hyenas. I haven't seen any family except my mom in more than three years. I'm having a little trouble relating to them right now."

It looked like anger to Harriet, but it was obvious he wasn't ready to deal with it. She opened her purse and pulled out her wallet. Jorge was stacking menus by the front entry podium. He shook his head at her.

"Your money is no good," he said in thickly accented English.

"Thank you," she said and looked at Aiden.

"Jorge kind of took over the dad job when mine died. He's more like family than some of my blood relatives." He stood up and stretched. "I don't feel like going home. You want to go for a drive?"

"I wish I could," she said, mostly because she knew she couldn't. "I have to drop some quilts off at a meeting Marjory is having. I'm not sure how long it will take."

"I could go home and feed my dog and then meet you back there."

"Are you sure you want to be with me right now?"

His eyes searched her face.

"I guess you wouldn't have asked if it was an imposition," she said, feeling a need to fill his silence. It was the least she could do for Avanell, she told herself, but admitted instantly this had nothing to do with Avanell.

Aiden walked her back to her car then strode off down the block toward the vet clinic.

The bags of baby quilts were undisturbed. She grabbed both, clicked the Honda's remote lock and entered the store.

A group of young women sat in a semicircle around an easel that held a flannel-board. Marjory had step-by-step samples of binding techniques pinned to it. Marjory, DeAnn and a woman Harriet didn't recognize were in the small room, cutting strips of fabric in pastel colors.

"Hi," Marjory said. "Thanks for bringing the quilts. I know you've got a lot on your plate right now."

"I'm not sure I found all of them. I have nine. I had one more, but I'm pretty sure it wasn't part of this group."

"You did fine. We need six for the girls, and we did have a few more for general donation. I'll be able to recognize them by the fabric—our distributors donate bolts of overstock, and then people bring leftovers from their stash, and we take whatever else we need from the store. They usually have the distributor fabrics for backing. Let me take a quick look." She pulled the quilts out of the bags. "These are them," she said.

Now that Marjory pointed it out, Harriet could see that each of the quilts had one of two fabrics for its back.

"Come meet my girls," Marjory said, and led her to the easel.

"This is Harriet Truman," she said to the group. "Her aunt did the machine stitching on the quilts you just made." She looked at Harriet then turned back to the girls. "We hope after you finish your own quilts and receiving blankets that you'll make at least one to donate to charity. When you do, Harriet here will quilt it for you.

"We're going to wait a few more minutes for a couple of people to arrive. You can come into the kitchen and get something to drink and have a treat before we start."

The girls got up as one and headed toward the food. Marjory stopped Harriet before she left the big room.

"I realized as I was saying it that I'm being a little presumptuous. Beth has always done the quilting for this project, but you are under no obligation to continue to do so."

"Don't give it another thought. Of course, I'll do their quilts." She paused. For as long as I'm here, she thought. "Does that girl with the black hair work at the Vitamin Factory?"

"Yes, she does. She had her baby a couple of years ago, but she's been coming back and helping the others. Lately, she's been bringing another girl with her—Misty, I think, is her name. I've been stalling to give Misty time to get here. I put peanut butter-and-jelly sandwiches and milk out with the cookies. Misty's one who needs to eat as much as she needs to stitch."

Harriet went into the kitchen.

"Carla?" she said. "Hi, I'm Harriet. We met the other day. I was having lunch with Mrs. Jalbert." Carla's gaze was so firmly downcast Harriet had to crook her neck to make eye contact. Her body language screamed whipped puppy and made Harriet wonder what sort of abuse had left her like this— nobody this painfully shy came from a happy loving home.

Carla finally looked up. "Yeah, that was awful, what happened to Miz Avanell." With her boarding school education, Harriet wasn't sure she'd ever get used to the West Coast custom of using first names, even in business situations. After all these years, it was still uncomfortable to her, even with the addition of "Miz."

"Yes, it was." Harriet wasn't sure how widely known it was that she'd been the one to find Avanell, and decided now wasn't the time to share that piece of news. "She told me she was working overtime in shipping. Did she do that often?"

Carla looked at her feet. She hesitated so long, Harriet wondered if she was going to answer.

"She didn't used to, but lately, yeah."

"What made her start?"

"I don't know. It's crazy, but we been shipping vitamins hot and heavy for a couple years. We usually hire temps at the end of the month to try to make our goals. Then all of a sudden, they can't afford to hire temps no more. Tony said they lost money when we had a recall a couple months ago. He said we shipped bad product. They fired our lead guy, Mack, and since then, Miz Avanell helps us with the shipping after regular hours. It just seems weird."

"What seems weird?" Harriet asked, even though she could think of several possibilities.

"I been working there since I was in high school. One time back then we got a bad batch of potassium tablets. Something had leaked into the package and ruined them. Thousands of 'em. Miz Avanell told us to throw 'em all out. She said they was so cheap it wasn't worth the stamps to mail 'em back. We threw 'em out and just ordered replacements. Nobody got fired or nothing. It's hard to believe prices would have changed that much in a few years."

"That does sound strange."

Carla cast a furtive glance toward the door. "I wish Misty would get here," she said.

"Isn't she the girl who was fired last week?" Harriet asked.

"Yeah, and now I can't find her."

"What do you mean?"

"She left Monday. Miz Avanell sent the sheriff home, but Mr. Tony still fired her. I talked to her Tuesday after work and she was talking about coming back to get something she left at work. I told her I didn't think that was such a good idea, but she wouldn't listen. And now I can't find her." She glanced at the clock and sighed. It was a quarter after seven.

"Thanks," Harriet said.

Carla turned and went back into the classroom.

"I'm going to take off," Harriet told Marjory. "I'll come next week."

"Don't worry. You get your studio back together and take care of yourself a little. Then you can worry about charity work."

"Thanks." She gathered her empty bags and went out the door.

Chapter Fifteen

AIDEN WAS LEANING ON THE WINDOWSILL OF THE PRINT SHOP NEXT DOOR TO PINS AND Needles. He stood up and fell into step with Harriet. When she clicked the doorlock on the Honda, he opened the door. She tossed the bags in, and he shut the door again.

"My car is down the block," he said. "That is, if you haven't changed your mind."

"No, if you're willing to get in a small enclosed space with the woman who clocked you with a sprinkler, how can I refuse? And, frankly, my house is a little depressing right now."

"Come on, then."

He turned. She was ready for his ground-eating pace this time and matched him stride for stride. He held open the passenger door on his rental car, and she climbed in. She wondered what she was doing driving off into the night with this unusual young man.

"Anywhere you want to go?" he asked.

She had mixed feelings about being back in Foggy Point. Without her time here with Aunt Beth she would have had no happy memories of childhood, but dropping in and out of a small community several times had not been without its own problems. The last time she left she'd promised herself it was for the last time.

"Not really. As long as it isn't my trashed studio, I'm good."

"Okay." He pulled onto Main Street and headed for the strait. The route took them out of downtown Foggy Point and through an industrial section that included an area of docks. Foggy Point was not by any measure a major shipping port, but ships did dock; and that made this the kind of place you wouldn't want to get a flat tire in if you were alone.

Beyond the docks, the terrain changed to rocky beaches.

"You care if we stop?" Aiden asked.

"Whatever you want is fine."

"Don't ever say that to a guy," he said, but Harriet could tell by the flatness in his voice his heart wasn't into teasing tonight.

He pulled off the road at a wide spot and got out of the car. She followed, and after she shut her door, it was completely dark. Aiden pulled a mini-Maglite from his pocket; it cast a small circle of light.

"Here, give me your hand," he said and grabbed it in his free one. "Be careful," he added.

Good advice, she thought, and once again wondered what she was doing walking on an isolated beach with a man she'd only met two days ago, and who was at least ten years her junior.

He led her to a large flat rock that stuck out toward the water.

"Here, put your foot up here." He pointed the light onto a step-like flat area on the rock. He lit the next one and the next—the rock had three natural steps leading to a broad flat ledge. She sat on the ledge and scooted to her left to make room for him. In two strides, he was beside her, sitting close enough she could feel the heat of his body in sharp contrast to the cool rock.

He turned the light off. Her eyes adjusted, and in the moonlight, she could see the expanse of the Strait of Juan de Fuca in front of her.

"This is amazing," she said.

"I've always come here when I needed to think, or to get away from everyone."

"I've never been here. I didn't even know this rock existed."

"My dad used to bring me here when I was little. It's a good spot to sit and fish. And then, later, I would ride my bike here." He was silent for a long moment. "I just can't believe she's gone now, too," he said. His voice sounded small and far away.

Harriet patted his arm. She wasn't good at this sort of thing. He leaned forward, elbows on knees. She was pretty sure he was crying, but his long hair concealed his face. She rubbed her hand in slow circles across the hard muscles of his back. They sat like that until he had control of his emotions again.

"Come on," he said, and stood up. He stepped down in the dark then guided her. He took her hand and led her back to the car.

They drove in silence until he turned away from the coastline and started up an incline.

"Bertrand said the police think my mom was killed during a robbery," he said at last.

"Is that what you think?"

"I don't know what to think. No one wants to believe their mother was killed because she got in the way of some petty criminal for a few hundred dollars. But I don't have a better answer. Face it. I missed the last three years of my mother's life."

"Don't even go there. Believe me, I've gone down that road, and there's nothing there."

Aiden turned his head to glance at her but didn't ask.

"I don't believe it was a simple robbery," Harriet said. "Something was bothering your mom for several days before..." She trailed off.

"Like what?"

"I'm not sure, but my aunt noticed and asked me to check on her. And she did look like something was going on. I went to lunch with her on Monday, and one of her employees came and got her just when we finished. It was something about a girl getting fired for stealing vitamins. Nothing that seemed like something anyone would get killed over."

He sighed.

"I'm sorry. I wish I could tell you more."

They fell into silence again.

The road rose steeply.

"Do you recognize where we are?" Aiden asked.

"We have to be on my hill. It's the only place this steep on the strait side of the peninsula. But I don't think I've ever been up this side before."

"This road might not have been here when you lived here before. Some developer in Portland had the idea he was going to build a group of McMansions up at the top of the hill."

"Why didn't he?"

"Same reason no one else has ever built there. If that hilltop were build-on-able, you can bet some of the old Foggy Point pirates would have done it. It's too steep."

"Can you get to Aunt Beth's house from here?"

"That's what we're going to find out. I went to your house just after six last night. I read your note, and then I decided that while I was waiting for you to get back, I'd go door to door and see if I could find out who owned the dog I'd carried off. I finally found the family in that pink-and-blue gingerbread house down the street. I talked to them for over an hour, assuring them their dog was fine and talking about aftercare. As I was going back to my car, I saw a buddy of mine from high school. I talked to him for about forty-five minutes. I saw you and your friend drive up your hill, and then saw him come back down, so I went up.

"The point is, no one else went up your hill in all that time. And obviously, no one parked at the bottom and walked in, either, or I would have seen them. I'm guessing trashing your studio took more than the few minutes that must have elapsed between your leaving and me arriving."

"So, they had to have come from the back side of the hill," Harriet deduced. "There are four houses besides Aunt Beth's on our street. After the last house, the street terminates with a guard rail, with a wooded area beyond it."

"Well, let's see how far we can get from this side."

The road narrowed as they climbed the hill. The pavement was riddled with potholes and, eventually, gave way to gravel. They bounced on until the road ended in a small rocky parking area. A trail marker announced an overlook in one-tenth of a mile.

Aiden picked up his MagLite and got out of the car. "You coming?"

Harriet had seen too many slasher films in her youth to be willing to sit in a car alone in a dark, wooded parking lot. She followed him up the path.

The woods opened onto a clearing at the top of the hill. Under other circumstances, she might have stopped to take in the panoramic view of Smugglers Cove and downtown Foggy Point beyond it. Tonight she was more interested in the clearing itself, and what other paths might lead from it.

"Look," she said. "Over there." She pointed to a shadowy area on the opposite side. A gust of wind rattled the old fir trees overhead. Harriet shivered. When she was young she had believed the trees were fighting when they rattled together like that. It still seemed sinister.

Aiden joined her at what appeared to be a path leading down the hill. He shined the light into the dark tunnel in the trees.

"Come on," he said. When Harriet hesitated, he took her hand in his firm grasp and led her down the path.

"Oh, my gosh," she said when a short time later they popped out of the woods at the end of her street. Aiden had pushed a large, low-hanging tree branch out of the way to create the final opening. "So anyone could come and go freely from this street, and the people living here would be none the wiser."

"I'm not sure this helps much. We still don't know who came and went this way, but at least we know how they did it."

"And we know it wasn't a spontaneous act. Someone planned it."

He looked at her. "You didn't really think it was a random act, did you?"

"No, I guess not. That one policeman had suggested it was drug users looking for something they could turn for a quick profit. But they probably would have taken the computer and television if that was the case. I wanted to believe him, because I don't want to think about someone coming back if they didn't get what they were looking for the first time."

"Have you had any ideas about what that might be?"

"Not a clue."

They stood together looking down the street, each lost in their own thoughts.

Aiden snapped the flashlight back on. "We should get back. As much as I don't want to, I've got to face the family."

Harriet wished she could tell him things would be okay but she knew better than anyone the damage lies could do.

Chapter Sixteen

HARRIET SPENT THE FOLLOWING DAY CLEANING AND ORGANIZING HER STUDIO. IN THE morning hours, she folded fabric and quilts and matched them up with their work orders. The afternoon went slower. Thread, pins, chalk pencils and other small notions had been scattered all over the room, as if the thief had thrown a temper tantrum and hurled the containers against the walls. The big spools of thread for the long-arm machine were hopelessly tangled. She cut out the tangles where she could, but in the end several spools had to be thrown out.

She'd spoken to Aunt Beth's insurance man, Bill Young, and he'd asked her to do an inventory of what was missing and damaged, so she dutifully wrote down each lost item.

For his part, Fred chased bobbins around the floor, rolling on his back and tangling his legs in the thread. The third time she had to stop and cut him loose, she picked him up and shut him on the other side of the kitchen door.

She was about to give up and join him when the phone rang.

"How is the clean-up coming?" Mavis asked.

"I've got the big stuff organized, but now it's going a lot slower. I'm down to picking up pins and untangling thread."

"Do you feel like a change of pace?"

"Yes, please, anything."

"Well, if you're up to it, Michelle asked if the Loose Threads could come over and deal with Avanell's stash."

An important part of the quilting process is the collection of a stash. Every serious quilter will make a practice of gathering pieces of fabric for undefined future use. Stash building can be a regular part of their weekly trip to the local quilt store, or can be done scavenger hunt-style by taking tours to various other communities in groups or alone. It's also a critical part of any vacation trip, usually to the dismay of husbands, children or other non-quilting companions. People vary in their approach. Some people collect in half-yard quantities, some in multiple-yard cuts, just to keep their options open. Harriet could only imagine how large a stash someone who had been quilting as long as Avanell would have.

"It's kind of soon, isn't it?"

"Honey, Avanell is dead. Michelle needs to take care of things while she's here. In Loose Threads, we joke about taking care of each other's stash if something happens, but it really isn't a joke. Avanell told her daughter if anything ever happened to her we were to take care of hers. Michelle called me an hour ago and asked if we could come tomorrow. If this is too much for you, just say so and I'll understand."

"No, I'll be there," Harriet said, and tried to make her voice sound like she meant it. "What time should I be there?"

"I told her we'd be there at nine."

"Do I need to bring anything?"

"If you can find any of those cotton project bags your aunt has, you can bring them. When someone passes, we usually finish up any UFO's." Harriet knew that this meant *unfinished objects* in quilter's parlance. "Usually, we know who they were for. If not, we just give them back to the family if they want them, or donate them if they don't."

"Are there really people who don't want their loved one's handwork?" Harriet asked.

"We've only lost two or three people who were still active in the group when they went, and in at least one case, the woman was ninety-three, and she had given her family so many quilts over the years they really had all the keepsakes they needed."

"Is there any word on the memorial service yet?"

"Yes. There will be a viewing on Monday night and then a service at the Unitarian Church Tuesday morning and then the interment following that. Are you going to attend?"

"She was one of my aunt's oldest friends. Since Aunt Beth can't be there, I feel like I should go to represent her."

"Honey, I think people would understand if it was too hard for you."

"No, Aunt Beth is right. I have to start living again, and attending a friend's funeral is an unfortunate part of life."

"I'm glad to hear you say that. Would you like me to pick you up tomorrow?"

The two women agreed on a plan and ended the call.

Harriet knew her aunt was trying to help her move forward with her life, but even Aunt Beth couldn't have envisioned how her plan was going to play out.

SHE WAS CONTEMPLATING DINNER WHEN THE PHONE RANG AGAIN. SHE ANSWERED, AND heard an unfamiliar man's voice.

"Harriet," he said, "it's Harold."

"Harold, how nice to hear from you again," she responded, and wondered if it was true.

"I couldn't help but notice how much you enjoyed the Chamber dinner the other night."

Was the man insane?

"Well, not the event," he went on. "But you did seem to enjoy the food."

That much was true.

"I heard about a new restaurant that opened last week down on Smuggler's Cove. The owner used to be the head chef at the Hilton in Portland. I thought I'd give it a try tonight and, as you appear to be a connoisseur of fine food, wondered if you'd care to join me."

It wasn't the most romantic invitation she had ever received, but since she wasn't interested in romance that suited her.

"Shall I meet you there?"

"I'll be coming from the factory, so I could swing by at seven and pick you up, if that works."

"That will be fine. I'll be ready."

She hung up and went back into the kitchen.

"Come on, Fred," she said, and the cat got up and followed her upstairs. "We have to put together an outfit for our dinner date."

The choices hadn't gotten any better in the last two days. She still had the basic black dress and Aunt Beth's scarves. Aunt Beth had a decidedly different shape than she did, making most of her wardrobe improbable; but Harriet was desperate enough to give it a try.

The floral jersey dresses Aunt Beth favored were a definite no even if they did fit. She passed them by and moved on to the skirts and blouses. She tried a skirt, but it was about three inches short and was too wide in any case.

The blouses showed more promise. She pulled out an off-white silk with a tie collar. She tried it on, twisting the two scarf-like ends of the collar into a bow. She looked at her image in the mirror. The blouse could be worn tunic-style over her sleeveless black shift. She found a soft leather belt on a closet door hook. She wrapped it around her waist and tied it instead of buckling. She twirled in front of the mirror. Her outfit made her look like an executive secretary. Or at least what she imagined an executive secretary would look like. It would be the perfect counterpoint to Harold's business togs.

She took a shower, towel-dried her hair and quickly blew it dry. She dressed and was waiting in her front room when Harold arrived.

"You look lovely," he said when she opened the front door. She handed him the tan trench coat she'd found in the entryway closet. He held it while she slipped it on, overlapping the front and securing the extra width with the belt. If she was going to go out at night, she would have to go shopping, and not at Wal-Mart, either.

She quickly chased that thought from her mind. She wasn't going to be here long enough to need a dating wardrobe.

Harold was the perfect gentleman. He opened and closed doors, made polite small talk about the weather in Foggy Point and drove a consistent five miles under the speed limit. What he didn't talk about was Avanell, the Vitamin Factory or any other topic that might elicit an emotional reaction.

Harriet felt both relief and guilt that he didn't want to discuss Avanell. She'd spent every waking hour since she'd found her obsessing about what she could have done differently that might have changed the outcome. So far, she hadn't come up with anything but a headache.

When they arrived at the restaurant, he had reserved a table by the window. The owner of the restaurant, James, greeted them at the door, surrounded by the faint aroma of baked garlic.

"How nice to see you, Harold," he said. "And who is this vision of loveliness?"

Harold introduced Harriet. He had neglected to mention that he and James had been fraternity brothers. James seemed pleased to see Harold with a date in a way that made her uncomfortable.

James seated them and immediately brought a plate of crostini with a pork liver pate.

"So, tell me about the quilting business," Harold said when James had retreated into the kitchen. "The chamber dinner wasn't really conducive to conversation. You said you work at a studio in your home, but what does that entail?"

Harriet proceeded to tell him all about the long-arm quilting business—or at least as much as she knew about it with her month of experience. He asked intelligent questions and leaned attentively forward as he listened. She explained how her first week on her own in the business was made more difficult by the Tacoma quilt show.

Not wanting to appear self-centered, she asked what he did for fun.

"Calculations," he replied.

"Uh, what sort of calculations?" She tried to think what she could possibly ask as a follow-up.

"Differential equations, usually, although I do branch out into combinatorial analysis sometimes for fun," he replied.

I'm a dead woman, Harriet thought.

"That sounds interesting," she said.

She was saved by James bringing a steaming poached salmon dish to their table. He followed this with roast squab; and then, after a palate-cleansing course of grapefruit sorbet, petit filet mignon with a blue cheese peppercorn sauce. The beef was served with garlic mashed potatoes and sauteed string beans. A salad of fresh wild greens was served after the beef.

Harriet had to assume either Harold or James was a tea-totaler. Italian sparkling water was served at the start of the meal, followed by an excellent French sparkling cider. The usual coffee and tea selections were offered, and they both chose tea.

The flow of food had made conversation not only impossible but also unnecessary. When James offered to bring a dessert tray for their perusal, Harriet spoke up.

"This dinner is the best I've had in years or maybe even in my lifetime, but if I eat another bite, I'll burst. I'd love to come by another time and maybe just have dessert and coffee."

James brightened, and she realized he was thinking she was suggesting another date with Harold.

Harold handed him a charge card.

"I'd like to pay for mine," Harriet said.

"That isn't necessary. Besides, this was my idea. When you invite me out, if you insist, you can pay."

"Thank you, then. The food was truly delicious."

"It's been my pleasure. Now, however, I'm afraid I have to return to work."

Harriet imagined herself flopping onto her bed and lying immobile, reliving the pleasure of the meal until she fell asleep. She couldn't fathom going back to work after a six-course meal.

Harold delivered her to her doorstep at exactly ten o'clock. He got out of the car and walked her up the steps and onto the porch. Any fear about awkwardness at the front door was quickly laid aside. He squeezed her hand, thanked her for coming to dinner and left.

"Fred!" she called. The cat came running downstairs. "Dinner was really, really good, but can you see us with a guy who does differential equations for fun?"

She kicked off her shoes, picked up the cat and went to bed.

Chapter Seventeen

Harriet was in the studio when Mavis arrived the next morning. She'd gathered a bundle of cotton quilt bags, a pad of sticky notes and a couple of markers. She wasn't sure what the usual procedure was for the group, but she believed you could never go wrong with sticky notes and permanent markers.

"Avanell probably has a shocking amount of fabric in her stash," Mavis said when they were settled in the front seat of her powder-blue Town Car. "Most of us have either husbands or budgets that prevent us from going overboard. After Ed died, she had neither. She made plenty of money, and stitching was her only vice."

"So, what do you usually do with the fabric?"

"There is no usual, thank the good Lord, but the Loose Threads are mostly seniors, so the subject naturally comes up now and then. Avanell made it clear that while she was willing to donate a fair share to the charity projects, she wanted her best stuff to go to members of our group who would appreciate it."

The car groaned as it climbed the long, steep road that led to Avanell Jalbert's home. The Queen Anne Victorian house had been built by Cornelius Fogg in 1851; its location overlooking the tip of the peninsula was no accident. It was rumored that, before he became the beloved founder of Foggy Point, Cornelius had been the notorious pirate Silver Beard. Some local historians believed he never gave up his thieving ways but used his ongoing proceeds to fund the development of his namesake.

The house had views of both the hidden inlets of Pirate's Cove and the deepwater channel of the Strait of Juan de Fuca. When Harriet was young, the local children told her there were tunnels from the basement of the house to the cove below. She had eagerly believed the tales back then but as an adult knew that almost every coastal town had rumors of tunnels that were nearly never true.

Jenny's black BMW was already parked in front of the house when Mavis pulled to a stop. Jenny took a large stack of clear plastic bins from the backseat and handed them into Aiden's waiting arms.

"Hi," she called out when Mavis and Harriet got out of the car. "Connie and Robin are inside, and we're still waiting for DeAnn and Lauren."

"What about Sarah?" Mavis asked.

"She had a meeting she couldn't get out of." Jenny rolled her eyes skyward as she said it. "Michelle has us in the upstairs parlor. We were just getting our stuff organized while we were waiting for you."

Aiden carried the boxes into the house, his broad shoulders disappearing as he climbed a narrow staircase off the entry. Jenny followed him up the stairs.

"Hi," said a petite dark-haired woman as she crossed the polished marble entry. "I'm Michelle." She held her hand out. "You must be Harriet."

Harriet took the offered hand. It was cold and hard, and the fingers circled hers in a claw-like grip.

"I'm so sorry about your mother," she said, and had to force herself not to rub her hand to restore the circulation.

"Yes, I understand you were the one who found her." She said it as if it were an accusation.

"Are you coming?" Mavis called from the stairwell. Harriet turned and climbed the stairs, leaving Michelle where she stood.

"Don't let Michelle get to you. She's grown a bit prickly since she left Foggy Point, but she's a good girl under all that."

Harriet wasn't so sure. She'd met dozens of good Foggy Point girls during her childhood whenever her parents got tired of playing the parental role and dumped her here. She had learned that kids can be cruel to anyone who is different, and when you spend your formative years bouncing between the capitols of Europe and Foggy Point, Washington, you were definitely different.

"Harriet," Connie yelled from across the room. "Come here."

Connie met her halfway across the large room and embraced her in a warm hug. It had to be a conspiracy. These women were trying to make up for a lifetime of missed hugs in Harriet's life all in a few weeks.

"Are you getting things straightened out in the studio?" Connie continued without waiting for a reply. "It must have been so awful for you, finding Avanell like that." She patted Harriet's hand. "Come over here." She led her to an ornate sofa table behind a forest green velvet settee. "I brought some tea."

She pulled a cardboard cup from a stack and picked up a black carafe, poured dark liquid into the cup and handed it to her. A spicy aroma invaded Harriet's nose.

"This is my own special blend," Connie said as Harriet took a sip of the orange-flavored tea.

She didn't really like spiced teas, but she smiled and thanked Connie anyway.

"Lauren called and said she was going to be a little late," DeAnn informed them as she joined the group. "Have you started yet?"

"No, we were waiting until everybody was here," Jenny said. "Michelle thought we could set up folding tables in this room to do our sorting."

Aiden chose that moment to arrive.

"Michelle said something about moving furniture for you ladies," he said, his cool gaze on Harriet. She felt heat creeping up her neck.

"If you could move the sofa and table against the wall and then bring down two of those eight-foot folding tables, we can put them end-to-end in the middle of the room and put folding chairs around them," Jenny suggested. "Maybe Harriet can help you with the chairs."

"Will do, chief." Aiden _saluted her. "Come on," he said to Harriet. "Mom's workroom is on the third floor."

He led her down a long hallway that had three closed doors on each side. At the end was a dark flight of steeply pitched stairs.

"Mom used the servant's quarters for her quilting. Apparently, old Cornelius didn't worry too much about his servants' comfort—at least not when he put the stairs in. Michelle was afraid the climb would be too hard for some of the ladies, in case you were wondering why we're dragging everything down to the parlor."

She had been curious but had decided not to ask. The stairs were a hard climb, but they opened onto a spacious landing.

"I'm not sure how many servants the old man had, or even if this was the original configuration of the space, but they seem to have had the whole floor. Mom uses their parlor..." He caught himself. "She used the parlor," he corrected. "Anyway, she had her machines in here, and then back there is a kitchen she used for wet stuff. There are a couple of bedrooms and bathrooms over there."

He pointed toward a short hallway. Harriet wasn't sure what direction they were facing.

"Come over here," he said. "You have to see her office."

He led her to a round room that opened off the parlor. This had to be the tower she'd seen from the outside. The room had windows all the way around. Each window had a stained glass header that had to be Tiffany, or at least one of his imitators. The clear leaded glass pane in the center of each panel revealed an incredible vista. She could see across the strait to Vancouver Island.

She crossed the room. From the opposite side, she could see the cove Aunt Beth's house looked onto, but from a different angle.

Aiden came up behind her. His proximity sent a warming shiver through her. He rested one hand on her left shoulder and pointed over her right with the other.

"See that dark area where the water disappears into the wood?"

"There where it looks like a river or creek or something?" she said, trying to focus on what he was showing her.

"That's where Cornelius kept his pirate ship. Or at least, that's the local legend."

"Do you believe the legend?"

"I believe anything's possible," he said, and with a hand on each shoulder, spun her around.

Harriet was pretty sure they weren't talking about pirates anymore. She lingered a moment longer than she should have then broke away and escaped across the room.

Aiden retreated to the next room, and she heard what she imagined was the sound of folding tables being moved. She took one last look at the view and started to leave the tower.

Avanell's ornately carved dark cherry desk sat in the center of the room. It must have allowed her to enjoy the view without being so close she would be chilled by the draft off the single-pane windows. Harriet couldn't help glancing at the two neat stacks of papers on the blotter. The top one on the left looked like a balance sheet. She wasn't an accountant, but she knew what red ink meant.

THE OLDER WOMEN IN THE QUILTING GROUP SAT AROUND THE FOLDING TABLE SORTING Avanell's fabric into piles. Harriet and DeAnn had carried box after box from the attic workroom down to the parlor, and they still hadn't touched half of Avanell's stash.

They used the center of each table to hold the sorted piles; Harriet's sticky notes came in handy labeling the various categories. One table held batiks, hand-dyed fabrics, Asian prints, Civil War reproduction fabric and other premium cuts that would be re-divided among the Loose Threads members. The second table held groups of fabric that would be donated to several charity quilt projects.

The end of the second table held what made up the dark underbelly of every stash—the "what was I thinking?" pile. Avanell had been old enough this last group not only included neon colors but polyester. These would be taken to the Goodwill store in Port Angeles. Harriet vowed to herself that, when this was all over, she and Aunt Beth were going to purge this category from the studio stash before their friends had a chance to see the extent of their mutual bad judgment.

DeAnn brought out a plate of tea cookies she'd made. Robin carried them around to everyone, Connie following her with the tea carafe, refilling cups as needed.

"Harriet," Robin said, "was that you I saw last night in a black Cadillac heading toward Smuggler's Cove?"

Harriet flushed. "Yes, it must have been." She stumbled over her words. "I went to dinner at Pirate's Treasure down there."

"Don't make us beg, chiquita," Connie said. "Spill it. Who was the guy?"

"And what is Pirate's Treasure?" Mavis asked.

Harriet wasn't used to discussing her private life in a group, but then, she hadn't made enough good friends in California to comprise a group.

"The man was Harold Minter. He's some kind of finance guy at The Vitamin Factory. I went to a Chamber of Commerce dinner with him in Avanell's place on Wednesday. A friend of his opened a new restaurant called Pirate's Treasure, and he wanted to try it out. He'd noticed my appreciation for good food and asked me if I'd like to go with him."

"And?" Connie said.

"And nothing," Harriet said. "We ate, he brought me home, end of story."

"Are you going to see him again?" Connie pushed.

"I don't know. I haven't really thought about it," she lied. She had thought about it. She imagined going out to delicious dinners and then going home to Harold's house and working differential equations together. A small part of her was attracted to the scenario.

She and Steve had shared a love of fine food, and the Bay area had no shortage of options. Their evenings were spent at bistros and cafes, dining rooms and trattorias enjoying beef Wellington and chicken cacciatore, pad Thai and provolone, all followed by rich wines, liqueurs and chocolate in every shape and form you could imagine—and some you couldn't. They would return home talking and laughing and collapse into bed, where they would make love until dawn.

What they hadn't shared was the knowledge Steve had a terminal disease.

Harriet knew she and Harold would never share a passion like she'd had with Steve; but then again, he would never be able to hurt her as deeply.

She shook her head. What was she thinking? She'd been on one date with the guy.

"Are you okay, honey?" Mavis asked and glared at Connie. "You want some more tea, or another cookie?"

"I'm fine," Harriet said stiffly.

An awkward silence fell over the group. The women returned to their work, heads down, focused on the piles they were sorting. Harriet went upstairs to retrieve another box, and when she returned, she had the distinct impression a discussion had taken place in her absence.

"Anyone feel like pizza?" Mavis asked.

DeAnn sat back and looked at the piles on the table. "I hate to stop now. I feel like we're just getting rolling," she said.

"I could go down to Mama Theresa's and pick up pizza for us to eat here," Harriet volunteered.

"Are you sure you don't mind?" Jenny said.

"Not at all. I'll just bring another box down from the workroom first so you won't run out while I'm gone."

"That sounds like a plan," Mavis said. "I'll call in our order while you're doing that."

Harriet got up, went down the dark hallway and climbed the steep stairs one more time. She started toward Avanell's workroom but found herself drawn to the tower room. She looked around, as if someone might have sneaked up behind her, then entered the round room.

With one more glance over her shoulder, she went to the desk and picked up the first stack of papers. She quickly ruffled through them. They seemed to be some sort of monthly balance sheet. She scanned the categories.

There seemed to be the usual ones you might expect to be associated with running a vitamin business. Raw materials purchases, labor expenses, utility costs, transportation payments were in one column, and payments for deliveries received in the other.

What didn't make sense was a series of write-offs that were taken each month. One month it was damaged goods, the next it was depreciated equipment. Every month had a write-off, and they were all five- or six-figure amounts. With those added to the mix, The Vitamin Factory was losing money at an alarming rate. No wonder Avanell had seemed troubled.

Harriet quickly scanned the other stack of papers. They were receipts for goods shipped. Without knowing more about the business, she couldn't tell if they were significant or not.

She set the papers back on the desk and tried to remember if they had been neatly aligned or not. She heard a noise and quickly arranged each stack then went into Avanell's workroom to get another box. She had just started for the stairs with a large plastic tub in her arms when her load was suddenly lightened.

"I'll get it," Aiden said. "Mavis thought you might be lost, so I came to check."

"Very funny," she retorted, trying to think of a reason she would have taken so long. "I was in the bathroom."

She hoped he hadn't been close enough to notice the lack of plumbing noises.

"Jenny said you were going to pick up pizza for the group. I didn't see your car out front. Were you going to walk?"

"I rode with Mavis and assumed I could take her car."

"That boat? Do you have your captain's license?"

She couldn't help smiling.

"How about I drive you?" he offered. "I need to stop by the clinic and pick up my schedule anyway. It'll only take a minute, and it's on the way."

He disappeared down a back set of stairs that must have been the servants' route to the first floor. Harriet stopped in the upstairs parlor to collect her purse and get last-minute instructions from Jenny. She came down the main staircase but found the entry hall empty. A quick glance through the etched glass insert in the front door verified that Aiden hadn't gone out without her. His rental car was still in the driveway.

She paced the length of the foyer. The downstairs parlor was empty. Several doors opened off the entry on the opposite wall. The second one she passed was slightly ajar. She could hear raised voices coming from an interior room.

"You put Mom's house on the market without even telling me?" Aiden said. "She's not even buried yet, and you've scheduled an estate sale? What about Marcel? Does he know about this?"

She didn't hear the reply, but from what he said next, it sounded like

Marcel did know.

"Were either of you going to tell me? Or was I just going to drive up one day and find my stuff gone and someone else living here?"

"Look, Aiden, you haven't been here. Don't play the injured party with me. You've been half a world away playing Dr. Dolittle while the business has been crumbling out from under us. Mom was going to have to sell the house anyway. And frankly, we need the estate sale to pay for the funeral. They want cash, and Mom doesn't have any. Uncle Bertie is barely keeping the business going while he looks for a qualified buyer. He can't help—he already sold his house. He and Sheryl are living in a two-bedroom apartment over Green's Tavern out on Shore Road."

"How could this happen?" Aiden demanded. "When I left we were getting quarterly payments that were substantial."

"Things change, little bro. That was three years ago. Have you looked at your statements lately? We haven't gotten anything in a year and a half. While you were off chasing Simba through the brush, Marcel was loaning Mom money so she could meet the payroll."

"What about the insurance money from Dad? And I know Mom had insurance. What about the money from Grandma Binoche?"

"Are you thick? It's gone," Michelle said, her voice rising in pitch. "All of it—spent, borrowed against, gone."

"Everything?" Aiden said in a tone of disbelief.

"Not Grandma Binoche's money, but that didn't do Mom any good, because Grandma set it up so Mom couldn't touch it, so it doesn't matter. If you ask me, it's a good thing Mom died when she did."

"Shut up," Aiden shouted. "Just shut up."

"Don't be naive. After Daddy died, Mom lived for The Vitamin Factory. It was failing, and she couldn't bear to go down with the ship."

"You're not trying to tell me she shot *herself* in the back of the head, are you?"

"Of course not. I'm just telling you how things are."

Harriet heard footsteps. She returned to the front door and was gazing out at the driveway when Aiden stormed into the entryway.

"Come on," he said, and went out without waiting for her.

He climbed into a black Jeep Cherokee. Harriet got into the passenger seat, and he accelerated down the steep driveway as she buckled her seatbelt.

"Is everything okay? I mean, I know it isn't okay, but is there anything I can do?" Her words sounded false in her ears. She knew nothing she could say or do would change the pain he was feeling.

He pierced her with an icy glance but said nothing. They were off the hill and driving down Main Street before he spoke.

"I can't believe Mom's business could go into such a steep decline in just three years. Has the economy been that bad while I've been gone?"

"Things were slow when the dot-com bubble burst, but that's been more than three years ago. It's hard to imagine that would impact the vitamin business. I don't know what to tell you. Can you look at the company books?"

"Technically, I suppose I could—when my dad died he left us each a share of the company. His will stated we didn't get to participate in the management unless Mom became disabled or invited us to participate. Uncle Bertie has the other share of the company, though."

"Is that a problem?"

"Well, let's just say he and I aren't on the best of terms."

"You could do some research on the internet. I assume The Vitamin Factory was privately held, but you might be able to find a public competitor and get an idea of how the industry has been over the last few years."

She wanted to tell him he needed to look at some rather large losses the company had incurred over the last year, but she couldn't figure out a way to work it into the conversation.

"Could you talk to the family attorney?"

"Do you think he would tell me anything? I've had nothing to do with the business. And then there's confidentiality. Isn't that the excuse lawyers always use so they don't have to answer any uncomfortable questions?"

"He's your lawyer, too, though. That should count for something, shouldn't it?"

He pulled up in front of the Main Street Veterinary Clinic.

"Want to see where I'm going to work?" he asked, ending the discussion.

Harriet followed him around the building to a side door. They entered into what looked like the employee breakroom. A long wooden table was pushed against the wall with the street-side window. The opposite wall held a sink, microwave and two-burner stove.

They passed through into a hallway. Harriet's nose was immediately assaulted with the pungent odor of disinfectant.

One wall had doors spaced evenly along its length. Aiden went to the third door, opened it and entered. She followed him.

"This will be my office," he said and spread his arms to indicate the small space. A scarred wooden desk dominated the room. A mismatched bookcase filled one wall, battered file cabinets the other.

"It's…" She paused searching for the right word. "Charming," she finished.

His mouth curved into a wry smile.

"The low man on the totem pole gets the leftovers," he said. "I have to pay my dues." A few papers were scattered on the surface of the desk. He picked them up and looked at each one in turn. "I'll have to go up front. None of these are my schedule."

He led the way down the hallway and through another door into the front office and reception area.

"Aiden," called a high-pitched voice from the waiting room. "Over here."

Harriet looked across the reception counter and saw Sarah Ness clutching a fabric-and-nylon-netting pet carrier containing a yowling cat. She was waving to Aiden.

He went to the counter. "Hi."

"I brought Rachel in to have her sneezing looked at. You said you weren't going to be here, so I made an appointment for her with Dr. Romig, but I have to wait because they are fitting her in. Can you examine her instead?"

Aiden looked around for help.

"I haven't really started working yet," he began, but was interrupted by Helen Martin, the veterinary technician who ran patient intake.

"Dr. Romig's schedule is stacked, and it would be doing us all a favor if you could look at the cat." Her expression finished the thought.

Aiden looked at Harriet.

"I'll call Mama Theresa's," she said and pulled out her cell phone.

"Here, use ours," Helen offered and pushed a desk phone toward her. "Come on back here, and I'll get you a lab coat and an exam room," she said to Aiden, and took him through another door into the bowels of the clinic.

"What are you doing here?" Sarah asked as soon as Harriet hung the phone up.

"Aiden's giving me a ride to Mama Theresa's to pick up pizza. Some of the Loose Threads are going through Avanell's stash today, and I'm on a food run."

"Mavis left me a message, but I had a meeting."

Harriet decided not to point out that she wasn't in a meeting now.

"You certainly seem to be getting cozy with Avanell's son," Sarah said.

"He just gave me a ride to get pizza, that's all."

"Oh, please. I saw the way you looked at him. Isn't he a little young?"

"I'm almost certain he's old enough to drive."

Whatever Sarah was about to reply was cut off by Helen. She opened a door labeled EXAM TWO and called Rachel's name. Sarah went into the room with her cat bag and shut the door.

Helen gave Harriet a copy of *Cat Fancier* magazine and led her back to the breakroom.

"That one's a piece of work," she said and shook her head as she left for the front desk.

Aiden found Harriet fifteen minutes later.

"Let's get out of here before she comes up with something else."

"What was wrong with her cat?"

"As near as I can tell, the only thing wrong with that cat is her owner."

Harriet smiled. "So, what did you tell Sarah?"

"Oh, I told her to change to dust-free cat litter and to keep a journal of when her cat sneezes. She's to record all the environmental conditions every time Rachel makes a nasal noise. That ought to keep her busy for a while."

"You're bad."

They drove to Mama T's, picked up the pizza and returned to the house, limiting their conversation to a generic discussion of how much Foggy Point had changed since they'd each last lived there, avoiding any mention of Avanell or her finances.

The quilters worked another three hours after their pizza feast. They filled bags with the sorted fabric and agreed there was at least another days'-worth of work left.

"Can everyone come back tomorrow?" Mavis asked.

Connie said she could come after church. Harriet, Jenny, Mavis and DeAnn agreed to meet at nine. Robin's mother-in-law was coming for the day so she had to pass, but she said she'd track down Lauren and find out why she was a no-show. If possible, she'd line her up for the next day.

Mavis and Harriet got into the Town Car and headed down the hill.

"We made a fair amount of progress today," Mavis said.

"Yeah, it makes me want to go home and do some stash-thinning."

"I know what you mean, except I'm too tired to do anything but put my feet up and veg in front of the tube."

"I hear you. Those stairs to the third floor were killer."

"Not so killer you didn't go up there with Aiden more than once."

Harriet's face turned pink. "Purely a coincidence."

"I saw the way he looks at you with those big blue eyes of his. He's definitely smitten."

"He's a child. Well, practically."

"He's not that young. And you're not that old. And don't you try and tell me you haven't given it a thought."

She felt her face transition from pink to flaming red. "So I can appreciate a good-looking guy. A too-young good-looking guy. I'm sure he sees me as a big sister."

"Listen, missy, I raised five sons, and believe me—Aiden does not look at you like he does his sister."

"Well, certainly not how he looks at his sister right now," Harriet conceded. "I overheard them arguing when we were leaving, and she was pretty harsh."

"They usually get along well enough. Avanell's death has got them both out of kilter." She shook her head. "I can't say as I blame them for acting out a little. It must be an awful thing to have your momma murdered."

"Did Avanell ever talk about her business?"

"Oh, she'd say something once in a while. If a new product made a big splash or sometimes if her employees were fighting she might ask the group their opinion when we sat around stitching."

"Had she said anything lately?"

"No, she hadn't." Mavis paused. "Something's been wrong for a while, though."

"In what way?" Harriet asked.

"Nothing you could really put your finger on. Just small stuff. She wasn't buying fabric. I know—with a stash like we just saw she could have gone years without buying fabric, but until lately, she didn't. She usually bought pretty regular. And her car. She always said her car was her one vanity item. She bought a new Mercedes sedan every year. Except this year. This is the first year she skipped since George died."

"Do you know why?"

"I assumed she must be having money problems, but she never did say."

Harriet knew all about families who kept secrets.

91

Chapter Eighteen

FRED WAS PACING IN THE KITCHEN WHEN HARRIET ENTERED FROM THE STUDIO.
"Did you eat all the food I left in your dish already?" She picked up his empty dish and poured a carefully measured half-cup of kibble into it. She glanced at the clock on the stove—it was ten after five. Pins and Needles stayed open until six on Saturday night.

She grabbed her purse from the chair by the door; the studio was in good enough shape she could afford to skip a night. A hand-piecing project would be just what the doctor ordered, and she'd seen a new cat print series that would make a nice kitty quilt for Fred. He had adopted a green wool-upholstered chair in her bedroom and was leaving a covering of cat fur in his wake. If they were going to be here for a while, it would need some protection. There was a movie rental store at the bottom of the hill, too; her Saturday night was shaping up nicely.

"I'll be back in a few," she yelled to Fred, who didn't look up from his dish.

She went out into the damp early-evening air, got into her car and drove into downtown Foggy Point.

The bell on the door to Pins and Needles jingled as she crossed the threshold.

"Be right with you," Marjory called from behind a row of fabric bolts. "Oh, hi, Harriet," she said as Harriet rounded the end of the display.

Carla Salter stood beside Marjory, studying her tattered canvas shoes.

"Meet my newest employee, Carla Salter. She's going to start working for me a few hours on the weekends."

"We met the other night," Harriet said. "How are you doing, Carla?"

Carla mumbled a reply, but Harriet couldn't make out what she'd said.

"I've got the studio pretty much back together, so I thought I'd take a night off and start a hand-piecing project. I saw some cat fabric you were unpacking when I was here on Tuesday. I thought I might make a small quilt for my cat Fred."

"Carla can show you where we put that," Marjory said. "You know which fabric she's talking about?"

"The Makower UK cats?"

"Yes," Harriet said.

"Over here."

Carla led her two rows over to a section that had several lines of stylized animal fabrics.

"Thanks." Harriet pulled several bolts off the shelf.

Carla had moved back a few steps but was still in the aisle.

"What do you think of these?" Harriet asked her.

"I like the blue-and-brown one," she said, so quietly Harriet almost didn't hear her.

"I do, too. What do you think about the orange for accent fabric? Is it too much?"

"Depends on your cat. If it's got a strong personality it probably would like the orange. If it's the kind that sleeps all day the off-white would probably be better." She spoke a little louder this time.

"Fred is definitely a strong personality, so orange it is."

"Do you want me to take these to the counter for you?"

"Yes, thanks. I'm going to look around a little more."

Carla's eyes widened and her cheeks turned red.

"I'm sorry. I didn't mean to rush you."

"No, it's fine. You are doing fine. By the way, did you ever find your friend the other night?" Harriet asked, trying to distract her from her distress. Doing a customer service job had to be a big stretch for her.

Carla twisted her hands in the hem of her faded blue T-shirt.

"She never showed," she said then looked up. "I'm getting really worried. I got Jason from work to drive me by her place on Friday, but it doesn't look like she's been there."

"Does she have family she might be staying with?"

"She doesn't talk to her family." Carla paused. "She's had problems they can't understand."

Or maybe they understand all too well, Harriet thought. "What kind of problems?"

Carla was silent, and Harriet was afraid she'd overstepped the boundary of their tenuous relationship. She turned back to the fabric bolts.

"She has problems in her head," Carla finally said in a soft voice. "That's why I'm so worried about her. She needs to take her medicine. As long as she does it real regular she's fine. Miz Avanell helped her with her medicine. She just got some last week, but I don't think she took it with her when they fired her. It was in her toolbox, and Tony didn't let her take her toolbox when she left. I tried to find it on Friday, and it was gone already."

"Maybe she got a new prescription from the pharmacy," Harriet suggested.

"She doesn't have money, and the thing is, when she's late taking her pill she starts getting weird ideas. And she starts thinking she don't need to take any medicine anymore. Then she gets hyper and—I'm just worried about her. She's a good person, really. She can't help the way she is."

"Well, she's lucky to have a friend like you to worry about her."

Carla's cheeks turned a deeper red, and she busied herself picking up the bolts of fabric.

"These'll be at the front," she said, and carried them to the cutting table.

Marjory cut the fabric and sent Harriet on her way with promises to see her the next day at Avanell's. Harriet continued down the block, turned the corner and walked another block to Foggy Point Video.

"DeAnn?"

"Oh, hi, Harriet."

"Do you work here? Of course you do. Why else would you be behind the counter? I'm sorry."

"Harriet, it's okay. Why would you know where I work? My family owns this place. I work here part-time."

"I'm sorry. I must seem like a fool. I'm still getting used to being back in Foggy Point. I'm not used to seeing people I know running every other business I go into."

"Well, it has its good points and its bad points. Here everyone knows everyone else's business. Most of the time, anyway—and we protect our own," DeeAnn added.

"What are people saying about Avanell's murder?"

"So far, no one seems to know much. Tony, the supervisor, fired a girl who had worked there for a while a few days ago, and now she's missing along with the contents of the safe. The police are working on that theory, but I haven't heard anything more."

"So, they think this girl killed Avanell and then robbed the place? Or Avanell caught her in the act? Does that seem possible?"

"It's the only thing they've got, according to my cousin who works in the sheriff's department."

"It's just so sad. Avanell and my aunt Beth were friends for as long as I can remember."

"The community is going to miss Avanell, too. She was a generous benefactor for a lot of civic projects around here."

"Had she donated much lately?" Harriet asked.

"Hmmm. You know, now that you mention it, I don't think she has been involved this year. Of course, we haven't had anything big going on, either. I'm the secretary of the Foggy Point Business Association. Avanell made a substantial donation to the skate park and playground equipment project two years ago. And of course, there are the scholarships, but then I guess she set those up when George died. Why do you ask?"

"I just wondered. My aunt seemed to think she was worried about something, and you know money is always one of those things people worry about."

"I can't imagine Avanell having to think about money. In our business association meetings she seemed pretty sharp where that was concerned. For our projects, she was always getting suppliers to sell us materials at cost, and she got the skate park ramps donated outright. I can't imagine she would be different in her own business."

"It must have been something else, then," Harriet said, deciding she had learned all DeeAnn could tell her. "I'm starting a new hand-piecing project tonight and was hoping to find a good movie to watch while I do. Something light and fluffy."

She had developed an embarrassing addiction to romance movies. She always cried at the happy endings.

"Follow me." DeAnn led her in the direction of a sign that read ROMANTIC COMEDY.

A half-hour later, Harriet had two comedies and a historical romance in her bag and a week to watch them in.

Dusk had turned into dark while she was in the video store. She knew Foggy Point was safer than Oakland, but she still hurried up the deserted block toward her car.

As she turned the corner she heard a shuffling noise behind her. She sped up, and the sound turned into the distinct rapping of boot heels on pavement. The footsteps sped up as well.

"Hey," Aiden called. "Wait up." A strange-looking dog danced around his feet. "Randy, sit," he said, and the little dog obeyed.

"Aiden," she said in relief. "You scared me to death."

"I'm sorry. I saw your car parked up by Pins and Needles, and I was on my way to the Rice Bowl when I saw you go into the video store. Randy and I were waiting for you to come out, but she got distracted by a rat back there," He pointed to a narrow alley. "And you got by us."

"What did you want?"

"I was going to offer a deal I hoped you couldn't refuse."

"I'm listening," she said, and reminded herself again that Sarah was right, Aiden was way too young for her to be having heart palpitations over.

"Okay." He nervously rubbed his well-muscled left arm with his right hand. "How about I buy dinner, and then we go back to your place and watch your movies," he said in a rush.

"You don't even know what movies I have in here," she said as she held up the bag.

"I don't care. If you like them, I'll like them."

"You mean to tell me you want to sit through an educational video on women and menopause? You *are* an evolved young man."

"Very funny. I think we both know that isn't what you have in there. For one thing, you're not old enough."

"You don't know that."

"Yes, I do. My brother Marcel told me you were one class ahead of him in high school. And I do know my mammalian biology. By the way, he had a crush on you back then."

"I was, and I knew that."

"But you were a mysterious older woman who wouldn't give him the time of day?"

"He was a Star Trek geek who went around making secret hand gestures and speaking Klingon to his friends."

"I'd like to think you were saving yourself for his charming younger brother."

"Listen to what you're saying. When I was in high school you were in second grade."

He closed the distance between them, and her breath caught in her throat as he gazed deep into her eyes.

"I'm not in second grade anymore."

He cupped her chin in his hand and brushed his mouth lightly over hers. The touch of his lips shocked her to her core, but she didn't break away.

"You're definitely old enough," she said when they separated.

"Do I get to come watch movies, then?"

"I'm not so sure that's a good idea," she said and absently rubbed a finger across her lips.

"If I promise to behave myself?" he asked. "Unless you don't want me to, that is."

"I have a feeling I'm going to live to regret this, but okay. You buy dinner, I'll show movies and we'll see what Fred thinks of Randy."

Dinner turned out to be fast food Chinese take-out. Harriet dropped Aiden and Randy at his apartment so he could get his car then went on up the hill. She carried dinner into the kitchen.

"Fred," she said. "This could be a big mistake. He's too young, and even if he were old enough, I'm not ready to consider getting involved with anyone. And frankly, Fred, I don't think I ever will be. Your daddy was it for me."

She had filled two bowls with rice and was arranging the beef and broccoli on top when she heard a soft tap on the kitchen door. She opened it, and Randy bounded inside, followed by Aiden.

Randy was similar in size to a beagle, but shaped more like a shoebox. Her head was round and her ears small triangles that looked like they had been glued on as an afterthought. Her color was a tan-and-grey mix that was highlighted with bluish freckles. She jumped up in front of Harriet, and for the first time she noticed the dog's eyes.

They were the same yellow-blue as Aiden's.

She looked at Aiden and then back at Randy.

"That's weird," she said.

"Not for her. It's not unusual for dogs to have white eyes."

"So, you're the weird one?"

"Didn't your mother teach you to be nice to guests? Especially when they bring you dinner?"

"Aunt Beth may have mentioned something about that, eons ago when I was young."

"Not the age hang-up again. Do you realize that if I were ten years older than you instead of the opposite we wouldn't be having this discussion?"

"Yes, we would. Ten years is ten years no matter which way it goes. Besides, no matter what our age difference, we shouldn't be having this kind of discussion."

"You're not a lesbian, are you? I mean it's okay if you like girls, I just didn't pick up that vibe from you, and usually I have pretty good gaydar."

"I am not a lesbian. I'm not an anything. I'm not on the dating market."

"Oh, God, you're not married, are you? Do you have an estranged husband stashed away somewhere?"

"No, nothing like that. If you must know, I'm a widow."

His face lost its smile. "I'm sorry. I didn't know."

"It's okay, there's no reason you would have known. My husband died five years ago."

"I'm sorry," he said again.

Randy sensed the change in mood and instantly went to her master's side. He reached down and scratched her ear.

"How about we just eat and watch the movies and not worry about anything else," Harriet suggested. "Here." She handed him the two bowls and picked up the bag of movies. "What do you want to drink? The options are pretty much water or tea."

"Water is fine."

She grabbed two bottles of water from the refrigerator and led him through the kitchen and dining room and up the stairs to the second floor, with Randy bringing up the rear. Aunt Beth had set one of the upstairs bedrooms up as a TV room—a burgundy leather sleeper sofa was oriented opposite a large television with a small side chair next to the window.

Aiden set the food on the large ottoman situated between the sofa and TV.

"This looks cozy," he said. He pushed a fluffy pink afghan out of the way and sat down.

"It is. It's where Aunt Beth comes to unwind."

Fred had apparently been sleeping upstairs and chose that moment to join the party. He didn't have much experience with dogs.

What happened next would have made a good highlight reel for one of those funniest home videos shows, Harriet thought later.

Fred came in the door and in one leap landed on Randy's back. Randy yelped and jumped onto the ottoman. Chinese food flew everywhere. Fred hissed, Randy cried, and Aiden and Harriet each tried to grab their respective pets. The cat jumped up onto a bookshelf, a clump of broccoli dangling from his head. The dog ran down the stairs, trailing rice as she went. The two adults collided and then rolled off the ottoman onto the floor in front of the TV.

Harriet found herself on top of Aiden. She looked down at the surprised expression on his face and burst out laughing. He smiled. She picked a clump of sticky rice off his eyebrow. He grabbed her hand and licked the rice off her fingers. Her fingers twined in his.

Aiden took her other hand and pulled both over his head. "Okay, you have me where you want me. What are you going to do now?"

Harriet's heart hammered in her chest. A shiver rippled through her. With a sudden movement, Aiden flipped them both over. He lowered his head and brushed a gentle kiss across her lips. She closed her eyes, and he kissed her again, questioning this time. She was shocked at her own eager response.

The kiss deepened, and Harriet lost all sense of time and place as his body melted onto hers. She felt abandoned when he finally pulled away.

"If we don't stop now, we won't be stopping at all," he said and looked hopefully at her.

She blushed. "We aren't that kind of friends…" She paused.

"Go ahead and say it," he said. "We aren't that kind of friends *yet.* That means there's hope eventually we will be."

"I wouldn't hold my breath. You caught me in a weak moment, that's all."

"Yeah, right. Don't kid yourself. You wanted it as much as I did."

Harriet pulled her hands from his grasp and pushed him off and onto the floor. Standing, she retrieved the two bowls and started picking up bits of broccoli and beef. Aiden rose and brushed smashed rice off his jeans.

"Go downstairs and bring the yellow sponge from beside the sink and paper towels from the rack under the cabinet," she ordered and continued collecting the bigger pieces of remains and putting them into the bowls.

Aiden returned and began wiping up what was left of the mess.

"Did you see Randy while you were down there?"

"No, but I can guess where she is. She always goes low. She'll be under a bed or sofa somewhere."

"I'm sorry Fred attacked her. I've never seen him do that before."

"That's okay. I'm sure Randy will be fine after a few years of therapy."

"The bad news is that dinner is ruined, and all I have here are salad makings."

"Don't worry. I'll call Jorge and see if he can whip up a batch of nachos for us, if that's okay with you."

"That sounds great."

Aiden made the call, and they both went down to Tico's Tacos to pick the order up.

"The white cup in the bag is guacamole for the señorita," Jorge said, and looked hard at Aiden. "The boy doesn't share too well," he explained to Harriet.

When they returned, she held the kitchen door open for Aiden, who carried their bag of food and the two bottles of Dos Equis Jorge had thrown in. Randy sat on the floor below Fred, who was studying her from the kitchen table.

"Looks like they've patched things up since we left."

"I'm sure Fred remembered his manners and apologized."

"Naw, Randy made the first move. She's like that."

Thankfully, their second stab at ethnic dining went better than the first. The nachos were crisp and cheesy. They were smothered in beans and shredded chicken, and topped with onions, jalapenos and chopped tomatoes.

"I may never eat again," Harriet said, and threw her crumpled napkin onto the ottoman near the nearly empty nacho platter.

"Jorge is definitely a good cook," Aiden said in a lazy voice. He set the plate on the floor, where Randy cleaned up the remains.

"So, you went to school with my brother. Now you've met my sister and me. And your aunt and my mom were best friends. What about you?"

"What do you mean, what about me?" She felt her full stomach tightening.

"I'm just getting to know you. If we're going to be that kind of friends we need to get better acquainted. You know a lot about me, and the only thing I know about you is that you have a mean cat, broke my brother's young heart and you've been widowed."

"You have some nerve," she said with a smile. "Fred will probably need years of therapy to recover from his visit to Foggy Point. Your brother was a stalker who needed to be reined in. We are not going to be 'that kind of friends,' and my marriage is none of your business."

"Okay, we'll start with the basics. What about your family. Where do your parents live? And how did you come to be living with your aunt?"

"I'm not certain where my parents live," she said, and realized that fact no longer bothered her. "I heard my father took a job in Singapore."

"You don't know?" Aiden said, his shock apparent in his voice.

"Well, I read a *Time* magazine article that said he'd taken a job in Singapore, so I suppose that means they moved there. I'm sure *Time* checked their sources before they printed the article."

"Wow," he said and leaned back against the cushion of the sofa. "Are you not speaking to them? Did you have a fight or something?"

"Nothing so dramatic. They have their lives, I have mine."

"That's pretty harsh. How can you not talk to your parents?"

Harriet stiffened. "How can you pass judgment when you know nothing about the situation?"

He reached for her hand. "You're right. I'm sorry," he said. "I've just never known anyone who didn't talk to their parents."

She pulled her hand free. "You keep saying that like I have a disease." Her voice was hard. "It's not that I refuse to speak to them, or that they refuse to speak to me. It just never comes up. I talk to them whenever they bother to make contact, which is admittedly not often. They relocated several times when I was in college, and once I was twenty-one their secretary quit updating Aunt Beth as to their ever-changing contact information. When they call, I talk to them."

"Are they some kind of spies or something?"

Harriet looked at him. "You've got quite the imagination. No, it's nothing that interesting. My mother is a physicist who invented something that has to do with particle acceleration years ago. I think she might do something with nuclear fission, too—I've never really known, to tell the truth.

"My father works in genetics. He was on the team that cloned Dolly the sheep, and now is doing stem cell research. At least, that's what the article said. It's hard to pursue their kind of research in the United States, so they have almost always worked abroad."

"Wow, that's kind of cool," Aiden said. "Your parents are famous."

She looked at him without smiling.

"Your childhood must have been exciting. Where did you live when you were a kid? Before you came here, I mean."

"Do we have to talk about this?"

"I'm just trying to understand who you are," he said and smiled.

"You're just trying to get in my pants, and I can save you some trouble. It's not going to happen."

He looked hurt. "I want to get to know you. I'm evolved—really."

"Yeah, right. If you must know, I didn't grow up anywhere. I was born in London. My parents were living there while one of them was doing a fellowship."

"You have dual citizenship? Cool!"

"After London my parents moved to Switzerland then Japan, I think, then Scotland. It's hard to remember. In any case, I was sent to New York with a nanny. If they wanted to be parents, they sent for me. When they got tired, I went back to New York. When I was school age, New York and the nanny were replaced by boarding school, sometimes where they were working, sometimes not. Aunt Beth intervened when I was eleven and she and Foggy Point replaced boarding school."

"That must have been better," Aiden said.

101

"It was great. Do you have any idea how odd you seem to the rest of the school children in Foggy Point, Washington, when you're fluent in four languages and passable in three more? How do you relate when the other kids are trying to learn the capitols of Europe and you've ordered room service in most of them? I was a freak. Plus, I came and went a few times on top of everything else."

"You speak seven languages?"

She gave him an exasperated look.

"So, what movies do we have?" he asked, finally letting her off the hook.

It turned out that it didn't matter—he fell asleep before the opening credits. She covered him with the fluffy afghan. At the end of the first movie, she took Randy downstairs and let her out into the yard. She did her business and came right back.

"Good girl," Harriet said. The little dog waggled her body.

She made it to the first break-up between the hero and heroine in the second movie before she, too, fell asleep.

Grey light was streaming in the window when she woke.

"Aiden, wake up," she said and shook his shoulder.

Randy jumped onto the sofa and started licking his face. He awoke, spluttering and spitting, and pushed her down.

"What time is it?" he asked. "Did I miss the movie?"

"It's ten after seven, and, yes, you did miss the movie," Harriet told him and laughed.

"Did you take advantage of me while I was asleep?"

"You wish. But I did take your dog out."

"You're still wearing last night's clothes, so I guess we did sleep together, huh? Was it good for you?"

"You've got a one-track mind, buddy boy. I need to get dressed to go back to your mother's house."

"Do I at least get a cup of coffee before you throw us out?"

"Yes, you can have a cup of coffee, but then you have to go so I can get ready."

He was still sitting at the kitchen table drinking coffee and reading the paper when she came down from her shower. She was dressed in jeans and a red T-shirt. Randy was licking the floor around the empty bowl Harriet had filled with cereal for her before she went upstairs. She looked hopefully at Harriet.

"I thought you were leaving," she said.

"I am. I'm just not anxious to go to my mom's house. My brother's arriving today."

"Don't you get along with your brother?"

"We don't *not* get along. Since he's the oldest he expects everything to be his way. He thinks he knows what's best for all of us no matter what the subject. And he hates Foggy Point. He couldn't wait to leave when he got out of high school, and he'll blame Mom's death on the fact that she lived here. He wanted her to relocate to Seattle when he got out of college, but she wouldn't consider it. He's sure she stayed here because of me. He might be right. Maybe if we'd moved to Seattle all those years ago she'd be with us today."

"You can't know that. She might have died in a car accident or been hit by a meteor."

They were still arguing when the studio doorbell rang.

"Are you expecting company?" Aiden asked.

"Not that I know of." She got up and went to the studio, Randy close on her heels. She opened the door. Sarah Ness walked in without waiting to be asked.

"Hi, Harriet. I hope it's okay that I came this early. I knew you'd be up since you're going to Avanell's at nine. I made a quilt for my sister's birthday and need you to stitch it for me by Monday."

"You do know it's Sunday, right? And you know I'm going to be at Avanell's all day."

"It's not that hard." Sarah said. "My sister's birthday is Wednesday."

"I can have it for you by the end of the day on Monday, but it'll cost you."

"I don't remember asking for a discount."

"Give it to me," Harriet said.

"It's in the car, I'll go get it."

"Who's here?" Aiden asked as he came into the studio.

"Be careful," Harriet said. "There are probably still pins on the floor, and believe me, you don't want to step on one in your bare feet."

"Dr. Jalbert," Sarah said. "What are you doing here? Is there a problem?"

"Miss Ness," he said with a smile. "We're just fine here, thanks for asking."

Sarah stiffened. She looked from Aiden to Harriet and back again.

"I'll be back Monday at four," she said and turned on her heel and left.

Aiden grinned.

"You're not helping things, you know," Harriet said. "She's a customer. According to Aunt Beth, a very good customer."

"She needs to know how things are, and the sooner she does the better for all of us."

"And just exactly how are things? Never mind, forget I asked."

"I know how things aren't, and she's my customer, too. Or at least her cat is, and the sooner she understands what isn't going to happen the better off we'll all be."

Harriet opened her mouth to speak.

"Stop right there. I don't want to hear about how she's my age and all."

"How do you know what I was going to say?"

He raised his eyebrow and stared at her.

"Okay, so maybe I was going to mention age," she admitted. "She *is* closer to your age, you know."

"Yeah, and she's a self-centered neurotic. Is being my age supposed to make up for that?"

"No, and it's none of my business, anyway. I need to go to your mom's house."

"Want to go with me and Randy?"

"I think not. Besides, I'm picking up Mavis."

They went back into the kitchen. Fred was eating his kibbles and keeping a wary eye on Randy, who sat under the kitchen table watching his every move.

Aiden gathered Randy up and left. Harriet went upstairs, brushed her teeth and then left to pick up Mavis.

Chapter Nineteen

D ID YOU GET SOME REST?" MAVIS ASKED AS SHE GOT INTO THE CAR. SHE WAS WEARING faded pull-on jeans and a purple sweatshirt with three squirrels painted on the front.

"I rented a couple of movies. I discovered DeAnn worked at the video store."

"Welcome to small-town America. I can tell you, I didn't make it very late last night. I ate a frozen dinner, watched one TV program and went to bed."

"The stash dispersal has to be more draining for those of you who knew Avanell well."

"That it is. I can remember when she bought most of those fabrics. I bought many of them myself. Every one of them is a memory of times we've lost." Mavis looked down at her lap. "I'm sorry," she said after a few minutes. "I didn't mean to be so maudlin."

"Hey, don't apologize for missing a good friend." Harriet wondered what it was like to know someone that many years.

They rode in silence for the rest of the trip. Harriet pulled into the driveway, let Mavis out then parked in front of the large detached garage that had probably once been a carriage house. She got out and was about to walk around the house to the front door when the back door opened.

"Hey, toots, want me to show you a shortcut?" Aiden called. Randy ran out between his feet and started dancing around her.

"How can I refuse such an offer?" she said and followed him into the house.

He led her across an enclosed porch and into a butler's pantry. A narrow hallway led to a breakfast room, which in turn led to a large formal dining room.

She was in the room before she realized there were people seated at the table eating breakfast.

"I'm sorry," she said to Michelle and a man she recognized as Marcel. "I didn't realize anyone was in here."

"It's an easy mistake to make," Michelle said "Why would you expect there to be people eating in their own dining room in the morning?"

"Ignore her," Aiden said, and started for the door on the wall opposite the one they had entered through.

"Harriet?" Marcel said. "Is that you? I'd heard you were living in California."

"I was, but I've decided to move back here," she told him with more conviction than she felt.

"You couldn't pay me enough to come back here to live."

"Doesn't seem like that's going to be a problem," Michelle said.

"I better go join the other quilters. I can find my way from here," she said to Aiden. "It's nice to see you again, Marcel. I'm just sorry it has to be under such sad circumstances."

"Yeah, right."

She climbed the stairs to the second floor. Jenny and DeAnn must have arrived while she was in the dining room. They were bent over a box of calico print fabric across the room when she stepped onto the landing.

"I'll go get some boxes while I'm up," she said.

She climbed the stairs to the third floor. She couldn't resist going into Avanell's tower office. A layer of mist covered both land and water in all directions out the window; the house was above the fog line. Soft lamplight from Foggy Point shops and streetlights glowed yellow through the fluff that covered the downtown.

She dragged herself away from the view. She glanced at Avanell's desk. The stacks of papers were gone. She pulled the drawers open and looked inside, but they were all empty. Someone had cleared the desk out since last night.

She made three trips carrying boxes before she sat down with the other women to sort fabric. Her job was to fold batiks. Avanell didn't always keep her own hand-dyed fabric apart from the rest of her stash, so it was sometimes hard to tell which ones were hand-dyed and which were commercial batiks.

She'd been at it for about an hour when her cell phone rang.

"Hello," she said. "Yes, I'm Harriet."

"Good morning, ladies," a voice boomed from the landing. Harriet covered her free ear and stepped into the hallway in order to hear her caller. She saw

Avanell's brother Bertrand come into the parlor with a plate of doughnuts.

"I brought you some doughnuts to have with your tea," he said. "I do appreciate what you're doing here."

Harriet finished her phone call and rejoined the group.

"That was weird," she said to no one in particular.

"Is there a problem?" Bertrand asked.

"I'm not sure. That was the woman in charge of hanging the quilts at the Puget Sound Quilt Show. She was informed of Avanell's passing, and it raised the question of whether her quilt still qualified to be hung in the group category or not. Technically, the quilt is now being shown by an owner, not a maker, and that's a different category.

"She realizes this is a rather unusual circumstance and said she'll get back to me as soon as she can get the board of governors together to make a decision."

"That's ridiculous," Bertrand said, a faint hint of his French accent apparent for the first time.

"Well, I'm sure they'll sort it out. According to Aunt Beth, Avanell has won the grand prize for quite a few years running. That has to count for something."

"I'll leave you girls to your work, then," he said, and turned with a flourish and went down the stairs.

"I'll bet he was a real Cassanova in his day," DeAnn commented.

"In his own mind, anyway," Jenny said. "He was in grade school when his parents moved here from France, but he always tried to impress the girls with his European heritage."

"Did it work?"

"Not really. He married a mousy little girl who was two years below him in school. Does anyone have a pile started for metallic overlays?" she said, effectively ending the topic.

Harriet went upstairs for another box; and while she was gone, Connie arrived. The shorter woman pulled her into a hug when she came back downstairs.

"How are you doing today?" she asked.

"I'm good." Harriet pulled awkwardly away.

Connie set her carafe down on the table.

"Anyone want tea?" she asked. "It's peppermint today."

Harriet held up her empty cup and allowed Connie to fill it with hot liquid.

"So, has anyone heard anything about Avanell's case," Connie asked after she'd gotten settled in her spot at the table.

"Shh, not so loud," Jenny said. "The whole family is downstairs."

"I'm sure they want to know as much as we do," Connie countered.

"Darcy came in for a movie last night, but if she knows anything more she's not saying," DeAnn offered. "She said the sheriff is still working on the premise it was a robbery gone wrong."

"He knows better than that," Mavis protested. "When have we ever had a robbery where they killed someone? That may happen in the city, but not in Foggy Point, Washington."

"That's what I say," Connie agreed.

"If not robbery, then what?" asked Harriet.

"I'm not sure," Jenny said. "But I for one don't believe that your break-in and Avanell's death happening on the same night was just a coincidence."

"But who would want Avanell dead?" Harriet persisted. She looked into the serious faces of her aunt's friends.

"On TV they usually say it's the person who has the most to gain from the death."

"That's easy," said Lauren.

"Who?" several others chorused.

"Aiden, of course."

"What does he have to gain from it?" Harriet asked.

"He inherits a big pile of money from his grandmother."

"What does that have to do with Avanell?" Jenny wanted to know.

"Grandma Binoche was a crazy old lady. And she hated Avanell. She had the room next to my grandma Oliver at the Muckleshoot River Assisted Living Center. She would come to my grandma's room when I came to visit. I don't think she had many visitors.

"Anyway, she told me the lengths she'd gone to so she could be sure Avanell would not benefit in any way from her death. She left her estate to Aiden, but it's held in trust until Avanell's death. So he not only inherits whatever Avanell left him, but he also gets whatever Grandma Binoche left, and from the way she talked, it wasn't a small amount, either."

"That's it?" Harriet said. "That's the evidence you have against Aiden? What about Michelle?"

"That, and the fact that he lives by himself and has no alibi," DeAnn added. "Michelle didn't come to town until Thursday afternoon."

"Darcy did mention that no one related to Avanell had an ironclad alibi. She heard the beat officers complaining because it was more work for them trying to find people who had chanced to see them, since they did pretty much nothing all night."

"That sounds pretty thin," Mavis scoffed. "And besides, Aiden has a skill that will earn him a good salary once he gets established. He wouldn't kill his momma for money."

"You never know what motivates people, though. Money does funny things to folks," Jenny said.

No one spoke after that. She was right—money did do funny things to people.

"DOES ANYONE CARE IF I TAKE SOME OF THE THIRTIES REPRODUCTION PRINTS FOR ONE OF the girls in Marjorie's Thursday night group?" Harriet asked, referring to a group of pastel fabrics printed with images that had been popular in the 1930s. She looked around the table.

"I think that would be fine," Jenny said. Connie nodded agreement.

"Let's put these stacks back in the boxes and label them. Harriet and I can take the Goodwill boxes and the ones that go to Foggy Point Assisted Living Center. Connie, could you take the box for the Friends of Seasonal Workers?" Mavis asked.

Connie nodded again.

"I can take the charity boxes that go to Marjorie's. I'll put them in my car and then bring them to Pins and Needles on Tuesday, if that's okay with everyone," offered DeAnn.

"That sounds great," Jenny said. "If everyone takes some of the boxes with them, we'll only have the project bags to deal with."

"I vote we take the bags with us, too, and finish deciding about them at Loose Threads or Harriet's or somewhere that isn't here," suggested Mavis.

"We can take them to my studio," Harriet said.

With a plan in place, the women said their goodbyes and agreed to meet at Pins and Needles on Tuesday and carpool to Avanell's memorial service.

"I'm glad that's over," Harriet said when she and Mavis were in the car and headed down the driveway.

"Me, too," Mavis agreed. "I asked Michelle if she needed help going through Avanell's clothes. She's got the house on the market, so she may have to deal with it sooner than she thinks. She said she'd get back to me."

"It does seem kind of weird that she's got the house for sale before Avanell's even buried."

"Everyone grieves differently, honey. Some hang on to stuff and some can't get rid of it fast enough, almost like death is a disease you can catch."

"I think I'll go to the quilt show tomorrow morning," Harriet decided. "It sounded like they took Avanell's quilt down. I'm not sure if they'll leave the spot blank while they decide what to do, or if they'll move one of our others. It could cost the group votes in the Most Popular category. I thought I'd rearrange the rest if they're going to keep Avanell's off display for very long. What do you think?"

"I think that's a good idea. You want some company?"

"Sure. I need to leave early, though. I have to stitch something for Sarah Ness tomorrow when I get back."

"I get up with the birds, so you just let me know when you want to leave and I'll be ready."

They agreed to meet at seven the next morning.

Harriet was tired after her poor night's sleep the night before, but she knew she'd rest better if she started Sarah's quilt. It took more than an hour to load. She knew Aunt Beth told quilters to leave a generous fabric border to allow for the natural take-up that occurs when lines of stitching are put into the fabric and batting layers, but Sarah had left a very minimal edge for her to work with. She ended up having to take the top off the machine and start over two times before she got it to line up with the backing. She resolved to charge Sarah for the extra set-up time.

Once she had the quilt in place, Harriet decided to go ahead and finish it. She stopped at eight o'clock for a quick salad and boiled egg then continued stitching until she was done.

At ten o'clock, Fred pushed through the door from the kitchen into the studio and meowed.

"I know—it's time to go to bed, and this time by ourselves."

She clipped the thread and turned the long-arm machine off. She could unload it when she got home from Tacoma tomorrow.

She was tired, but glad she was done. She picked up Fred and carried him upstairs.

Chapter Twenty

Shall we swing by Dannay's Donut Shop on our way out to the highway?" Mavis asked. "I'll buy."

"Fine with me," Harriet said. "Just don't tell Aunt Beth—she's got me on a diet of lettuce and water."

"Your aunt Beth is one of Dannay's best customers."

"Aunt Beth also believes in the old 'do as I say, not as I do' brand of parenting."

"This'll be our little secret," Mavis said and smiled.

Traffic slowed to a crawl as they approached the city, and it was nearly nine-thirty by the time Harriet pulled into the parking lot of the show hall. A sign on the entrance door indicated the show didn't open to the public until ten.

"Good," Harriet said and pointed at the sign. "We have time to make whatever changes we need to before the show opens." She pulled the door open. No one was in the ticket booth.

"Hello?" she called.

Mavis crossed the lobby to the office door. She tapped on it with her knuckle and, receiving no response, opened it and leaned her head in.

"Nobody's home," she said and shut it again.

"Let's go fix the display, and then we can try to find someone," Harriet suggested.

The safety lights were the only illumination in the cavernous hall.

"It's kind of creepy in here without the big lights on," Mavis said.

Darkened quilts swayed gently in the air current created by the building's ventilation system. She moved closer to Harriet.

"What's that noise?" she whispered.

Harriet stopped. A dull thwack was followed by a metallic jangle.

"Hear that? It sounds like it's coming from the next row."

"That's where our exhibit is," Harriet said. "Come on."

She strode into the next row. The center quilt in the Loose Threads display was jerking and bucking. The rod pocket ripped.

"Stop!" she yelled.

The quilt went limp. She heard a scuffling sound. Each quilt in the display billowed in turn, as if someone were pushing it out from behind.

She ducked behind the row but was only in time to see a door swing shut. She pushed her way back out between two quilts.

"This is really weird," Mavis said. "Looks like someone was trying to rip Lauren's quilt down from the display."

"Lauren's quilt?" Harriet said. "Lauren entered her quilt as an individual display, remember? We hung it up at the front."

Mavis held up a corner of the large quilt with its bottom edge now sagging to the floor.

"This is definitely Lauren's. There's no mistaking the image of Kathy the Kurious Kitty."

"I wonder what it's doing back here."

"Well, wherever it belongs, it needs to be repaired before it can go on display anywhere. Here, help me get it down."

"Wait," Harriet said. "Let me get a chair so we can unhook the rod from the hanging chains." She went to the end of the aisle and pulled one from a cart that had been placed there for the use of exhibitors.

"Who's there?" a voice called. A woman in a wheat-colored denim jumper came down the main aisle toward her. When she got closer, Harriet could see it was Jeri, the registrar they'd met on their previous visit.

"It's Harriet Truman, and Mavis Willis," she said. "We're with the Loose Threads display."

"No one is supposed to be in here until ten o'clock." She crossed her arms tight across her chest, her alligator loafer tapping a nervous rhythm on the cement floor.

"We stopped at the office on our way in, but no one was there."

"That didn't make it okay for you to come back here."

Well, excuuuuse me, Harriet thought.

"It wasn't clear from our conversation yesterday if you were taking Avanell's quilt down or not," she explained. "We wanted to rearrange the display if that was the case."

"You need to talk with your group members." Jeri paused to allow her contempt to envelope them. "Lauren Sawyer already spoke to me last night. She instructed us to remove her entry from the individual display and put it on the rod Ms Jalbert's had been hanging on. She said the group agreed that quilt should be off display until a decision was made about its classification."

"Excuse me, *Jeri*," Harriet said, emphasizing the woman's first name. "I think it's you who needs to talk to *your* group—your security group. When Mavis and I came in here this morning, someone was in the process of trying to steal Lauren Sawyer's quilt. It's been damaged, and believe me, I'm going to let her know on whose watch it happened. We're going to have to take it down and repair it, if it even can be repaired. I'm sure you'll be hearing from Lauren shortly."

"But it's too late to make a substitution," Jeri spluttered. "The public will be entering in fifteen minutes. We can't have an empty rod. It will spoil this whole row."

"Look, lady..." Harriet was ready to unload her frustration on this narrow-minded woman.

"Where is Avanell Jalbert's quilt?" Mavis interrupted.

Harriet glared at Jeri but kept her mouth shut.

"We have it in the office," Jeri said and stiffened as she guessed the implied solution.

"The group just decided it wants Avanell's on display while you make your decision about its classification," Harriet said. She could see from Jeri's face the woman didn't like that idea but knew she couldn't oppose it without the consent of the show committee.

Jeri turned on her heel. "I'll get the quilt from the office," she said over her shoulder as she stalked away, squaring her shoulders in an obvious attempt to regain her composure.

"She's just a breath of fresh air," Mavis said with a smile that was little more than a grimace.

"Here," Harriet said. "Hold my chair, and I'll get Lauren's quilt down."

Mavis held the folding chair steady while Harriet stood on it to release the hanging rod from the chains suspended from the ceiling. She bundled the quilt to her chest and stepped down.

"Boy, someone really wanted this down," Mavis said as she ran her fingers over the torn red batik on the back. The rod pocket had been pulled loose along nearly half its length. It wouldn't have been so bad if the pocket had become unstitched, but this wasn't the case. The pocket had been torn from the backing where it had been stressed.

Harriet laid the pocket back in its proper position. "I suppose she could take the binding off the top edge and then reapply a larger rod pocket to cover the damaged area."

Mavis ran her gnarled fingers over the pocket and the torn fabric under it.

"It will have to be a fairly large pocket, and if she does that, it might show when the quilt is actually hanging on it. We'll have to think about this a little. She might have to put a new piece of backing on along this top edge."

"But then she'd have to pick out her stitching in that area and re-do it."

"I didn't say it was going to be easy. Here, take the other end. Let's fold it up."

Jeri returned with Avanell's quilt clutched to her chest.

"You realize the committee is meeting at one o'clock this afternoon, and they may well decide to take this right back down again."

"We'll take our chances," Mavis said, and pulled the quilt from her grasp. Mavis turned her back on the woman and pulled the folding chair back into place under the display hooks.

Jeri stormed back down the aisle toward the office.

"I thought she'd never leave," Mavis said. "I was hoping I wasn't going to have to get up on that chair."

Harriet handed her the wooden dowel that would slip into the rod pocket. They fed the rod into the opening, and when it was in place, Harriet climbed onto the chair and placed it into the hooks.

"How does it look?" she asked.

"Scoot it a little to the left."

She did as instructed.

"That's better," Mavis said.

"Funny, I never noticed before that Lauren used the same backing fabric Avanell did."

"Yeah, it's funny, all right," Mavis agreed. "Lauren tends to attract coincidences like that."

"I guess it was all for naught. I don't see how she can get her quilt repaired in time to make any kind of showing here."

"You never know with that girl. I guess we'll see."

"Can we look at the other displays, as long as we're here?"

Mavis looked at her watch. "It's still a few minutes until opening, but what the heck. The worst old Jeri can do is throw us out, but I don't think she'll bother."

Harriet was amazed by the variety in the exhibit. It was hard to believe that quilters could continue to come up with new and different ways to combine color and shape, and render the result in fabric.

Several groups were following the popular trend of combining a book club with quilting. The members read a book chosen by the group then designed and created quilts that depicted the designers' take on the story. Journal quilts also continued to be popular. She stopped in front of a clothesline-style display of journal pages.

"I don't see how they have time to do a quilt every month all year."

"They're a lot smaller than a bed quilt," Mavis pointed out.

"Yeah, but they're a lot more dense with imagery and stitching, plus they still have to back and bind them, and that's time-consuming no matter the size."

"It's all about priorities, I guess."

They spent another half-hour looking at the exhibits, paying special attention to the other groups in their category. Jeri was nowhere to be seen, which suited Harriet just fine.

"I worked on Sarah's quilt last night. All I have to do is take it off the machine when we get back, so I'm sure I have time to stop for lunch, if you're interested."

"I know a really great cafe in Gig Harbor," Mavis said.

"Sounds good to me."

"Good. That'll give us time to talk about your love life while we're driving."

"That's going to be a short discussion, given that I don't have a love life."

"Honey, I know you were thinking of your late husband when Connie was asking you about your date. It'll never be the same. No one can replace Steven, and no one expects you to try, but there is a lot of room between that and sitting home. Steven wouldn't have wanted you to sit home for the rest of your life, would he?"

"I don't know," Harriet said, tears welling up in her eyes. "It turns out I didn't really know him at all."

"No man wants his wife to mourn him forever. Besides, I'm not saying you need to go out and get married again. You just need to go out. So, how was Harold?"

"You probably know more about him than I do."

"Generally that's true in Foggy Point, but Mr. Harold Minter is new to the area. He moved here from Seattle last year when Bertrand hired him."

"Hmm," Harriet said. "How was Harold? Well, we had a really great dinner.

His friend is a good chef. His poached salmon was moist and flaky, and the grapefruit sorbet was to die for. We were too stuffed to eat dessert, but I saw the tray on our way out, and they looked very chocolate and very tempting."

"So far you've made a great case for marrying the chef. Now, how was *Harold?*"

"He was..." She paused. "Polite. Punctual. He drove the speed limit."

"Just what I always look for in a man," Mavis said and looked out the window, preventing Harriet from seeing her expression.

A light rain began to fall, and within a few miles, the sky opened up and it poured in earnest. Visibility dropped, and the wind picked up. Harriet needed all her concentration to keep the car on the road.

At last, she pulled into the graveled parking lot of a log cabin-style building.

"Here we are," Mavis said. The sign over the door read ALICE'S LOG CABIN RESTAURANT.

Inside, painted wooden picnic tables were covered with red-and-white checkered cotton tablecloths. Small tin buckets held paper napkins and mismatched pairs of ceramic salt and pepper shakers graced each table. A large brick fireplace filled one wall, its cheery flames providing welcome warmth.

"What do you recommend?" Harriet asked when they were seated.

Mavis recommended the Reuben sandwich, and it turned out to be delicious. The bread was dark, the sauerkraut crisp and tart. The corned beef was flavorful and not too salty. Best of all, the cheese was melted but not greasy.

"How did you find this place?" Harriet asked when they had finished eating.

"Oh, you know how word travels in a community like ours. People are always driving back and forth to either Tacoma or Seattle, and eventually, someone in Foggy Point has been to every place there is along the route."

"This was a great find, whoever found it."

The rain had let up while they were in the restaurant. The wind gusted in puffs but had lessened. Harriet hoped both wind and rain would hold off until they were safely back in Foggy Point.

"Do you believe what Lauren was saying about Aiden being the most likely suspect in Avanell's death?" she asked after they were back on the highway.

"I don't want to believe it," Mavis said. "But someone killed her, and likely as not, it will turn out to be someone we know. Those police shows I watch say you're more likely to be killed by a loved one than a stranger."

"Aren't crimes of passion usually between a man and a woman in a romantic relationship?"

"Crimes of greed aren't."

"From what people are saying, it seems like Avanell didn't have anything left to be greedy over," Harriet countered.

"You can't believe what you hear on the gossip line. Avanell might have had money stashed away that we don't know about."

"Aiden just doesn't seem like the kind of guy who would be hung up on money."

"You sound pretty sure for someone who isn't interested in him."

Mavis then changed the conversation to the safer topic of the quilt show for the rest of the trip.

It was just after one o'clock when Harriet drove down the wooded driveway and into the clearing in front of Mavis's cottage.

"I'll see you tomorrow at Pins and Needles," Mavis said. "Try and get some rest."

"I'll do that."

Chapter Twenty-one

Harriet realized she'd forgotten to ask Mavis how to get hold of Lauren to return her damaged quilt—Lauren did her own quilting, so Aunt Beth wouldn't have her in the business address book. She decided to swing by Pins and Needles on her way home. Marjory was sure to have contact information.

She glanced at her watch. There should be time for her to drop Lauren's quilt and still be ready for Sarah.

A class was in progress in the large classroom when she entered the shop. From the front aisle, she could see seven women sitting at sewing machines, their attention on a small dark woman at the front of the room. She headed toward the room; and as she got closer, she could see that Lauren was one of the students.

She retreated back to her car and got the quilt, folding it over her arm as she started down the aisle toward the classroom. She had planned to wait until the teacher stopped lecturing before she entered, but Lauren caught sight of her—and the quilt—before that happened.

Jorge at Tico's Tacos three blocks away could have heard the shriek she let out.

"What are you doing with my quilt?" she screamed, knocking her chair over as she leapt toward Harriet. "Why isn't it in Tacoma? You're ruining everything! Take it back there right now!"

She stomped her foot to emphasize her demand. Her classmates froze, and then all began talking at once. No one left the table to join Lauren.

She was shouting too loud to hear anything Harriet tried to say, so Harriet flipped the quilt open and held up the torn strip of rod pocket.

"How dare you! Is Avanell winning so important to you you're willing to destroy my work to insure it?" Lauren shrieked. Her face was a purplish-red.

The thick veins on the side of her neck stood out like piping on a formal pillow.

"Would you please get hold of yourself," Marjory whispered and pushed her into the small classroom. Lauren pulled Harriet along with her.

"What on earth is going on?" Marjory asked.

Lauren started to wail. Marjory put a hand on her arm and said, "Harriet first."

"Mavis and I went up to Tacoma to see what they were doing with Avanell's quilt. Apparently, Lauren had called them already and asked to have her quilt put where Avanell's had been. When we arrived, someone was trying to pull the quilt down. They took off, but they had torn the rod pocket. I couldn't see who it was."

"Could you not stitch the pocket back in place while you were there?" Marjory asked.

Harriet turned it over and showed her where the backing and stitching had been torn.

"Of course, we would have done a simple repair if that would have worked, but as you can see, the backing fabric is torn and some of the batting has been pulled out. Look how the quilting stitches are pulled tight in the area, too. And that shows on the front side." She flipped the corner of the quilt back over. "It seemed like the best thing to do would be to bring it back to Lauren as quickly as we could and let her decide what to do."

"I'll be ruined," Lauren wailed. "My patterns were going to be a sellout when my quilt won the best in show." She looked at Harriet. "This is your fault. I'm ruined just so a dead woman can have one more win she wouldn't care about even if she were alive to see it."

"I think that's quite enough," Marjory said.

"You'll pay for this," Lauren snarled, her voice low. "You will definitely pay for this." She pulled the quilt out of Harriet's arms and stormed out of the room.

"I'm sorry," Marjory said.

"I guess she believes in killing the messenger."

"She's upset. She spent all her money finding a publisher for her patterns and then getting them printed. She really wanted that win. I've never seen her act like that. I'm sure she'll apologize once she's had time to calm down."

"I wouldn't count on it."

"I've got to get back to the class, but is there anything I can do for you before I go? A cup of coffee, maybe?"

Harriet declined the offer but on impulse asked for Misty's home address. The woman had filled out a registration card for the Thursday night group, and Marjory was happy to give her the address if she promised to let her know if she found her.

The address was an apartment number in the docks area of Foggy Point. It had been dark when she and Aiden drove through there before; but from what she had seen, it wasn't the kind of place a woman would want to go alone, even in the daylight. Then again, Misty lived there and presumably came and went unmolested.

Harriet pulled out her cell phone. She dialed Avanell's house. The phone rang eight times, and she hung up when Avanell's recorded voice came on. Of course, she realized. The family would be at the funeral home for the viewing.

She pulled away from the curb and headed for the docks. She turned toward the water and slowed as the road became bumpy with railroad tracks. She checked the address again then stopped and looked for a street sign.

She was about to give up when she saw a faded wooden sign that said RIVER VIEW APARTM. The end of the word was missing where the wood had broken. She eased down the unpaved street.

The apartment building was a single-level with a sagging roof and badly chipped paint. Six doors opened onto a broken cement sidewalk. Moss clung in green gobs to the roof, siding and any other surface it could penetrate. Cardboard and duct tape filled the spaces where windowpanes had broken. A faded artificial rose hung limply from a tack on the third door down. A stick-on sign underneath read MANAGER.

Harriet parked and stepped carefully on the broken sidewalk. She stopped at the door marked number four. She looked for a doorbell and, finding none, rapped sharply. She listened and hearing nothing, rapped again. This time, the door swung open slightly.

"Misty?" she called. "Can I talk to you?" She listened again. "Misty?" When she received no answer, she pushed on the door.

It opened into a dark, damp room. The fruity smell of rotting bananas assaulted her nose. She held her hand up to her face but stepped in.

"Misty, are you in here?"

She heard the rustle of movement behind her. She started to turn, and everything went black.

SHE WOKE UP IN HER CAR. IT WAS DARK. SHE FELT HER HEAD.

"Ouch," she said out loud as her fingers found the goose egg at the back.

She pulled her fingers away. They were slippery with what she assumed was blood. Her head was pounding, and she felt like she was going to throw up.

She groped around the console and found a partially full bottle of water in the passenger's cup-holder. She held it to her face and soaked in its coolness then uncapped it and took a sip. She found a napkin, dampened it and wiped her fingers clean. She wouldn't try to deal with the lump until she got home.

Whatever was happening in Misty's apartment, the woman was on her own. Harriet wasn't getting out of her car.

She wasn't sure how safe she was going to be driving, but she sure wasn't staying at the docks any longer. She straightened in her seat and buckled her safety belt. Her head throbbed, and a wave of dizziness was followed by a wave of nausea. She eased the car away from the sidewalk and slowly turned a wide circle. Turning her head was not an option, so she prayed no one had parked on the street since she'd arrived.

She completed the turn and breathed a sigh of relief when she reached the road. She drove toward town at twenty miles an hour.

It seemed to take forever to cross town and reach her hill. As she started up the incline, she realized there was a car following her.

Terror shuddered through her, causing the hammer in her head to pound with renewed energy. Her skin felt clammy, and her stomach contents threatened revolt. A part of her wanted to just stop and give in to whoever was behind her—anything to make her head stop pounding.

She looked helplessly around. She had several boxes and bags of fabric along with two books on tape, a travel mug and a half-full bottle of water. Her cell phone should have been in the center console, but was no where to be found. Her head hurt too much to think about whether she had put it somewhere else before going into Misty's.

She locked her doors and pulled into her circular driveway before she remembered you were supposed to avoid your own house and go directly to the police station if you were ever being followed. She sighed. She couldn't possible drive anywhere else, and in any case, she wasn't sure exactly which street the police station was on.

She picked up the travel mug as she parked. The mug had dregs of hot chocolate in the bottom. As weapons went, it was probably useless, but then again she'd done reasonable damage with a sprinkler.

The car behind her stopped. If she loosened the mug's lid, it would fly off and perhaps startle her stalker and then the muddy liquid would blind him. She wasn't quite sure what came next, but it was the only plan she had.

Adrenaline coursed through her body as cold sweat trickled down her spine. She waited.

"Are you okay?" she heard through her closed window. She looked up without moving her head. A curtain of black clouded her vision. Anger quickly chased it away. Aiden stood beside her car, his hand on the door.

He repeated his inquiry. She clicked the locks, and he opened her door. He crouched down beside her

"What happened?" he asked.

Harriet slumped toward him and began to cry. He held her until she stopped shaking.

"You scared me," she finally managed as she pulled herself out of the awkward embrace.

He was dressed in a black suit that had probably fit him before he'd gone to Africa. Now it was slightly baggy, but on his hardened body and with his tan and long hair, it made him look like he'd just stepped off the catwalk in Milan. Harriet's head hurt, but she wasn't blind.

"I was driving back home after Mom's viewing and I saw you creeping through town. It looked like you were kind of weaving. I got worried, so I followed you."

His voice was soothing. She could see why he made a good vet. He was used to dealing with patients who couldn't talk back or say where it hurt.

"Someone hit me in the head," she rasped, her throat suddenly dry again.

"Where?" he said.

"Down by the docks."

"No," he said, a small smile playing across his lips. "Where on your head?"

She pointed. "Don't touch it. It hurts."

He ignored her request and gently worked his fingers from the sides of her skull toward the bump. He stopped each time she gasped.

"Look at me," he said.

She slowly turned, moving her whole upper body. He pulled his Mag-Lite out of his pocket.

Her eyes burned, and she blinked as he shone the light in each eye.

"Look at my finger," he said and moved it across her field of vision. "Your pupils look okay, and your eyes are tracking, so that's good, but I think we need to get you to the emergency room. We'll take my car. Let me pull up beside you so you won't have to walk far."

He moved his car then supported her as she shifted from the driver's seat of hers to the passenger seat of his.

"It's going to take a little longer, but I think I'll drive you directly to the Jefferson County Hospital in Port Townsend. There's an urgent care clinic in Foggy Point, but I'm not sure if they can do a CT scan or not."

Harriet didn't have the energy to argue. She was so glad someone else was in charge at this point she would have gone anywhere with him.

She wanted to sleep during the hour-long drive, but Aiden said he couldn't let her sleep until she'd been checked over. She felt as though she were permanently stuck somewhere between asleep and awake. She knew Aiden talked to her but couldn't remember the next day what they had talked about.

At some point during their drive, he must have called the hospital. He pulled into the ambulance circle, where they were met by a nurse with a wheelchair. Harriet was pushed into the triage area while Aiden parked the car. She was in cubicle one when he returned. A white-haired doctor with a golf-course tan was examining her, pretty much repeating the tests Aiden had done.

"You're a very lucky young woman," the doctor said. "That's a nasty lump on your head. We'll take a few pictures to make sure you didn't crack your skull and keep you overnight to see if we can knock that headache down a little. We can also give you something for the nausea. I don't expect to find anything. I think you'll probably have a headache for a few days, but that should be all. I'll leave you a prescription for some pain medication to help with that when you get to your room."

"Thank you," she whispered.

The doctor smiled and left the room.

A nurse in teddy-bear-print scrubs came in and gave her an injection in her hip; Aiden turned discretely away. When the nurse was gone, he came over to where she sat on the gurney and gently put his arms around her.

She tried to talk. She wanted to explain why she'd gone to the docks and about Misty.

"Hush," he said. "We can discuss this tomorrow. For tonight, just try to relax and let the medicine take effect."

Chapter Twenty-two

Harriet's sleep was punctuated by hourly wake-up visits by the night nurse. The nurse would take her temperature and blood pressure, and by the time she fell asleep again it would be time for the next hourly check.

Each time she woke she saw Aiden, who didn't seem to be bothered at all by the night nurse, as evidenced by the slow, steady breathing she could hear coming from his chair.

When grey light filtered through the slatted blinds on the narrow window in her room she gave up all pretenses. The next time the nurse came in, Harriet was sitting on the side of the bed, her legs dangling over the side.

"Okay, I'm finished with this game," she announced.

Aiden sat up. "What's going on?" he asked, and looked around as if he didn't know where he was.

"I'm out of here, that's what's going on. Ouch!" Harriet said, and winced as her feet hit the floor.

The nurse took a good look at her and went for the door.

"I'll call the doctor," she said as she left the room.

The doctor came in, pronounced Harriet able to travel, gave her a prescription for pain medication and instructed her to return for a check-up in one week. Aiden brought his car around to the front entrance, and a nurse wheeled her into the misty morning.

"Where to now, milady?" he asked when he had her safely buckled into the passenger seat.

"Home," she said. "I just want a hot shower and a couple of hours sleep in a bed that doesn't have a plastic sheet."

"Do you think that's wise?"

"Right now I don't think anything."

"First someone breaks into your studio and wrecks everything, and then someone whacks you on the head and leaves you for dead. I'm no detective, but I have to think someone isn't too happy with you. The last thing I think you should be is a sitting duck, and that's exactly what you'll be if you go home."

"I don't really have a lot of options. Besides, I have a business to run."

"Let me think a minute," he said. "My studio would be a little cramped."

"And not obvious at all," Harriet said. "Sarah Ness would have it all over town before my bag was unpacked."

"There's tons of room at my mom's house."

"Oh, yeah. That would be real comfortable for all of us. Your sister hates me. You hate your uncle. We could have a great time together."

"Have you got a better idea?"

"Yeah, I go home to Fred, and you go back to your family." She leaned her head against the car window. "And I really can't talk about it anymore."

She closed her eyes. When she opened them again, Aiden was guiding his car down the wooded drive that led to Mavis Willis's cottage.

"I can't just drop in on Mavis like this," Harriet protested in a voice barely above a whisper. "It's only what o'clock in the morning besides."

"It is seven-fifteen, and we both know Mavis gets up earlier than that."

Mavis greeted them at the door in a plaid flannel bathrobe that had once belonged to her husband.

"What have we here?" she said and took Harriet's free arm. Aiden let go of her other one and followed them into the sitting room of the cottage.

"Sit," Mavis said, and guided Harriet into a tan corduroy recliner. "Go get a pillow from the bed in that room next to the bathroom," she ordered Aiden and pointed toward a short hallway.

He returned with a down pillow, and Mavis gently wedged it under Harriet's head, taking the pressure off the lump and relieving her pain considerably.

"Go put the kettle on," she continued in that voice mothers use and kids of every age obey without question.

"Now," she said to Harriet as soon as he was out of earshot, "tell me what happened before he gets back."

Harriet told her the basics: she gave Lauren her quilt then tried to find Misty; Misty didn't answer the door, it opened and Harriet stepped in. The next thing she knew, she was in her car with a big headache. She drove home. Aiden saw her driving erratically, followed her and took her to the hospital. She finished with the fact that Aiden didn't think she should go home.

"I'm not sure I agree with his theory about your safety, but my boys played football and I do know that after a blow to the head you shouldn't be alone for a few days. You can stay in my spare room for a day or two until we're sure your head is okay."

"Water's ready," Aiden called from the kitchen. Mavis went in and returned in a few minutes with a tray loaded with a pot of tea, two mugs, a sugar bowl and small pitcher of cream.

"I better take off," Aiden said.

"Thank you," Harriet told him. He leaned down and kissed her gently on the forehead.

"No problem," he said and went out the door.

"I'm telling you, that boy is sweet on you."

"I'm not so sure about that," she said, but in a small corner of her heart, she hoped it was true.

"He sure has been handy when you've needed a friend."

"I know, but I can't help but think about what Lauren said yesterday. You know, when we were talking about who stood to gain from Avanell's death, and she said Aiden was the one who inherited money when Avanell died."

"You can't believe gossip like that."

"But who was right there when the studio was broken into? And who found me after Misty's place? Aiden—both times. And he's been on me like a glove. He finds a reason to come over almost every day."

"That's not unusual if the boy has a crush on you."

"Even that doesn't make sense. I'm at least ten years older than him. He's a young professional with a bright future. He could have any woman in Foggy Point. Why me?"

"Let's look at the other side. Why would Aiden break into your studio and trash it? And why would he hit you on the head only to turn around and bring you to the hospital when you came to?"

"I think Misty is the key to this," Harriet said. "Nobody's seen her since she was fired from her job at The Vitamin Factory on Tuesday. I take that back— Carla saw her right after that. Then my studio was broken into, after Misty went missing, with Avanell being killed that same night, maybe at the same time even. Now, when I try to find Misty, I get hit on the head. It has to be connected."

"But what does any of that have to do with Aiden?"

"Misty must know something about Avanell's death," Harriet decided.

"That doesn't explain your studio, and maybe what she knows about

Avanell's death is that she killed her. Did you think of that?"

"I haven't figured out how the studio fits into anything yet, but I don't believe in coincidence. And I have a hard time believing Misty would kill Avanell. Carla said Avanell had helped Misty."

"But Avanell didn't keep her from being fired. Maybe she was mad at her," Mavis suggested.

"When Carla came to get Avanell at lunch, she said *Tony* fired Misty. It's not clear that Misty saw Avanell. Tony fired her, not Avanell."

"Here, drink your tea," Mavis said, and handed her a mug. "We aren't going to solve this right now, and you shouldn't be getting worked up about it while your head is hurting." She picked up a lap quilt and tucked it around her. "Try to rest a while. Then, if you feel well enough, we'll get cleaned up and go meet the group at Pins and Needles to go to Avanell's memorial."

Harriet couldn't help but notice the pattern on the lap quilt. It was a sawtooth-style block made in Civil War fabrics. The pattern's name was *Kansas Troubles*.

Chapter Twenty-Three

MAVIS DREW THE DRAPES IN HER LIVING ROOM AND RETREATED TO THE KITCHEN. "You try to get some sleep, honey. I'll be in the kitchen if you need anything."

Harriet reclined the chair, adjusted the pillow and fell into a deep sleep. She woke two hours later when the doorbell rang. Mavis shuffled to the door, and when she opened it, Harriet could see Officer Nguyen.

"Is Ms. Harriet Truman here?"

Mavis nodded and led him into the living room.

"You are one hard lady to find," he said. "I'm Officer Nguyen. I was at your house earlier this week."

"Yes," Harriet said. "I remember. How can I help you?"

"Dr. Pattee reported you came in with a head wound last night. He said it looked like you'd been hit with the proverbial blunt object. Strictly speaking, he only has to report gunshot wounds, but Jefferson County is a small hospital in the middle of several small communities. We all work together." He paused. "Is there anything you'd like to tell me about? This is your second incident in four days. That makes you a one-woman crime spree around here."

"I really don't know what I can tell you," Harriet said. "I went to find someone in an apartment down at the docks. I shouldn't have gone there by myself, and I paid the price. I don't think there's any big mystery."

"It's true you should have known better than to go down to the docks alone, but you were still assaulted. It's a crime, and you need to report it."

"Fine, as long as I can do it from this chair."

Officer Nguyen sat in a dining room chair Mavis placed next to the recliner. He opened a black leather flip-top notebook.

"Tell me what happened," he said. "The long version."

She told the story again, including approximate times. He took notes and asked a few questions. When they were both satisfied she could recall nothing more, he closed the notebook and stood up.

"This isn't much to go on, but at least it will be on the record if anything else happens. And if you want my advice, until we figure out what's going on, you should stay here with Mrs. Willis."

Mavis appeared again from the kitchen and showed him out.

"Well, that's settled, then. You'll stay."

"I'll stay until my head stops spinning, but I have a cat to feed and Aunt Beth's business to run. I can't stay in hiding indefinitely."

"We'll see about that." Mavis glanced at the clock. "I'm going to go rinse off and get dressed, and then we can go back to your house so you can get some clothes and get ready for the memorial. You can either put out food for the cat, or if it would make you feel better, you can bring him along."

Harriet closed her eyes and slipped into a drug-induced sleep until Mavis came out and awakened her, dressed in black and holding her purse and car keys.

Fred was frantic when Harriet opened the kitchen door. She immediately put food in his dish, but he kept weaving between her legs and meowing. She groaned as she bent down to pick him up. He began to purr.

"Did you miss me?" she asked, and he head-butted her in reply.

"Let me talk to the cat," Mavis ordered. "You go take a hot shower and get into something black."

Not a problem, Harriet thought.

She came back down stairs twenty minutes later in the same black dress she'd worn on her two outings with Harold. This time she'd draped a large black silk scarf with a tiny grey pattern over one shoulder and held it in place with a black enameled pin.

Fred was reluctant to be left behind, but the two women retreated to the studio and escaped out that door. Mavis drove them to Pins and Needles and parked in front of the store.

"Honey, are you all right?" Connie said and pulled Harriet into a hug as she walked in the door. Harriet's head hurt too much to protest. "My daughter-in-law works the night shift at the hospital. She told me Aiden brought you into the emergency room last night with a head injury." She held her at arm's length and looked into her eyes. "Are you okay, mija?"

"I'm fine—really. It was just a little bump on the head."

"It's a goose egg, Connie," Mavis interjected. "Luckily, she inherited her aunt's hard head. She's going to stay with me for a few days, just to be sure."

"Good," Connie said. "You listen to Mavis and do what she says."

"I plan on it." Harriet looked around for something to drink so she could take a pain pill. All this hugging and moving was making her head hurt again.

She noticed Carla in the small classroom folding fat quarters she had just cut.

"I'm going to get a drink of water," she said and headed for the breakroom. She got her water then stopped in the training room.

"Carla," she said, "can I talk to you a minute?"

Carla got a deer-in-the-headlights look but nodded assent.

"Do you know where Misty is? I'd really like to talk to her. I went to her house and someone knocked me out. I think she's in trouble, and I'd like to help her."

Carla looked down. "She came to my house yesterday," she said to the floor. "She wasn't doing too good."

"In what way?"

"She really needs her medicine, and she don't have any. I told her to go to the free clinic for now and that I could help her on payday. I couldn't tell if she was going to do it or not."

"Tell her I have some fabric for her baby quilt and tell her I will get her some medicine."

"I don't know where she is. She's hearing voices. She said a man is coming to get her, and then she took off. I don't know if she'll be back or not."

"Listen, can you call me if she shows up again? I'm serious—I'll get her medicine for her. I'll get her enough to last until she gets a new job."

Carla looked up at her with clear blue eyes. "I'll try," she said.

Harriet returned to the group of women. DeAnn was relating a bit of gossip about a woman named Barbara whom Harriet had yet to meet when Lauren came in.

Robin put her arm around Lauren's shoulders. "I heard about your quilt. I'm so sorry. Can I do anything to help?"

Lauren glared at Harriet. "You can't, but she can," she said and gestured toward her. "I stayed up all night and repaired my quilt. There isn't time for me to re-quilt it on my sewing machine, but it wouldn't take anytime at all on the long-arm."

"Fine," Harriet said. "I'll do it. Right after the memorial service."

Mavis started to protest, but she silenced her with a glance.

"Where is *my* quilt?" Sarah Ness demanded as she entered the store.

"My day is complete," Harriet muttered to Mavis.

"I went to your place of business and waited and waited and you never showed up," Sarah yelled.

Harriet's head began to pound in earnest. "Could you please lower your voice?" she asked. "Your quilt is done. I just need to take it off the machine frame."

"You leave her alone," Mavis scolded. "She hit her head and had to spend the night in the hospital, that's why she wasn't there for your appointment."

"I can't believe there weren't two minutes to call me," Sarah complained. "You probably waited forever in the waiting room."

Mavis glared at her. Sarah finally noticed and stopped talking. She stuck her bottom lip out. Mavis sighed. Her third son had raised pouting to an art-form; Sarah was a rank amateur.

Sarah looked at Mavis as she spoke to Harriet.

"I'm coming over as soon as this memorial thing is over. Have my quilt ready." She turned her back and flounced off to the breakroom.

"Don't you worry about her, honey." Mavis rubbed Harriet's arm. "Okay, everyone," she said to the group. "Who's driving, and who needs a ride?"

The women quickly divided themselves among three cars and drove toward the strait to the Unitarian Church. The gravel parking lot was half-full when they pulled up to the low, glass-fronted building. Harriet hoped the chapel inside was more inviting than the cold exterior and was not disappointed.

They entered an open reception area. Wooden racks held colorful pamphlets with titles like "Why Should I Try Your Church," "Securing the Future" and "The Front Steps." A somber-looking woman with long grey hair pulled back and held with a silver clasp was handing out funeral programs in front of two ornately carved wooden doors. Mavis looked at her watch.

"We're a few minutes early," Michelle said as a lanky blond man in a black suit came into the vestibule from a hallway that led off to the left. Mavis walked up to her and clasped her hand.

"I'm so sorry for your loss," she said. "Jackson, I'm so sorry to see you again under such unhappy circumstances," she added to the blond man.

Harriet assumed Jackson was Michelle's husband.

Bertrand de LaFontaine emerged from the same hallway, accompanied by a small, pale woman with red-rimmed eyes and two equally pale young women who had to be his daughters.

Mavis and DeAnn went to the family.

"I'm so sorry for you loss," Mavis repeated, and took his hand in her two.

"Our group won't be the same without our most prolific prizewinner."

"She loved making beautiful quilts. That and the business were her life," Bertrand said.

"She loved her family, too," DeAnn added.

"Did that show ever decide what they were going to do about Avey's quilt?" Bertrand asked. "If they aren't going to display it, we'd like to get it back. Some of the employees want to put up a memorial display in the building lobby. They asked for one of her quilts to be the backdrop. I thought since that show quilt was the last one she ever made, it would be the right choice, if we can get it back."

"Harriet and I just went to Tacoma to get it—"

"Uncle Bertie, the chaplain needs to speak to you," Michelle interrupted.

Bertrand pulled his hand from Mavis's with a look of apology and followed Michelle. Lauren and Robin were deep in conversation with the program woman. Harriet looked around at the clusters of people and felt alone. The one family member she knew wasn't in evidence. Her head was pounding again.

She touched Mavis on the arm. "I'm going to go find the restroom."

"Are you okay?"

"Yeah, I'm fine. I just want to freshen up a little." She turned away before Mavis could protest.

She peeked down the hallway the family had come out of and saw a small sign sticking out of the wall at the other end. It had to be a restroom. She walked slowly down the hall, trying not to jostle her head. The sign turned out to be for a library, but the hallway angled to the right, so she continued on. Finally, at the end of the second hallway, she found the women's room and went in.

Two large white baskets filled with lavender and pink silk flowers were to the right of the door. Just beyond was a large open closet with a variety of choir robes, aprons and worn-looking flannel shirts splattered with paint, all on wire hangers. A box marked CANDLES sat on the shelf above the closet pole. A vanity table with hairspray, deodorant, cotton balls, breath spray and hand lotion was to the left of the door.

She went through an interior door that led into the actual lavatory, dampened a paper towel with cool water and held it to her forehead. She went back out to the dressing room area and sat on the vanity chair. She rubbed lotion into her hands then shut her eyes, propped her elbows on the table and rested her head in her lavender-scented palms. She took a few deep breaths and willed her head to stop hurting.

She wasn't sure how long she'd been in the room when she heard a noise in the hallway. She knew Mavis would worry if she didn't return, so she got up and headed back to the vestibule.

"Calm down," she heard a male voice say from an open doorway. She flattened against the wall and inched closer to the source of the sound.

"You don't get it," Michelle said, her words broken by sobs.

"So, tell me," Aiden said. "I get that Mom was out of money. I don't understand it, but I get it. But you're a lawyer; your husband is an environmental scientist. You must make plenty of money between you."

"It's simple, really. You see, it turns out that it doesn't matter how much money you make, it's all about how much you spend."

"So stop spending so much."

"Stop spending so much," she mimicked in a snotty little-girl voice. "How am I supposed to do that? You tell me how to stop spending. Do I take the girls out of the only school they've ever known? Or do I let them come home alone after school and sit around and watch television all night? Or should I resign from the club, so we can all get fat and die of heart disease? Are you suggesting I can go to my job in one of the most prestigious law firms in Seattle in thrift store clothes? Take my clients to lunch in a used Toyota?" She started to sob again.

"Stop crying," Aiden said. "I told you I'd take care of it. Just give me another week. The bank needs to process the paperwork. Then we'll both have all the money we could ever need."

Harriet stepped away from the wall and went back to the entry hall. She'd heard enough.

Harold had arrived while she was gone.

"Harriet," he said when she came back into the foyer. "I'm sorry to be seeing you under such unfortunate circumstances."

"It's very sad," she said. "I suppose we all expect to bury our parents someday, but I think we hope it will be when we and they are all very old and that our parents will have gone gently in the night."

"It has been quite a shock for the family," Harold said. "Say, I spoke to James earlier. He said he's trying a new 'Death by Chocolate' dessert recipe and suggested we might come by and try it out. I'll need to make an appearance at the coffee the church ladies are hosting after the burial, but then maybe we could slip away for some dessert and coffee. If you think it's inappropriate, considering why we're here, I'll understand, and we can do it some other time."

"No, I think it's a fine idea. I just need to get a project from one of the other people. It was damaged at the quilt show, and I need to help with the repair."

"I'll wait to hear from you, then," he said, and pantomimed tipping a hat. Then he turned to speak to Bertrand and his wife.

She looked around the room and located the Loose Threads.

"There you are," Mavis said as she joined them. "Jenny just went to the ladies room to try to find you. It's about time to go in and get a seat."

The carved wooden pews were filling up. Lauren and DeAnn were holding a space for the group. Harriet filed in between Mavis and Jenny, who had returned, and sat down on the hard wooden seat.

The pews were adorned with clusters of cream-colored lilies and pale yellow roses. Large baskets of hothouse azaleas, hydrangeas and mixed bouquets of white chrysanthemums, baby's breath and green sword fern filled the area behind Avanell's closed casket. Every business and association in Foggy Point and beyond must have sent an offering.

An ornately carved oak table at the back of the chapel held a basket that was overflowing with condolence cards. A matching basket held envelopes and cash. A small sign noted that donations would go to Avanell's scholarship fund for deserving local students.

The chaplain came in, and a hush fell over the group. Sarah Ness rose and went to the front of the church. Harriet wasn't sure why she was surprised. Being annoying didn't preclude the possibility of having a beautiful voice.

Sarah sang a moving rendition of "Take Me Home to Jesus" and sat back down. The chaplain read several Psalms then introduced Marcel, who delivered a short eulogy. Sarah sang "Amazing Grace," and it was over.

People were offered the option of filing by the closed casket and about half did. Marcel announced from the back of the room that everyone was invited to join the family in the cemetery behind the church for the graveside portion of the service.

A fine mist had been falling earlier but had ended sometime during the service. The funeral attendees exited the church into a pale sunlit afternoon. The cemetery was separated from the church by a copse of trees. Pea gravel on the path crunched under Harriet's feet as she walked with Mavis through the trees, up a small rise and into the grassy burial area.

A blue canopy with white chairs underneath had been erected at the far side of the lawn, a mound of earth covered with sheets of Astroturf just beyond the seating area. The first row of chairs surrounded a large rectangular hole in the ground. The family were already seating themselves when she and Mavis arrived.

"If it's okay with you, I think I'll stand at the back," she said.

"I know this is hard for you," Mavis said. "You do what you need to do."

Harriet stood behind the last row of chairs. Darcy came over and joined her.

"It's really sad, you know? My mom used to work at The Vitamin Factory when I was in middle school. Avanell had a deal where employee's kids could come to the factory and work on their homework in the breakroom. She hired teenagers to act as tutors. They got scholarship money, and we kept out of trouble. Avanell would buy healthy snacks for us, too. She was just a cool lady."

"Has there been any progress on her case?"

"Not really."

Before she could say more, Michelle left the front row and stormed down the short aisle.

"What are they waiting for?" she demanded of Darcy. She glared at Harriet and strode down the path toward the chapel.

"What is her deal?" Harriet asked. "I know I found her mother, but she gets ruder every time I see her. I'm sure she's upset about her mom, but it seems to be more than that where I'm concerned."

"According to Officer Nguyen, she claims Avanell stayed late at work to finish binding her quilt so she could get it to you for the show. If you believe the burglary theory, and Michelle does, then it follows that if Avanell hadn't been at work finishing her quilt she wouldn't have been there when the thieves arrived. She thinks her mom stayed at her office to finish it because she was almost done, and her office was closer to your place than her home was."

"She wasn't working on her quilt that night," Harriet corrected. "Aiden already had her quilt. In fact, her quilt was at the dry cleaners Wednesday." She related to Darcy how Aiden had used the quilt and the resulting repair and cleaning.

"That's really weird. Michelle obviously wasn't here, so she'd have no direct knowledge of what happened," Darcy said. "I wonder why she thought Avanell was stitching."

"Her pincushion and some of the backing and binding scraps were in her office. Avanell *did* work on her quilt in her office Tuesday. Maybe Michelle just assumed since the sewing stuff was in the office, Avanell must have been working on it on Wednesday." Harriet worried, too late, that Darcy might wonder how she would know that, but Darcy didn't seem to notice.

"In fact, it probably doesn't matter what she was or wasn't doing at work. I don't believe it was a random robbery—Foggy Point just doesn't have this type of crime. We're not big enough to attract the kind of people who plan this type theft. We have our share of drug problems down by the docks, but those people don't usually stray more than a half-dozen blocks in each direction. If they're stealing to feed a habit, they aren't doing it in Foggy Point."

"Still, it's kind of weird she's telling people Avanell was sewing. One of the factory workers told me Avanell often worked packing vitamins to save on paying overtime."

"Maybe Michelle doesn't want people to know about Avanell's financial difficulties."

"Was Avanell having money trouble?"

"I'm sorry, I've said too much already."

A short man in a dark suit came out of the trees and went up the aisle. He spoke in hushed tones to Avanell's family. Bertrand, Marcel and Aiden got up and followed the man back to the chapel. A red-faced Michelle passed them at the clearing.

"The tractor that is supposed to pull Momma's casket up here broke down," she said loudly enough for the group to hear. "They are going to have to carry her up." She plopped in her chair in a distinctly unladylike manner.

The crowd was growing restless by the time Harriet spotted the casket, carried by Avanell's sons, her brother and three men from the funeral home. The chaplain followed, and began a prayer as soon as the casket was in place at the front of the group of mourners.

Avanell was lowered into the ground, and family members each rose and one by one threw either a single rose or a handful of dirt on the casket. Harriet saw Mavis dab at her eyes with a tissue. She looked away and caught a brief flash of motion at the tree line.

She turned and surveyed it. Misty stood beside the trunk of a large maple.

"I'm going to go find something to drink," Harriet said and rattled the bottle of pain pills that were in her pocket. She turned toward the church, and Darcy drifted over to a group of women Harriet didn't recognize.

Harriet circled back and moved silently toward the path and the tree beyond.

"Misty," she whispered. Then, when she was away from the group, she said it again louder. "Misty? It's okay if you came to Avanell's funeral. Can I talk to you? I can help." She kept talking. The woman had to be on the other side of the tree. "I have some fabric at my house for your baby's quilt. And I can help you get your medicine."

"I don't need medicine" came from behind the tree.

"I can help you make a quilt for your baby." She tried to sound soothing. "You must have liked Avanell. I know she liked you."

"She said Tony shouldn't fire me," Misty said. "She said I wasn't stealing." She began to sing. "Hush, little baby, don't say a word..."

"Misty, did you go back to the factory after Tony fired you?"

"Mama's gonna buy you a mockin'bird..."

"Misty, this is real important. Were you at the factory when Avanell got hurt?"

Misty's eyes got big, and she started making a noise that sounded like *hum-mum*, repeated over and over. She turned and ran down the path into the woods.

Harriet debated following but didn't want to draw attention to the woman. She returned to the mourners.

"How are you holding up, honey?" Mavis asked.

"My head hurts, but no worse than it did this morning."

"If you want to leave, just say the word."

"I sort of told Harold I would go get coffee with him after this. I told him I had to get Lauren's quilt first."

"I can get the quilt, but are you sure you should be going out?"

"He promised me Death by Chocolate."

"What on earth is that? It sounds dangerous."

"I hope so. It's a dessert experiment by his friend James, the chef."

"Let's go eat our cookie and drink some tea and then you can get on to your 'chocolate death' or whatever it is."

The Loose Threads reassembled and returned as a group to the church reception. The tea was weak and the cookies doughy, but it was a kind gesture by the women of Avanell's congregation. Lauren had been one of the drivers, so she got the quilt from her trunk and brought it in to Harriet.

"Here," she said and thrust it into Harriet's hands. "When can I get it back?"

Harold chose that moment to join them. "Do you need more time?" he asked.

"Just let me put this in the car," she told him then turned to Lauren. "I should have it done sometime this evening. I'll have to see how much area has to be done before I can be more specific. I'll call you when I get it on the machine."

Lauren walked away without so much as a fare-thee-well. Harriet hadn't expected a thank-you but the woman could at least have been civil.

Lauren reminded her of a girl named Jeanne she'd gone to school with when she'd been dropped here in junior high. Harriet knew now that Jeanne had simply been protecting her territory—she had the other girls in their class convinced she was the most sophisticated, cutting-edge seventh grader Foggy Point had ever seen. She'd studied French the whole summer prior, and she would break into the language whenever a cute boy was in sight.

On her first day, Harriet made the mistake of responding to one of her comments, also in French. It was automatic. She hadn't done it on purpose. She hadn't been there long enough to realize that French was reserved for Jeanne and the boys, and no one else. Jeanne never spoke to her again, and for the rest of the year, no other girls did, either, if Jeanne was in the room.

Her problem with Lauren was that she hadn't done anything to the woman. There was no reason for her to be the focus of Lauren's anger. She hadn't destroyed anything. Lauren should be grateful she had been at the show and able to bring the damaged quilt back right away. She was going to point that out when Lauren came to pick it up.

"Here, honey, I'll take that," Mavis said when Lauren was out of earshot. "You know you shouldn't be working, with your head and all."

"Is something wrong?" Harold asked.

"Nothing a little chocolate won't help," Harriet replied.

"I'll go get the car and pull it up front."

He left, and she saw Aiden standing across the room, picking at a cookie. She walked over to his side.

"I'm really sorry about your mother," she said.

Tears filled his pale eyes. "It really sucks," he said.

Her heart went out to him, but she couldn't help but wonder just how far a brother would go to help his sister.

"You want me to get a movie and bring it over to Mavis's later?"

She didn't reply. Her pulse raced as she rapidly tried out and then rejected methods of ditching Harold. Could she drop to the floor in a fake faint? No, they might try to take her to the hospital. She couldn't plead a headache; she'd already said chocolate would help her headache. Her head throbbed.

"What?" he asked. "You have a hot date or something?"

"I have to fix Lauren's quilt," she said. She saw Harold's El Dorado pull up in front of the fellowship hall. Aiden's gaze followed hers.

"Is he waiting for you?"

"He asked me to go for coffee, and I said yes. His friend is a chef and is making a special dessert."

"You sound like you know the guy. Have you been out with him before?"

"Not that it's any of your business, but yes, we went to dinner."

"The Chamber meeting, right?" he said.

"No, dinner."

"So...what? You're dating Harold?"

She could see the disbelief in his eyes.

She put her hand on his arm. "It's just coffee."

He was still staring at her when she turned, walked out the front door and got into Harold's waiting car.

"Is the boy all right?" Harold asked.

"He's upset about his mother. Do you have any idea what form Death by Chocolate takes?

"Let's go find out," he said, and turned his car toward Smuggler's Cove.

Chapter Twenty-four

THE DESSERT EXPERIMENT TURNED OUT TO BE A SMASHING SUCCESS. THE CONCOCTION was a layered affair; the main sections were somewhere between really rich cake and a dark chocolate fudge, with the filling layers a heavy chocolate ganache. James drizzled raspberry sauce onto the chilled plates before arranging the perfect chocolate wedges on top.

"That was a nice service. Didn't you think?" Harold said when they had finished the dessert and were sipping cups of dark coffee.

"I don't think it's possible to have a nice funeral service. Maybe if you die at home at the age of a hundred and five. But I'll bet your children are still sad."

"Your children will be in their eighties by then, and their sadness will have more to do with what implications your death has for their own mortality."

Harriet actually smiled at this. "Good point."

"Of course, there won't be any children at my funeral," Harold said.

"Mine, either, it would seem." She sighed. She tried not to think about Steve, but it was impossible. They had made plans for a family. Of course, that, too, had been a lie. He knew he wouldn't live to have children, and if he did he had a fifty percent chance of passing on his disease to any offspring.

No, there weren't children in her future.

"Did I say something to upset you," Harold asked and took her hand across the table.

She pulled it away. "No, it's not you. It's been a hard day. Would you mind if we went home now?"

He glanced at his watch.

James came to the table before Harold got up.

"How did you like it?" he asked.

"It was wonderful," Harriet said. "And believe me, I know my chocolate."

"Okay, Miss Expert, what's your favorite chocolate candy."

"Are we talking high-end or grocery store?"

"Your choice."

"High-end, I like Ethyl M's, but they're hard to find here. In the northwest, I like Moonstruck and Dagoba."

He looked at Harold. "The woman has taste."

"Grocery store, I go for Lindor Balls, the blue wrapper. Seattle Chocolates, pink wrapper, are good when you can find them, too."

"You come here any time you need a chocolate fix." James put his hands up in a gesture of rejection. "Tonight's on me," he said as Harold went for his wallet.

"Thank you, this was a perfect end to a hard day," Harriet told him.

Chapter Twenty-five

Harold delivered her to Mavis's cottage. He opened the car door and escorted her to the small front porch. To her relief, he rubbed his hand on her back, urged her to get some rest and left.

"That you?" Mavis called from the kitchen.

"Yes," Harriet said and wandered in to join her. Mavis was pulling a baked chicken from the oven.

"I cooked a bird so we could have an early supper, but I'm afraid I can't stay here and eat with you. My daughter-in-law called and needs me to watch the baby so she can go to a class she's teaching. My son was going to do it, but he's stuck at work."

"I'm not hungry right now anyway," Harriet said. "Besides, I need to go fix Lauren's quilt. Could you drop me off at my place? Then I can drive my car back when I'm done."

"You aren't supposed to be alone at your house, though."

"Everyone knows I'm staying with you, especially after the memorial service. No one will go looking for me at my house. It's probably safer for me there. If someone comes looking for me, it will be here."

She could see Mavis was trying to work out a better plan in her head.

"I suppose if you call me every hour while you're there. And just stitch, nothing else. Then you come right back."

"Agreed."

"Okay, let me put this chicken in the icebox and then we can go."

Harriet used the time to call Sarah Ness.

"I have your quilt on the machine. I'm leaving now, so just give me a few minutes to get it off the frame." She rang off.

"You know, the more you accommodate her the more she's going to

142

expect," Mavis said and leaned into the coat closet to retrieve her purse, cutting off any response Harriet might have made.

Mavis drove around the lagoon and up the hill to Harriet's house.

"I'm still not comfortable with you being here alone," she said as Harriet got out.

"It's going to be fine. I'll stitch the quilt and probably be back to your house before you are." She retrieved the quilt from the back seat.

"Don't worry," she said as she shut the door.

Mavis drove away, and Harriet fished the house keys out of her pocket. A low window to the left of the door was covered with a cream-colored sheer lace curtain to allow a maximum amount of natural light into the studio. She froze as the curtain slowly rippled. She started to back up and slipped off the landing onto the top step. The curtain slowly pulled to one side, and a furry face pressed against the glass.

"Fred," she said and let out her breath.

She opened the door and stepped into the studio. The cat jumped off the windowsill and began to meow and rub his face on her shoes.

"I haven't been gone that long," she said.

Fred wasn't buying it. It had clearly seemed an eternity to him.

"Come on." She set her purse and the quilt on a chair in the studio and went into the kitchen. She poured a scoop of catfood into one ceramic bowl and filled the other with fresh water.

"There," she said. "Just don't think you get to go on a food binge because I'm spending the night with Mavis."

Fred made a purring noise and planted his face in his dish. Harriet propped the door open and went back into the studio.

At the long-arm machine, she attended to Sarah's quilt. She loosened the tension block and unclipped the elastic tension pulls then removed it from the frame and laid it on her cutting table. She picked up a small, curved pair of scissors that would allow her to clip any loose threads close to the fabric's surface without cutting into it. She pulled a floor lamp over to the table and bent over the quilt. She was almost finished when she heard the door open.

"It's almost ready," she said without looking up.

She heard footsteps approach the table then smelled a sickly sweet odor. She struggled to pull away the cloth that was clamped over her nose but only succeeded in breathing more deeply. She suddenly felt very heavy.

Chapter Twenty-six

H ARRIET," A VOICE CALLED FROM FAR AWAY. "HARRIET, CAN YOU HEAR ME?"
She could hear, but it was too hard to answer. She tried to open her
eyes, but it took too much effort. She slid back into the darkness.

When she awoke again, she was lying in a dark room. She wiggled her feet
and tensed her hands then released them. She could feel everything, including
the IV line attached to the back of her left hand. That had to be a good sign.

She moved her head, and a wave of nausea so powerful she couldn't quell
it swept over her. She threw up in a kidney-shaped yellow plastic pan someone
held for her. A cool cloth draped across her head.

"Try not to move," an unfamiliar female voice said.

She opened her eyes again.

"Don't try to talk," the woman's voice said. "You're in the hospital. Sarah
Ness found you slumped on the floor of your studio. She called nine-one-one
and they brought you here." She must have seen the panic in Harriet's eyes.
"Don't worry. Your head is fine. It says on your chart you were hit on the head
last night. Tonight, it would seem, you were drugged. From the smell of your
clothes when they brought you in, it was probably ether or something similar.
You'll have a bit of a hangover, but other than that, you should be fine by
morning. I'll call the doctor and see if we can give you another shot of
Compazine to control your nausea."

Harriet mumbled a thank-you and closed her eyes again. The woman
picked up the pan and headed for the door.

"I'll take care of this and be back to clean you up a little. Then if you feel
like it, there's a gentleman outside who'd like to see you."

True to her word, the nurse returned with a toothbrush and paste and a
warm wet washcloth.

"You just hold still and let me do the work," she said. "The trigger for nausea is motion."

She worked magic with a squirt bottle and several clean hand towels. Harriet had to admit, she did feel a tiny bit better.

"You ready for your visitor?"

"Give me a clue. Young? Old? Uniform?"

"No uniform, very good-looking."

Harriet nodded ever so slightly.

"What happened?" Aiden said as he rushed into the room. He pulled a wheeled visitor's chair to the side of her bed and sat down, scooping her hand into his as he sat. "Mavis called and said you were going to your studio and she was worried about letting you go there alone. She said she tried to call you to check up and you didn't answer. She asked me to run by and see if you were all right. I passed the ambulance coming down your hill. I checked your studio, and the police were there—I guess Sarah Ness found you. I found Fred and locked him out of the studio so the police could do their thing."

"Thanks," Harriet mumbled. She pushed her suspicions aside and closed her eyes, knowing she was being weak but unable to fight it.

The grey light of dawn made a pale rectangle of light on her bed the next time she woke up. A different nurse with a digital thermometer and a blood pressure cuff stood by her bedside.

"This'll just take a minute," she whispered. "I'll try not to wake your boyfriend. He can't have gotten much sleep wadded up in that chair." She nodded her head toward an upholstered chair near the window.

"He's not my boyfriend." He could be the reason I'm here, she added to herself.

"If he's not your boyfriend, he should be," she said. "He hasn't left your side since you've been here. That's not easy to find in a man." She wrote some numbers on Harriet's chart and left again.

Harriet knew all about men who left. But the nurse was wrong. She didn't need a boyfriend, especially one who kept showing up without an excuse.

She lay in her bed and listened to the rhythmic rise and fall of Aiden's breath. She must have dozed off again, because the next time she looked at the window bright light was streaming in.

"Welcome back," Aiden said. He was sitting in the wheeled chair beside her bed again. He held a cup of something steaming in his right hand. He swept the hair off her forehead with his left hand, his fingers trailing along the side of her face. "How do you feel?"

She moved her head away from his hand. The area of the lump was still tender, but no nausea greeted her movement.

"Better," she said. "What happened to me?" she asked for a second time. "This time I want the long version."

"I'd like to hear that one, too," Officer Nguyen said from the door. "I stopped by to question you last night, but you were..." He paused. "...busy."

Harriet moaned. She didn't remember much about last night, but she did know it had taken more than one dose of the anti-nausea drug before she had fallen into a drugged slumber.

"Let's start with Ms Truman's story. You can wait in the hall till I call you," he said to Aiden. He pulled the visitor's chair up and sat down. His spicy cologne filled the room with its masculine scent.

Harriet recounted the events from the night before. She started with her arrival at Aunt Beth's house and ended with waking in the hospital.

"So, let's back up a little further," Nguyen said. "It would seem that a lot of people knew you were staying with Ms Willis. Who knew you were going back to your house?"

She thought for a minute. "Mavis, of course. Lauren Sawyer—I was there to work on her quilt. Someone had damaged it at the show in Tacoma, and we were repairing it." She closed her eyes. "Sarah Ness. I had just taken her quilt off the machine when..." She trailed off.

"When you were attacked?" Officer Nguyen suggested. "Was there anyone else?"

"Aiden Jalbert. Mavis called him when she couldn't get hold of me—wait. I told him at the memorial that I was going to be working on Lauren's project. Oh, and Harold Minter. I went to coffee with him after the memorial service." And Misty, she thought. She'd told her she had fabric for her at home. Maybe Misty had decided to take her up on it.

"Can you think of anyone else?"

"The quilt group all rode to the memorial service together. It wouldn't be outside the realm of possibility that they talked about it on their way home."

"So, what do you have that someone wants bad enough to break into your home twice for?"

"If I knew that, I'd be the first to tell you. As near as I can tell, they didn't take anything when they trashed the place. They ruined a few quilts and messed up a bunch of stuff."

"Who would benefit if the quilts were damaged?"

"No one. Well, the other quilt groups in the show, I guess. Lauren, maybe. I just can't believe anyone wants to win the competition that bad. It's not like there's some big prize. It's mainly about bragging rights."

"Someone wanted something bad enough to come back for a second look." He stood up. "Okay, Mr. Jalbert, you can come in now."

Aiden returned and sat in the visitor's chair. Officer Nguyen moved to the wide windowsill.

"Start with what you were doing before you went to Ms Truman's."

"I was at my apartment—I have a studio over the vet clinic on Main Street. I was picking up my dog. I'd left her in the outside kennel at the clinic while I was at my mom's funeral. I took Randy for a walk around the block and had just poured her some kibbles when my phone rang."

"Did you talk to anyone, see anyone?"

"Only the dog," he said with a tight smile. "The phone rang, I put Randy back outside and went to check on Harriet. I passed the ambulance on my way up the hill. I'm sure your buddies told you what I did after I got to the house."

Officer Nguyen shut his notebook. "They did," he said. "I'm sure we'll have more questions for you later, but this is enough for now." He turned back to Harriet. "We'll have patrol cars swing by your house a couple of times a night, but I strongly recommend that you continue to stay with Ms Willis until we catch the guy that did this to you."

"Okay, everybody out," a square-shouldered doctor with a thin sandy-colored ponytail said from the door. "How are you feeling this morning, young lady?"

Harriet tried to smile. "Better than when I came in."

"You were lucky your friend found you so quickly. Ether is nasty stuff. It's pretty easy to overdo it. And they apparently left you facedown. You weren't breathing too well when we got you. Luckily, it wears off with time, and we gave you a few things to help the process. You should have no lasting effects. You were fortunate you didn't hit the bump on your head again.

"You did pop a stitch, though, which probably happened when they were putting the oxygen mask on you. I'd like to go ahead and do a little repair on that, and then I think we can let you out of here."

A nurse came in, and the doctor did a more thorough check of her vital signs then repaired the wound on the back of her head.

He left, and Mavis came in, alone. Apparently, Aiden had gone without a backward glance.

"Oh, honey," Mavis said. "I knew I shouldn't have let you go to your house alone."

"It's not your fault. I'm a big girl. Besides, it makes no sense that someone would come and drug me. How could you have anticipated that?"

"My mama radar was working overtime. I knew you shouldn't go there, and I went ahead and let you go alone. Your aunt Beth is gonna kill me."

"It's done and I'm fine, so how about we work on getting me out of here?"

Mavis held out a paper bag. "The police took your clothes as evidence. The nurse said I should bring you an outfit, or they would be sending you home in scrubs."

Harriet took the bag. She pulled out a new pair of jeans, a pink T-shirt and a purple sweatshirt. She could see packages of new socks and underwear in the bottom of the bag.

"What's this?" she asked.

"I wasn't about to go back to your house alone. I took a run to the Wal-Mart. You needed more clothes anyway."

Harriet appreciated the effort, but she vowed to go shopping somewhere else as soon as she was able. Her old clothes may have been loose and black, but they were designer label loose and black.

"You didn't need to go to so much trouble, but thank you."

She eased herself to the edge of the bed and stood up. She'd been to the bathroom with the nurse earlier and had learned after a few missteps that moving slow was the key. She slowly changed out of the hospital gown and, with a little help from Mavis, got dressed.

"Doctor wants to see you in a week," the nurse said when she came with the requisite wheelchair. "And you need to take it easy for a few days. Try not to come in through the back door again," she said with a smile.

Mavis was waiting in the Town Car when the young Hispanic attendant wheeled Harriet out.

"Nice ride," he said with a smile that flashed a gold tooth.

"Yeah, isn't it?"

The young man set the brake and held Harriet's arm as she got out of the chair and into the car.

"Thanks," she said and waved as they drove off. She lowered her window when they were underway. The air was heavy with the salty smell of open water, and she breathed deep. The moist air made her feel stronger.

"I'm taking you right home," Mavis said.

"I need to go to Aunt Beth's."

"No way. We're going home and only home."

"I have to get Fred. I can't just leave him. Aiden locked him in the kitchen.

He's probably scared. It'll be fine. There are two of us, and the police are driving by often in case anyone comes back."

"We just get the cat, and then we go home," Mavis insisted.

Harriet didn't argue. She had every intention of looking around her studio—there had to be more to the break-in. Whatever someone wanted, they wanted it bad enough to come back twice. And they weren't afraid to hurt her to get it.

She didn't want it to be Aiden, but once again he was Johnny on the spot when she was hurt. And he had no alibi for the time before she was found.

Mavis pulled up the hill and into the circular driveway.

"In and out," she ordered. "And we stick together."

They got out of the car, and Mavis pulled a key from her purse and unlocked the door. It swung open, and she stood frozen on the threshold.

"Will you look at that?" she said and pointed.

A fluffy pile of shredded batting and slivers of multicolored cotton fabric sat on the floor by the cutting table. The predominant fabric color was red.

"What is—or, rather, was—it?"

Harriet stepped around her and knelt down by the heap. She picked up a handful and ran it through her fingers. She repeated the action twice more.

"I think it used to be Lauren's quilt."

Chapter Twenty-seven

HARRIET GRABBED FRED AND HIS TRAVEL CAGE, HIS DISHES AND HIS BAG OF FOOD. Mavis all but walked in the heels of her shoes, which made the task take twice as long as it might have.

They were back at the cottage before they dared speak about what they'd seen.

"Lauren is going to have kittens when she hears the news," Mavis said. "In fact, I don't think you should tell her in person."

"I have to tell her. Her quilt was in my possession when it got ruined."

"But when it was damaged in the first place, you weren't there. In fact, if we hadn't arrived at the show when we did, it probably would have been destroyed on Monday."

"I just don't get it. What could anyone gain by destroying Lauren's quilt?"

"The real question is who would be willing to kill you to destroy Lauren's quilt?"

The kettle Mavis had put on to heat whistled, and she got up and poured hot water into their waiting mugs. She set the mugs on the table and was putting homemade gingersnaps on a plate when the phone rang. She handed the cookies to Harriet and searched for the cordless phone. She found it on the table beside her chair in the living room and answered just as the caller hung up.

"Dial star-six-nine," Harriet suggested.

She did, and Harriet could hear the phone on the other end ringing.

"Hello?"

Mavis listened, said a few uh-huh's and finished with "We'll be there."

"Aren't you just the clever girl," she said to Harriet when she keyed the phone off and returned it to its base. "That was Jenny. She said the Loose

Threads want to meet tomorrow to deal with the project bags from Avanell's. What she didn't say is that they all want a first-hand account of what happened to you. I hope it's okay that I said you'd come."

"If we're going to be joined at the hip, I guess I don't have a choice," Harriet said. She realized she sounded like a petulant teenager, but she was tired and feeling boxed in.

"I can call her back if you're not up to it," Mavis said, trying to hide the hurt in her voice.

"I'm sorry, it's not you. It's my life. Aunt Beth was right—I was hiding in Oakland. But I thought I came here to help her. Then I find out I'm really here to take over her business and start my life again. I was even starting to believe it could work when all hell broke loose. I'm living like a fugitive, afraid of I don't know what. My life in California might not have been perfect, but I was safe and free."

"Honey, life is never predictable. You can lock yourself away in an apartment in California with only a cat to talk to, but that's not living. I'm not saying getting hit on the head is normal, either, but that could have happened just as easy in California as here. In fact, it's probably less uncommon there." Mavis came over to her chair and rubbed her back like she would a child. "The police are going to get this sorted out and you'll be back at your aunt Beth's in no time. You've lived in Foggy Point before. You know it's a good place."

Yeah, she knew what a great place it was. That's why she had so many friends from her previous time here. Still, a small part of Harriet wanted to believe her, but it was hard to see how it was going to happen. As near as she could tell, whoever had trashed her studio, hit her on the head, drugged her and ruined Lauren's quilt was getting away scot-free, and neither she nor the police had any idea what was going on or why. And she didn't even want to think about Avanell's death. She was trying to convince herself her troubles were unrelated to that; but deep down, she didn't really believe it.

"It might be good for you to talk to the Loose Threads. Maybe they can see a connection with the quilt and your studio and Avanell's death that we don't."

"I suppose," Harriet conceded. "You're right about one thing."

"What's that?"

"We aren't getting it. Whatever *it* is."

HARRIET HADN'T BELIEVED THE DOCTOR WHEN HE PREDICTED HOW MUCH BETTER SHE would feel by the next morning, but she had to admit he'd been right. She wasn't ready to run a marathon, but the world no longer spun with her every movement, and her stomach had stabilized.

She opened her bedroom door to the smell of eggs cooking. Mavis had prepared scrambled eggs with Laughing Cow cheese and chopped chives. It was accompanied by toasted English muffins dripping with butter and homemade blackberry jam. The two women washed it down with steaming mugs of English Breakfast tea.

"You're looking better this morning, honey," Mavis said when they were finished.

"I do feel as though I might live, which is a definite improvement over yesterday."

"If you want to change your mind about facing the Loose Threads, you say the word and I'll call in our regrets and we can spend the day here."

"No, I need to face Lauren, and I do think you're right about talking to the group and seeing if they have any fresh ideas. And, as much as I like you, I think we'll drive each other nuts if we just sit here all day and night."

Fred jumped into her lap and gave her a friendly head butt.

"He seems to have adjusted just fine," she said.

"I expect he's happy anywhere as long as he's with you."

"He's going to have to get along without me for a few hours. I need to see Lauren and get it over with."

"You go take your shower and I'll rinse off these dishes, then we'll hit the road."

"Mavis," Harriet said when she came out of the bathroom a half-hour later dressed in the pink T-shirt and jeans from the day before. "Did you wash these while I was sleeping?"

"I always wake up with the birds, and you needed your sleep. I was washing a load of towels so I tossed your stuff in. It wasn't any extra effort. We'll have to figure out something about getting the rest of your clothes. I was thinking we could ask Aiden Jalbert to go pick up a few things for you."

"I'm not sure I want his help at this point. I can't get past the fact he's the one person who seems to have a convenient reason to be close by whenever something happens to me."

"I've known that boy his whole life. He could never harm anyone. He's a vet, for pity's sake. When he was a boy, he'd cry when he saw a dead squirrel in the road. And I've raised enough boys to be able to tell when one is sweet on a girl, and you mark my words—that boy is smitten with you."

"It's highly likely you're going to know *whoever* attacked me, and probably whoever killed Avanell, too. I don't want it to be Aiden, either, but until I figure it out, I can't take any chances."

Mavis didn't say anything. She picked up a plaid wool shirt jacket that had been her husband's and slipped her arms into the sleeves.

"Let's get this over with, then."

Harriet grabbed the purple sweatshirt and her purse and followed Mavis to the car. The silence during the ride was a bit strained. Mavis finally spoke as she pulled up to the curb a block away from Pins and Needles.

"You tell the group everything that's happened, and I'll bet they'll have some ideas about what's going on around here, and it won't be Aiden."

She got out of the car, locked it and headed up the block to the fabric store. Harriet had to hustle to keep up.

"Good morning, ladies," Marjory said as they came through the front door. "Connie's in the breakroom making coffee, but no one else is here. How are you doing, Harriet? I heard you spent the night in the hospital again."

"I'm fine. I've got a little bit of a headache, but I'm much better than I was. I just wish I knew what was going on."

"It does seem like someone's got it in for you, doesn't it?"

"Yeah, that's the easy part. The why is what I don't get." Maybe Jeanne still lives here, she thought.

"That's what we're going to try to figure out," Mavis said. "As soon as everyone gets here."

Right on cue, the door opened and Robin McLeod and DeAnn Gault entered, each with a colored canvas totebag bearing a faded logo commemorating a quilt show many years past hooked over her arm. They dropped their bags and coats in the big classroom and went into the breakroom for coffee. Jenny Logan arrived carrying a wicker basket in one hand and a travel mug with a teabag string pinched between the lid and the rim in the other. She dropped her black leather coat on a chair, put her basket on the table and set about extracting the teabag from her mug.

Harriet's neck muscles tightened a little more with each arrival. Sarah Ness arrived in a cloud of complaints, and Darcy called to say she would be joining the group a little later and to save her some cookies. That left only Lauren. Hollywood couldn't have scripted it better.

She and the other quilters moved the worktables around to form one big rectangle then sat down with their stitching projects and hot drinks. Harriet picked a green-and-yellow baby quilt from Marjory's charity shelf then found a pastel rainbow-stripe fabric to bind it with. She cut binding strips then picked up one of the two sewing machines Marjory kept in the store for students who weren't able to bring one when they took a class. Connie gave her a spool of thread, and Mavis provided scissors. She had machine-stitched the binding about halfway around when Lauren entered carrying a red totebag with a stylized cat appliqued on its side.

"Oh, Harriet, I'm glad you're here. I can reapply the binding to my quilt and then take it back to Tacoma this afternoon. That way, it can at least be on display for the weekend. They expect the largest crowd on Saturday."

The room had gone silent.

"What?" she said. She looked around the table. "Where's my quilt?"

Mavis looked at Harriet and then pulled a large Ziploc bag from her tote. She set the bag of scraps she'd scooped from Harriet's floor the night before onto the table.

Lauren looked around for an explanation. Mavis opened the bag and dumped the contents on the table in front of her. The younger woman picked a handful of the fluff up with stiff fingers. The color drained from her face.

"Lauren," Harriet began, "I'm really sorry."

Lauren dropped straight down, her tailbone hitting with a jarring thud on the edge of her chair. Her mouth opened and closed, but no sound came out.

"After the memorial service, I took your quilt to my studio," Harriet continued. She didn't think the other quilters needed to know about her date with Harold. "I had Sarah's on the machine, but it was finished. I took it off and laid it on the big cutting table and was trimming threads when someone knocked me out. The next thing I knew I was in the hospital. Mavis picked me up the next morning, and when we went back to the studio to finish your quilt…" She looked at Mavis, hoping she wouldn't expose the small lie. "All we found was this." She pointed to the pile of quilting debris.

"How could you?" Lauren finally choked out. "I can understand you wanted Avanell's quilt to win the competition, especially with her being dead and all, but why did you have to destroy mine?" She looked at Harriet and burst into tears.

"Get her a cup of tea," Mavis ordered Connie.

The small woman got up and hurried to the breakroom. DeAnn pulled a handful of tissues from her purse and handed them to Mavis. Mavis dabbed at Lauren's face then pressed the tissues into her hand. She patted it.

"It's going to be okay, you'll see."

Lauren looked up, her face red in uneven patches and wet with tears.

"It won't be okay, ever. This was my chance. I used my credit card to pay for advertising, and to have patterns printed up and I needed the win. Avanell didn't care if she won or not. Couldn't she have just stepped aside this once and let me have my chance? Was that so much to ask?"

"Diós mio," Connie said as she came back and set a cup of steaming tea beside Lauren. "You can make another one. And if you were silly enough to spend money you didn't have, well, that's your mistake. Avanell is dead. She didn't do anything to you."

Lauren turned back to Harriet. "I trusted you with my quilt," she accused.

Harriet stood up.

"I'm sorry about your quilt, but I can't do this right now." She turned off the sewing machine and left the room. She saw Connie start to follow, but Mavis stopped her.

"Just give her a few minutes," she heard her say.

She went into the retail area of the store and was looking at a row of new arrivals without really seeing the fabric when she glimpsed Misty outside the store window.

"Misty, wait," she called as she hurried to the door and stepped onto the sidewalk.

Misty turned the corner and disappeared. Harriet broke into a run and rounded the same corner. She stopped and didn't see anyone. She was about to turn back when she heard a soft voice.

"Hush, little baby, don't say a word," the voice sang tunelessly.

Harriet continued slowly up the block. Misty was huddled on the stoop of an abandoned office suite. A faint odor of rotting food permeated the area. Misty pressed her body against the doorjamb.

"It's okay," Harriet said softly. "I don't want to hurt you. I just want to talk."

"Mama's gonna buy you a mockin'bird…"

"Will you let me help you?"

She didn't answer. She stopped singing and started picking at a patch of raw skin on her elbow. A trickle of blood snaked down her forearm. Harriet took a step toward her, but Misty cringed away, so she crouched down in front of her.

"Misty, can you tell me what happened to Avanell at the factory a few nights ago? Were you there?" She felt a brief stab of guilt—Misty had enough problems of her own. But this couldn't wait.

Misty started humming, occasionally breaking into song for a few phrases. Harriet listened.

"What are you trying to tell me?"

Misty continued her humming.

"Hmmmm, my brown-eyed girl, hmm hmmm hmmm hmm," she sang.

Harriet thought she was hearing a rendition of Van Morrison's song "Brown-eyed Girl."

"Misty, did a brown-eyed woman hurt Avanell?"

"Bang-bang."

"Did you see who shot Avanell?"

"Hush, little baby, don't say a word…" she sang again, and started rocking back and forth.

"Harriet," called DeAnn from the corner. "Is that you?"

Harriet turned to look, and Misty jumped up and ran down the block.

Harriet stood and walked back to DeAnn.

"Mavis got worried when she couldn't find you in the store. I told her I'd come out and see if you'd gone around the corner for a soda." She pointed toward a mini-mart across the street.

Harriet fished in her pocket for coins.

"That's what I was doing, but I ran out without my purse," She held up her hand with thirty cents in her palm.

"Here." DeAnn handed her two crumpled bills from her jeans pocket. "I'll tell Mavis you'll be right back."

Harriet thanked her and crossed the street. If DeAnn wondered what she was doing talking to the straggly-looking waif in a doorway, she didn't say.

Harriet returned to the group and sat back down at the sewing machine, her untouched can of cola on display to the right of her half-filled teacup and her scissors. Lauren's place at the table was now vacant. Mavis caught her glancing at the empty spot.

"She decided she'd rather lick her wounds alone," she explained.

"That's a diplomatic way to put it," Connie said. "She had a tantrum, and Marjory offered her sympathies and ushered her out the door."

Harriet finished the machine-stitching part of the binding and moved the sewing machine back to the storage shelf. Mavis handed her a threaded needle.

"Why don't you sit down and tell everyone what's been going on, and let's see if we can make any sense out of it."

Harriet wasn't sure this was the route to go, but as she was living with Mavis, she knew word was going to get out anyway. At least this way, they would all hear the same story at the same time.

"Start with the day you moved here," Jenny suggested.

Harriet explained how she had come from Oakland believing she was going to operate Aunt Beth's business for the month her aunt was away on her cruise. She'd spent a little more than three uneventful weeks working alongside Aunt Beth, reacquainting herself with the quilting machine and learning Aunt Beth's recordkeeping system. There had been no indication of trouble in those first weeks.

She told them how Aunt Beth had given her the business. The group's lack of reaction confirmed they had known the plan before she had.

After a brief internal debate, she told them about the scene in the Sandwich Board the day she'd gone to lunch with Avanell. She reviewed the perils afflicting Avanell's quilt from the time she'd given it back to her through the injured-dog fiasco and ending with the quilt being delivered to the show on the morning of Avanell's death. She skimmed over the part where she found Avanell's body; and as far as she was concerned, no one needed to know she'd been through Avanell's and Bertrand's offices. She hadn't found anything, so it couldn't possibly matter.

"Don't forget what happened after we left the quilt," Mavis reminded her.

"I think most of you know I got a phone call from the quilt show committee telling me they had to meet to decide if Avanell's entry could remain on display with the group exhibit. Mavis and I got worried about what they would do with the quilt while they were deciding. We drove back to Tacoma, but Lauren had already talked to them and had instructed them to put her Kitties in the center spot of the group entry and to take Avanell's trapunto off display.

"As we were walking into the exhibit hall, someone was trying to yank Lauren's quilt down from the back. We yelled, and they abandoned their effort and took off; but they damaged the quilt in the process. We re-hung Avanell's and brought Lauren's home for repair."

"Why on earth would anyone damage Lauren's quilt?" Jenny said. "Avanell knew Lauren wasn't a threat to her entry, and besides, Avanell was dead before you delivered the quilts."

"You tell me," Harriet said. "You know all the people involved. Who would be threatened by Lauren's success?"

"Maybe it wasn't Lauren they were targeting," Sarah suggested as she stood and picked her coffee cup up. "Maybe whoever it was wanted to discredit all of us. You know my quilt was displaying all the new fabrics Marjory got in this spring. Maybe one of the other stores would be threatened if quilts made from Marjory's fabrics win all the prizes." She turned and walked toward the kitchen.

The group went silent.

"I'm sure that's it," Robin muttered low enough that Sarah couldn't hear.

Connie stood up. "Anyone else want a refill of coffee or tea?"

Robin wanted coffee, and DeAnn got up and said she'd make a pot of tea and bring it back with her. Jenny went to the restroom.

When everyone was back, Harriet picked up her story. DeAnn had refilled her cup, so she stalled a minute while she added sugar and stirred.

"I didn't mention the break-in at Aunt Beth's studio because most of you were there. For those who weren't, I went to a Chamber of Commerce dinner Avanell asked me to attend, and when I got home someone had broken in and damaged some of the quilts and generally messed things up."

She edited out the part where she hit Aiden in the head with a sprinkler. She felt a slight twist in her stomach at the thought of him but ignored it and continued her story.

"My part of the story picks up again Monday. Mavis and I returned from Tacoma with Lauren's quilt. I gave it to Lauren here and then went to look for one of the young women from the Thursday night group. I got to her apartment, and the door was slightly ajar. I pushed it open and that's the last thing I remember clearly until I woke in the hospital. I'm not even sure how I drove my car home."

"She's not mentioning that the girl's apartment was down in the dock area."

Jenny and Connie rolled their eyes.

"I know your aunt taught you better than that," Connie said.

"The girl lives there," Harriet countered.

"That doesn't make it a safe place," Jenny told her.

"Continue," Sarah interrupted. She was clearly bored with the conversation.

"I went to stay with Mavis when I got out of the hospital. We went to the memorial service and saw all of you. Then I went to my studio to take Sarah's quilt off my machine and re-stitch Lauren's."

"And I found her on the floor, passed out," Sarah interjected. "If I hadn't come along she'd probably be dead. Not that she thanked me or anything."

Harriet looked at her but couldn't think of an appropriate response.

"I took Harriet back by Beth's place so she could get her cat, and we found

Lauren's quilt, or what was left of it, in a pile on the floor," Mavis said.

Darcy came in and set her nylon stitching bag on the end of the table. She went to the breakroom and came back a moment later with a cup of coffee and two oatmeal raisin cookies.

"Don't stop talking on my account," she said as she sat down and pulled a quilted square from her bag.

"What are you making?" Robin asked.

Darcy held the nine-inch square up so the group could see it. It was a simple pinwheel variation in sage green and pink. She was sewing a dark-green binding on the block.

"It's a kitchen quilt," she said. "My sister is remodeling her kitchen, and I'm making her a set that will match her new colors."

"Kitchen quilt" was the group's euphemism for a potholder.

"It's cute," Jenny said.

"So, what were you guys talking about in here, looking so serious?"

Mavis spoke first. "We were going over Harriet's problems to see if we could make any sense of them. You probably know all about them anyway."

"I'll tell you what I do know—whoever drugged Harriet didn't leave us much to work with. We found the handkerchief that was used to deliver the ether, but it's absolutely ordinary. You can buy them in any variety store. Otherwise, there wasn't anything to work with. Of course, in a studio where fibers are the stock-in-trade of the business, it wasn't likely we were going to find much hair or fiber evidence. So, did you guys come up with anything?"

"We were just starting to work on that when you came in," Mavis said.

"Let's start with the first incident—the break-in."

Marjory had been listening to the discussion from the kitting room where she was cutting fabric for patterns that would be packaged with the appropriate materials to make a finished quilt top. She came in carrying an easel and flipchart with a couple of marking pens.

"This might help," she said and went back into the kitting room.

Robin took the green pen and wrote "Harriet's Break In" at the top. "Okay, what do we know?"

"Some quilts were destroyed and some weren't," said DeAnn.

"Nothing was stolen," Jenny offered.

"There was no sign of forced entry," Darcy said.

"I'm not sure how much that means. There are quite a few keys to Beth's studio floating around in the community. Most of us have them," Mavis pointed out.

"That's a comfort," Harriet said, and made a mental note to call a locksmith when she got back to Mavis's house.

"What difference was there between the quilts that were damaged and the ones that were passed over?" Sarah asked, initiating a long silence.

"I don't think we know that, do we," DeAnn stated finally.

"Make a column on your piece of paper," Connie said. "Let's go around the table. Everyone can say if your quilt was damaged or not. And maybe even say how badly damaged it was."

Each in turn described the quilt they had at the studio and what, if any, damage it suffered. The results didn't yield a ready answer.

"So, what could be gained by destroying the particular quilts that were ruined?" Harriet wondered.

"I'm not naming names, but maybe someone was trying to guarantee a win," Sarah suggested.

"That doesn't make sense," Jenny said. "Why would they destroy DeAnn's and leave Connie's and mine alone?"

"Would they even know it was DeAnn's they were destroying?" Harriet asked.

"All the show quilts are labeled, aren't they?" Robin asked.

"My label didn't show up very well," DeAnn said. The fabric I used wasn't high enough contrast. It faded into the background. I didn't have time to fix it before the show, though, so I just left it."

"I know at least two of the non-show quilts were ruined, and they didn't have labels because they weren't bound yet," Harriet added, and tried to remember what other work had been in the studio at the time.

"So, maybe instead of damaging show quilts, they were excluding them." DeAnn offered. "It's hard to imagine why they would do that."

"Unless it was someone who personally knew how much work had gone into them," Mavis suggested.

"Then we're back to why," Harriet said. "There's no reason for someone to damage a random assortment of quilts."

"Let's move on to the next event," DeAnn said. "Harriet finds Avanell." She wrote it on the flipchart sheet.

"What can you tell us about that?" Robin asked.

"Not much, I'm afraid. I went to Avanell's to get the entry form for her quilt. The receptionist told me she was in the back, so I went to there and found her. She was dead."

"What can you tell us about finding her?" Robin asked.

"It was really sad," Harriet said. And something she didn't really want to think about.

To distract herself, she scanned the group, looking for brown-eyed girls. Darcy and Mavis were blue-eyed, and Robin had green eyes. That left Sarah, Jenny, Connie and, if you counted hazel, DeAnn. Harriet should remember the color of Lauren's accusing eyes, but all she recalled was the anger in them.

"How was she killed?" Jenny asked.

"I don't know," Harriet said. "I saw her on the floor and there was a lot of blood around her head, an amount that it would be hard to do without. I touched her hand, and it was stiff. I called nine-one-one, and that was it. I tried not to look at her face, so I don't know what happened."

"Single gunshot to the head," Darcy supplied. "I think it's okay to tell you that, but don't ask me anything else, 'cause I can't tell you."

"What kind of gun?" Sarah asked.

"Sarah," Robin said, "she just said she can't tell us anything, let her be." She wrote on the chart "found in the early morning, shot in the head, stiff to touch."

"Was anyone else around?" she asked Harriet.

"Not where I found her, but there was a young woman in the reception area." Harriet would have to check her eye color, too. At least, if you believed the humming of a disturbed young woman.

"Let's move on," Mavis said. "It was hard enough on Harriet to find the body. She doesn't need to keep talking about it just to satisfy our morbid curiosity."

"Okay," Robin said. "What happened next? Harriet took the quilts to Tacoma and then came home. And then what happened?"

Nothing I'm telling this group about, decided Harriet as she mentally reviewed her impromptu dinner with Aiden followed by her proper dinner date with Harold.

"The next big event was getting hit on the head," she said, and Robin wrote "Harriet attack number one."

"Not much to tell there, either," Harriet said.

"If you aren't willing to tell us anything we aren't going to be able to help you solve your problems," Sarah complained.

"Look, if I knew more, you'd be the first to know. I went to find a young woman who hadn't showed up at Marjory's Thursday group. For my effort, I got hit in the head. I woke up in my car. I saw no one, I heard nothing."

"Harriet hit in head down by docks," Robin wrote. "Related or bad luck?"

she added in parenthesis.

"The next thing that happened to me was after I got out of the hospital," Harriet continued. "As I told you, after the reception, I went to work on Sarah's and then Lauren's quilts. I heard a noise, but I thought it was Sarah. Someone put ether on a handkerchief and drugged me from behind."

"Did you get any sense of how tall the person was?" Jenny asked.

"Not really. I was bent over a table, so I suppose the attacker could have been short."

"Well, this has been a real waste of time," Sarah said.

"I'm sorry. Next time I'm attacked multiple times within a few days, I'll take notes."

"Clearly, whoever drugged you did it to buy time to destroy Lauren's quilt," Jenny said, and Robin made a note to that effect. "So the break-in, and the drugging and, for that matter, the attempt to remove Lauren's quilt in Tacoma were all related to the Kitties." Robin put these notes under a heading labeled "Lauren's Quilt." She went back to the column marked "Harriet finds Avanell" and underlined it.

"But what about Avanell?" she said. "There has to be some connection between the attacks on Harriet and Lauren's quilt and Avanell's death."

Harriet looked at the list again. "This would make more sense if it was Avanell's they were going after. If someone were jealous of Avanell's wins at the quilt show then killing her and destroying her quilt would make sense, in a sick sort of way."

"But Lauren was the one with the most to gain if Avanell's quilt weren't in the show, and she wouldn't destroy her Kitties," Jenny said. "That would defeat the whole purpose."

"What if it wasn't anyone from your group?" Harriet wondered.

"Would anyone really kill over a quilt?" DeAnn asked no one in particular.

"People kill over pocket change," Darcy answered.

"I still have to wonder if Avanell's family might be involved," Harriet said.

"On TV they always say you're most likely to be murdered by a loved one," Connie said as she tied a knot in the thread she'd just stitched and clipped the end close to the fabric surface.

"Unfortunately, that's a fact," Darcy said. "Being related is the number one risk factor in murder. It's generally either money or an argument over something stupid. And there are a lot of spouses who think murder is easier than divorce, although that doesn't apply here."

"First, it's hard to believe Avanell's family would hurt her," Jenny said.

"And second, how does destroying the quilt fit into that scenario, assuming Avanell's quilt is the real target." She looked around the room, but no one had any answers.

"I think I can answer one thing for you," Marjory said as she came in from the kitting room. "They both chose a red batik for their backing. Avanell used it first, and then Lauren chose it, too. I know that for sure, because Lauren's so sensitive about what Avanell is or isn't doing. I did call Avanell and tell her, but she just laughed and said she wasn't going to start over at that point. If someone only looked from the back and not real close at the stitching, they might look alike."

"We're still missing something," Harriet said. "It doesn't make sense for someone to kill Avanell and then destroy her quilt. Once she was dead, why would they care?"

"So, we are no closer to figuring this out than we were an hour ago," Sarah said.

"That's not entirely true," Robin argued. "If we assume Harriet's attack down by the docks was the result of going into a bad neighborhood alone, then the other two problems were probably about destroying the quilt, whether it was Lauren's or Avanell's that was the target."

"If that's right, then Harriet shouldn't be a target anymore if Lauren's quilt was the thief's goal," DeAnn said.

"That's a big if," Mavis pointed out. "If Avanell's quilt is the one, then Harriet won't be safe until the police arrest someone."

"I think you're overlooking the obvious here," Sarah announced.

"Please," Jenny said. "Enlighten us."

"We go get Avanell's quilt, and leave it in some easily accessible place. When it's gone, we know Harriet's safe."

"Do we worry about catching this person, who is probably Avanell's killer?" Mavis asked.

"Are we supposed to do everything?" Sarah retorted. "Aren't the police supposed to be catching the killer? Besides, we don't know for sure the same person who is destroying quilts is the person who killed Avanell. It could be two separate incidents."

"Sarah has a point," Darcy conceded. "First, we can't assume the events are related until we have evidence to link them. And second, it isn't the group's responsibility to solve either crime."

"The police don't seem to be getting anywhere," Jenny said. She got up and took her cup to the kitchen. They could hear the sound of running water as she rinsed it and set it in the drying rack.

"At least Avanell's quilt is safe for a few more days," Connie said. She folded the pink-and-orange table runner she'd been binding and put it into her bag. "I took my mother-in-law to the show yesterday, and they had hired additional private security guards. It seemed like we saw a guard every time we turned around."

"If it stays safe, that will tell us something," Darcy said. "If someone in Avanell's family is behind this, all they have to do is wait until the quilt is returned to them on Sunday. If it's not a family member who wants the quilt, they'll have to make a move in the next two days."

"That's assuming Avanell's is the target," Harriet said. She finished the last stitches on the baby quilt binding and buried the knot in the batting, clipping the thread end close then pulling the cloth to make the thread withdraw below the surface.

Mavis stood up. "We're going in circles here. Everyone keep your eyes and ears open and call if you hear anything. I'm going to take Harriet back to my place."

Harriet folded the quilt into quarters and took it into the kitting room, where Marjory was now cutting and bagging fabric swatches that would be mailed to her block-of-the-month customers. She held it up for approval.

"That looks great," Marjory said. She took it from her. "Did the group help at all, or are they just adding to your stress?"

"The only real thing the group came up with is that since Avanell's and Lauren's quilts have the same backing, it's possible someone might have confused them. That, and the fact they all think I was asking for trouble going down to the dock area."

"If you ask me, this isn't about quilting. I heard a little of what you all were saying. I don't buy that someone is sabotaging quilts for personal gain. Frankly, I don't think anyone in the Loose Threads cares enough about winning to make it worth their time and trouble. And I can't believe any of them would kill Avanell. Not even Lauren. No, I think in the end it will be something else entirely."

"What do you know about Avanell's family?" Harriet asked.

"After her husband died, she developed the business into a going concern. She and Bertie have been generous to the community. They seemed to get along well. The kids all scattered when they grew up. Marcel couldn't get out of here fast enough, but he came back to visit on a regular basis.

"Michelle was more difficult for Avanell than the boys were. She's a bit of a drama queen, and Avanell didn't have much time for that. Aiden is the sensitive one. I think Avanell was a little more protective of him, since he was younger when George died. He came back to be close to his momma. I suppose that might change now."

Harriet drew in her breath and then coughed to cover it. It hadn't occurred to her that Aiden might leave. She mentally scolded herself for caring.

"You ready to go, Toots?" Mavis asked Harriet.

"I just need to rinse my cup."

"Connie did our dishes, so we're good to go."

She led the way through the shop and out the door. "Do you feel up to a stop at the grocery store? If you're too tired, Connie said she could come over at five and stay with you so I could go. The Foggy Point Market has whole chickens on sale, and I want to get a couple before they're too picked over."

Chapter Twenty-eight

I'M AVAILABLE."

Harriet hadn't heard Aiden come up behind them.

"I can take Harriet to your house and stay until you get back."

She tried to signal no to Mavis, but Mavis either didn't see her gesture or was ignoring her.

"If Harriet doesn't mind, that would be great," she said.

"That's not necessary," Harriet protested. "I can sit in the car while you stop at the store, I really don't mind." Her head was pounding again, and she knew she probably looked like death warmed over. She attempted a smile.

"You're practically out on your feet," Aiden said. "Come on." He put his arm around her shoulders and turned her toward his car. "I'll take you back to the cottage and fix you some of Mavis's herb tea. Then, you can nap, and I'll catch up on my reading." He held up a thick book. "I have to read up on the latest in canine prescription medications before next week."

Harriet felt like a lamb going to the slaughter. "Seems like it's decided."

"Good," he said, and opened the passenger side door on his rental car.

She got in and leaned her head against the back of the seat. She closed her eyes, and Aiden pulled away from the curb. When she opened them, he was pulling into the wooded drive leading to Mavis's cottage.

"Welcome back," he said.

"I guess I was a little more tired than I thought," she said and felt herself blushing slightly. She hoped her mouth hadn't gaped open while she slept or, worse, that she'd snored.

"You've been through a lot the last few days. Your body knows you need to rest even if you aren't listening."

"Yeah, well, I've had a few things on my mind lately. You really don't have

166

to stay here, you know. I'll be fine."

"You keep saying that, but so far that hasn't proved true, has it?"

"Lauren's quilt has been destroyed. Whoever hit me has now been through my stuff twice. They've either found what they wanted or they realize I don't have it. I don't think anyone has ever believed this was about me personally. Everyone in town knows I'm staying with Mavis. My aunt's place is fair game if they want to look again, so see, there's no reason for you to be here." She turned and headed up the stone path to the front door.

"Is it me or have things gotten a little icy around here? Did I do something? Is it that accountant guy? Have we broken up and you didn't tell me?"

She stared at him. "Broken up?" she choked. "We had nothing to break. And leave Harold out of this."

"What am I supposed to think? Saturday night we had a nice dinner, a movie and spent the night together. Now you treat me like I'm the delivery man or some other casual stranger you've encountered."

"You are delusional. Saturday we had take-out, and it took two tries to even have that, then you fell asleep on my couch and I watched a movie by myself. We didn't sleep together—or any other way, for that matter. And I hate to point out the obvious, but I barely know you." She slipped her key into the door lock.

Aiden grabbed her arm and spun her toward him. He lowered his head and pressed his lips gently to hers. His tongue traced the soft fullness of her lips; her body tingled from the contact. Her arms slipped inside his jacket, hands pressing on the work-hardened muscles of his back, pulling him closer. Disquieting thoughts seeped into her mind as her traitorous body responded to his.

He pushed the door open with one hand, the other cradling her close to him; his lips maintained contact with hers as he pulled her through, shutting it with his foot. He guided her onto the chintz-covered sofa in Mavis's living room.

"I can't do this," she said and pushed her hands against his chest.

He held her in place.

"Do what?" he asked and kissed her again. "I'm just what the doctor ordered. He said rest. I'm helping you relax so you can rest."

"It's more complicated than that, and you know it. I'm practically old enough to be your mother for starters."

"It's simple, and you're only a year older than my brother. Why don't you quit fighting for a little while? Lay your head down and sleep. If you want me to leave when Mavis gets back, I'll go."

He stroked his hand over her close-cropped hair. She laid her head on his chest and breathed in his masculine scent that was a unique blend of soap and fresh air. She supposed if he really wanted to do harm to her he wouldn't choose Mavis's living room; and besides, he felt so warm and strong it was as if invisible weights held her down, preventing her from moving or even…

She was asleep before she completed the thought.

HARRIET WAS ALONE ON THE SOFA WHEN SHE WOKE UP; THE KANSAS TROUBLES LAP QUILT was once again keeping her warm. Pioneer women believed that if you slept under a quilt with the word *troubles* in its name, you would surely experience them. She flipped the hazardous cover off. She didn't need any more of those, thank you.

She looked to the window, and the grey late-afternoon light seeping in around the closed curtains indicated the clock had advanced a few hours while she'd slept. She sat up and ran her fingers through her flattened hair. She could see Aiden sitting at the kitchen table, his book open in front of him, a mug gripped in his left hand. Mavis sat opposite him blowing across the surface of the steaming cup of tea she was holding.

"I had to clean out Mom's office at the factory this morning. It doesn't seem right, getting it ready for some hired stranger to take over her job. She was the heart and soul of the company. If it were up to me, I'd close the place down."

"What would your uncle Bertie do then?" Mavis asked. "He still has a family to feed."

"Maybe he could go get a real job. Mom has been carrying him for years. He huffs and puffs around the factory workers, trying to impress them with how important he is, but Mom made all the decisions. He was little more than a glorified clerk. And he's already hired someone to replace her. I don't see how he could find someone qualified under any circumstances, and yet he's got a replacement coming Monday, not even a week after we buried her."

"Maybe your mom had someone lined up already. I'm not saying she knew she would be killed, or even was planning on retiring, but she always interviewed qualified candidates if they approached her. She called it succession planning."

"Yeah, well, I don't like it. It's like he can hardly wait to remove every trace of her from the factory—and the town for that matter. And Michelle is just as bad. She's having an estate sale tomorrow. Did you know that?"

"I did see a notice at the market," Mavis said.

"In another week, it'll be just like my mom never lived. I don't see why Michelle's in such a rush. I don't understand why she has to sell the house in the first place. I told her I would pay for things."

"You know your sister. Once she gets something in her head she can't stop until it's done. She's always been like that. But this community will never forget your mother. There's a plaque in the high school thanking her for her scholarship program. The Community Church dedicated a whole pew to your parents when your mom paid for the children's nursery. Most importantly, there's your sister, your brother and yourself. You are her most important legacy."

Harriet was moved by Mavis's speech. Maybe Aiden and his sister were just worried about money in the aftermath of their mother's death. But if not them, then who?

"Welcome back," Aiden said, noticing she was awake. "I thought you were turning into Rip Van Winkle on us."

"She needs her rest," Mavis said. "How are you feeling, honey?"

"My headache is better. It's weird—even though I've just slept for hours, I feel like I could lie down and sleep for hours more."

"Too much sleep isn't good when you've had a bump on the head," Mavis said. She looked at Aiden. "I read that somewhere."

"That's true when someone has just been hit in the head and you're waiting for help. You don't want them to go to sleep. But after someone is released from the hospital, rest is the best thing you can do. In this case, though, I think if Harriet's up for it, a walk outside might be just what the doctor ordered."

"Would you two please stop talking about me as if I weren't in the room?"

"We're just trying to take care of you, honey," Mavis said.

"Come on, let's give Mavis some peace and quiet. Randy's out in the car. I picked her up while you were sleeping, and by now, I'm sure she's ready to get out and run."

Harriet didn't want to spend time alone with Aiden. She hadn't had time to sort out her feelings about him. And besides, her life was complicated enough without him in it. Mavis's steadfast belief in him was hard to resist, but there was still the age problem. Here in Foggy Point, women young and old alike seemed to worship the ground he walked on, but life existed beyond the confines of this peninsula. Was she ready to introduce a man almost eleven years her junior to Steve's friends in California, or her college roommate?

She felt guilty just thinking about her embarrassment, and realized the age issue was her hang-up, not his. Still, it wouldn't be fair to him to enter into a relationship she was only willing to acknowledge within the confines of Foggy Point.

She also wondered if Aiden's easy acceptance of their age difference would stand the test of time. Sure, he might find her attractive while she was not yet forty, but would he feel the same when she was fifty or sixty? Not that he had suggested a long-term relationship, but she'd already loved one man who'd promised her a future he didn't provide. She wasn't anxious to set herself up only to end up alone again. Her heart couldn't take it.

She looked back at Mavis. She did look like she could use a little rest. Harriet had brought a lot of excitement into her life in the last few days.

"Okay, I guess a little fresh air wouldn't hurt," she said.

"Randy will be happy to hear that. Do you have a coat?"

Harriet picked up her purple sweatshirt and put it back on.

"Let's go then."

He led the way to his rental car. Randy was curled up on the backseat next to the box of personal items Aiden had removed from Avanell's office at the Vitamin Factory. The dog bounded out of the car when he opened the door and ran into the bushes to take care of personal business.

"Kind of sad when your whole career at a place can be reduced to two cardboard boxes," he said, indicating them.

"Have you gone through the stuff to see if there's anything that could shed light on what happened to your mother?"

He looked at her long and hard. "I didn't fall off the turnip truck yesterday, you know."

"I'm sorry. I didn't mean to be presumptuous." She was silent for a moment. "Did you find anything?"

"My mother had very few personal items at the factory. She kept her awards and business gifts at her home office."

"So, what did you find?" Harriet asked. She was pretty sure she knew the answer, but she wanted to hear what he said anyway.

He unfolded the flap on the first box. "We have a tissue box cover decorated with seashells." He held it up then put it back. "Some sort of voodoo hat." He displayed the small stuffed pincushion, glass-headed straight pins stabbed in its crown.

"It's her pincushion," she explained.

He set it back in the box.

"Here we have a broken hand mirror and a hairbrush with glass fragments stuck in the rubber handle. I'm not sure why she kept a broken mirror, but it must have some significance."

"Wait," Harriet said. "Maybe she kept it because it wasn't broken. Maybe it only broke when whatever happened to her happened."

Aiden turned the mirror and looked at it from all angles. "If it means something, I'm not sure what it would be." He set it back in the box and picked up the brush. "I can't imagine this brush being involved in anything sinister. I think it had the misfortune of being in close proximity to the mirror after it broke." He replaced the brush and retrieved the mug with the faded casino logo on its side. "This is a mug Uncle Bertie and Aunt Sheryl brought Mom the first time they went to Las Vegas." He returned it to the box. "There's not much else here. A bunch of pictures of us kids, some red fabric scraps, not much else. I left the bathroom supplies. Whoever Bertie hired to replace Mom…"

His voice trailed off, and his eyes filled with tears. Harriet took the framed picture he had been holding from his hand, put it in the box and shut the car door.

"I think Randy's ready now," she said and took his hand.

She led him away from the car toward the edge of the woods. Randy was sniffing and pawing at the ground. When she saw Aiden moving toward her, she ran to him and danced around his feet, wagging her curved tail. He bent down, and she rapidly licked his face, wiping away the tears that had threatened to spill down his cheeks. He smiled and ruffled the hair on the dog's head.

"Let's follow this path down to the water. The founding fathers decided Foggy Point's beaches should have a buffer from civilization, so they created a long narrow green space that runs from Smugglers Cove all the way to the Point. We can connect up to a trail that goes to my mom's house."

"How do you know so much about the secret paths around here?" Harriet asked, hoping to distract him.

"Four years of running cross-country at Foggy Point High School. I think we ran every road, trail or animal path on this peninsula. It comes in handy now. There are short cuts through almost every neighborhood if you just know where to look."

Given recent events, she didn't find that fact very comforting.

"Follow me," Aiden said and headed down the path, Randy hot on his heels.

They'd gone less than a thousand feet when the woods thinned out and the path joined the trail that circled the end of the peninsula. Harriet could now see the water. Randy ran through the remaining brush to the water's edge. In this area, there wasn't anything you could call a beach. A weedy area led to a strip of round rock that led directly into the saltwater of the lagoon.

They stood and watched Randy as she dashed into the water and out again, barking and biting mouthfuls of the salty liquid.

"Has anyone asked you about your mom's show quilt?" Harriet asked.

"Wanting to buy it, maybe? Not a one. Why?" he asked.

"Just a theory the group came up with." She explained about the duplicate backing fabric. "So, it's possible that even though it was Lauren's that got destroyed, someone who wasn't familiar with the front image on your mother's could have confused the two."

He looked at her, his nearly white eyes wide. "That's it? That's the big revelation? Whether it's my mom's or Lauren's, what's so important about any quilt that someone would repeatedly break into your house to get at it and destroy it?"

"We haven't figured out that part yet, but I think it's significant that it could have been your mother's someone was after, given what happened."

"Is it worth a lot of money or something? I hate to admit it, but I'm totally clueless when it comes to quilts. I know Mom always won prizes, and a couple of hers appeared in people's books as examples of their style after she took classes or workshops."

"Her work is valuable, but if that were the reason someone was after it, it seems like they would have taken the ones out of your house. Aunt Beth said a couple of her quilts won awards at the International Quilt Festival in Houston. Those would be worth more than the one that's being shown now, just because they've already got a history."

"You know, now that you mention it, I can't say if Mom's other quilts are still at the house or not. Each of us kids has the ones she gave us, but the rest are in one of the bedrooms. She has them in these glass cabinet things that have little wooden closet poles to hang them on. Maybe we should go have a look. If we follow this trail for another mile, it will go right by the yard."

"I wonder if she's ever had them appraised," Harriet said and fell in step behind him as the gravel path narrowed.

"Do people do that? I mean, when they're alive? Are they worth that much?"

"Quilts can vary, but I wouldn't be surprised if your mom's were valued in the fifteen hundred to two thousand dollar range. The ones that won national awards could be higher than that. It's none of my business, but you should check about the appraisals before your sister sells any of them at the estate sale. I'd hate to see her give them away."

Aiden was silent. The trail turned away from the shore and wound back into the woods as it climbed. She had to concentrate on the path in front of her to avoid slipping on the damp rocks. There was a brief break in the trees, and she could see the water well below them now.

"Are you doing okay?" Aiden asked as he stopped, causing her to bump into his back.

"I was until you stopped without warning," she said. "My head is pounding a little as we're climbing, but I think that has more to do with my lack of conditioning than the bump."

"We're almost to the path that leads into my mom's property," he said and pulled her into his arms. Randy pushed between their legs. He reached down and rubbed the dog's furry head.

"You're still my favorite girl," he said to the dog and then straightened. "I want to apologize in advance for my sister."

"She does seem to dislike me."

"It's not you," he said, but Harriet was pretty sure it was a lie. "She doesn't really like anyone but herself and her demon offspring. But what she thinks doesn't matter. I like you, and that's what counts. Remember that, okay? No matter what she says."

Harriet had a feeling Michelle disliked any female Aiden showed the slightest interest in, including Randy. Anyone or anything that took his attention away from her was the enemy.

"Okay," she agreed.

They continued on the peninsula trail for another ten minutes then followed a path deeper into the woods. In another few minutes, the trees thinned and the underbrush began to look more purposeful. They passed a wooden bench hidden in a leafy glen.

"We're almost to the house," Aiden said just before they came out of the woods onto a broad grassy slope. They ascended the slope and then followed a stone walkway through a grove of mature rhododendrons. Another grassy area led up to the back of the garage.

He led her around the former stables and to the back door of the house.

Avanell's kitchen looked very different from the last time Harriet had passed through it. The contents of cabinets and drawers were on the countertops, orange tags attached to every item. The table in the breakfast room was covered in lead crystal glasses, pitchers and serving bowls. Bundles of silverware were tied with string in what looked like sets of six place settings. A grey-haired woman in a long-sleeved floral dress came into the kitchen.

"The pre-sale viewing doesn't start until tomorrow morning at seven," she said.

"Who are you?" Aiden asked.

"I'm the estate sale manager," the woman said. Her spine visibly stiffened.

"I'm Aiden Jalbert. This is my mother's house."

"I see," the woman said. "I understood your sister was the sole family member involved in the sale. She's upstairs, on the third floor. Will you be staying?"

"Only long enough to speak to my sister." He picked up a mug with the Seattle Mariners logo on its side. He peeled the orange sticker off and stuck it to the tabletop.

"I would encourage you not to move things. I've already arranged them for the liquidation."

"My Mariners mug is not for sale," Aiden said, and strode from the room.

Harriet had to hurry to follow as he stormed to the servant's staircase. He took the steps two at a time until he reached the third floor.

"Michelle!" he yelled.

"Stop shouting," she answered. "I'm in here."

He went through the open door of his mother's tower office. He held out his mug.

"You were going to sell my Mariners mug?" he said in a cold voice.

"This house doesn't run itself. It takes money—lots of it. We need to get as much money as we can as quickly as we can. And if that means selling your Mariners cup, so be it. It would take someone months to sort through every little thing just to find a few sentimental trinkets. Who's going to pay for that?"

"We could get a loan to pay a few months' expenses. I don't understand why you're in such a rush."

"That's because you're an idiot," Michelle said. "I've told you every way I know how. I have no money. My credit is maxed. I can't get a loan. Uncle Bertie isn't in any better shape, and whatever resources he has he's using to keep the business going. Marcel doesn't want to be involved. You aren't working yet. Someone has to take charge. Why should we pay who knows how many months' worth of utilities if we're just going to sell it anyway? It'll be better this way. We'll just get it over with then we can all move on."

"What about Mom's quilts?" Aiden asked.

"What about them?"

Aiden looked at Harriet as he spoke to Michelle. "Have you had them appraised? Do you even know how much they're worth?"

"I know how much bedding costs. The estate sale woman asked me to price them and I did."

"Did your mother specify any special bequests regarding the quilts in her will?" Harriet asked.

Michelle whirled around to face her. "That's really none of your business. What are you doing here, anyway? The sale isn't until tomorrow."

"She's with me," Aiden said and stepped closer to her.

"A little long in the tooth for you, isn't she?" Michelle sneered and arched a brow.

Harriet felt her face burn. She bit her tongue but remained silent.

"What about Mom's will? Did she say what she wanted to happen with the quilts?"

"Not really." Michelle looked away. "She said to use our best judgment."

Aiden stopped. "I know I'm not the executor of Mom's estate, but aren't we supposed to have a group reading of the will at the lawyer's office?"

"You watch too much television."

"I want to see the quilts," Aiden said. "Where are they?"

Michelle glared at her brother, and Harriet thought she wasn't going to answer.

"They're in the blue bedroom."

"Come on," Aiden said and took Harriet's hand. He led her to the main staircase and down to the second floor to a blue-walled room.

Show-quality quilts were stacked on the bed, folded on the dresser and draped over a small green upholstered chair and its matching ottoman. They varied in size from queen-size to lap quilts. Several still had their winning ribbons attached. Harriet picked up the corner of a large appliqued one. Purple Celtic knots made from narrow bias-cut fabric twined around a golden-yellow border fabric. The center medallion pattern resembled a Persian rug. The rich green, purple, red and blue fabrics Avanell had appliqued on the gold background appeared to be hand-dyed. Small perfectly round circles of fabric had been placed in various geometric shapes. Harriet preferred piecing to applique in her own work, but knew her preference had more to do with her lack of applique skill than anything else. It took a lot of patience to make the necessary tiny invisible stitches, and patience wasn't a trait she possessed in great quantity.

She flipped the corner of the quilt back to expose the next one in the stack. Red, yellow and green tobacco roses were stitched onto cream background blocks. The applique blocks were set on point and alternated with ecru-colored blocks. Harriet recognized the style from a book her aunt had on Civil War quilts. A paper tag was attached to the corner of the quilt with a small strip of plastic that had been punched through the fabric. TWO HUNDRED-FIFTY DOLLARS, the tag read.

"This is a travesty," Harriet said.

"What?" Aiden crossed the room to stand behind her. She could feel the heat of his body through the thickness of her sweatshirt. She had to remind herself to think about the quilt.

"This quilt is priced ridiculously low." She flipped through the rest of the stack, turning the tags and looking at each in turn. "You couldn't buy the fabric for most of these for the prices they've put on them. I'll bet you anything the estate sale manager knows that, too. She probably has a shill or two who will show up first thing tomorrow to snap these up. Then she'll take them out of the area and resell them at their true value for a tidy profit."

"You're sure about the values?"

"Oh, please. I'm in the business. Believe me—these prices won't even cover what Aunt Beth charged to machine stitch them."

"Really." He pulled out his cell phone and dialed the three-digit information code. "Nathan Bohne, please." He paused then hung up and dialed again. He must have been gotten an assistant, judging by his rather firm insistence that he needed to speak to Mr. Bohne now and he would hold while she interrupted him. After another pause for the man to come on the line, he proceeded to explain the basic situation.

He inquired about Avanell's will, and she saw his jaw tighten as he listened silently—the man's voice was loud enough she could hear it. She couldn't make out everything that was being said, but she did grasp that he said the sale should be stopped and that he would call Michelle and inform her to cease immediately.

Aiden snapped his phone shut. "That was weird."

"What did he say?"

"It's more what he didn't say. He said to stop the sale. He said that he is the executor of Mom's estate. Besides the executor, she apparently made a change to her will a few months ago as well. He wants me to come down to his office now—and Michelle, too. He said he'd been planning to call a meeting

176

next week to read the will, but since Michelle was so intent on taking action, he would move it up and talk to us individually if that's what it took."

"Did he give any hint as to what the changes to the will were?"

"No, he didn't. Knowing my mom, she could have decided to give her house or money or even everything she had to her scholarship fund. She was determined that every child who wanted to attend college and had worked hard in high school should have a scholarship. She donated money herself, but she also was a master at getting donations from both individuals and business people. You can bet that anybody who ever made it big in any venue after leaving Foggy Point heard from my mother."

"She was an amazing woman," Harriet said.

"You want to ride along to the attorney's office? We can take one of the cars from the garage so we don't have to walk back to the cottage first."

Harriet felt like she had enough on her plate without involving herself in the drama that was unfolding in Aiden's family, but she was curious at the same time. She wanted to know who would benefit from the new will and who would have benefited before the change, and—most important—who knew about the change.

The Vitamin Factory seemed to be in financial trouble, and if Michelle were to be believed, more than one family member had personal money troubles. It would explain a lot if the will left the money to the people who might benefit most. It wouldn't explain the damage to Lauren's quilt or the attacks on her, but then, it wasn't at all obvious those events were related in any meaningful way to Avanell's death, anyway.

Chapter Twenty-nine

AIDEN BACKED A BLACK LINCOLN NAVIGATOR OUT OF THE GARAGE AND LEANED ACROSS the passenger seat to open the door for her. She got in, buckled her seatbelt and ran her hand over the warm leather seat.

"This is a beautiful car," she said, wonder apparent in her voice.

"Yeah, Mom did love her cars. I think she has four, all of them top end. It was her one indulgence when the company took off."

Randy jumped into the passenger side foot well, and Harriet closed the door. The dog lay down and propped her head on Harriet's foot as Aiden guided the SUV down the long curved driveway and headed toward downtown Foggy Point.

They drove in silence for a few moments.

"I wish I knew more about the business," Aiden said. "Mom never talked about it when I was home. All she ever wanted to talk about was her latest scheme to get money for her scholarship fund."

"Are your sister or brother involved in the business?"

"I don't think so. I mean, Mom used to talk about the business belonging to all of us, and of us being on the board of directors, but I'm not sure she actually did anything formal. Marcel and Michelle didn't want to live in Foggy Point, and I did, but I also knew I wanted to be a vet from the time I was a little boy, so there was never any plan for me to join the business."

"It's too bad you were away the last few years. It's hard to imagine what went wrong—seems like vitamins are more popular than ever. How could they suddenly be losing money?"

"I have no clue, but maybe Mr. Bohne can shed some light on it."

The law offices of Bohne, Bohne and Bohne were at the opposite end of Main Street from the veterinary clinic. The patriarch of the Bohne clan had purchased the grand Queen Anne-style Victorian in the early fifties. The house had been carefully restored in the "Pink Lady" style of its youth and converted into a suite of offices he had then populated with his sons and grandsons. Harriet had been there one time with Aunt Beth while she was in middle school. She remembered a waiting room filled with what her young self considered to be hideously uncomfortable furniture. In later years, she realized they were probably priceless antiques. She hoped they were still in use so she could validate this conclusion.

"A penny for your thoughts?" Aiden asked.

She turned her face toward the window so he wouldn't see the blush that crept up her neck and spread onto her cheeks.

"I was just thinking about possible changes your mother might have made to her will," she lied. She wasn't about to admit that while he was worrying about the future of his mother's estate, she'd been daydreaming about really nice antiques.

"Well, you won't have to wonder much longer," he said, and put the car into park in the graveled area that took the place of the side yard. "We're here."

He instructed Randy to stay and came around to Harriet's door to help her out. She hadn't had a man hold her car door since her senior prom. Now it had happened twice in a week. Steve's funeral didn't count—those people were paid to open her door.

Michelle turned Avanell's Mercedes into the parking area and got out almost before she turned it off.

"Oh, God," she said as she joined them on the porch. "Why is she still with you?" She turned to Harriet. "This is none of your business."

The door opened into a spacious waiting room in what had once been the formal parlour. Nathan Bohne motioned the trio into a hallway. He opened a door and guided Michelle into a small book-lined conference room. He motioned Aiden and Harriet into his office.

"Would you please wait here while I speak to your sister?" he asked Aiden, although it was more a command than anything.

Aiden raised his eyebrows but didn't argue.

"I wonder why he's separating us?" he said when they were alone.

"I'm sure he'll tell you when he's ready. Maybe he knows your sister well enough to realize her reaction to whatever he's going to say might be better handled one on one."

She sat, and Aiden paced around the room in uneasy silence for a full fifteen minutes before Nathan Bohne finally came back.

"Your sister decided she'd go on back to your mother's place," he said and shut the door behind him. "Her presence isn't necessary for what I'm about to tell you in any case."

"Please, sit," he said to Aiden and motioned to the empty chair in front of his desk, next to the one Harriet was sitting in. "Can I assume by her presence that you'd like Miss Truman to hear anything I might reveal to you?"

"Yes," Aiden said and sat down next to her as requested.

"Let's begin, then." He picked up a file from the credenza behind his desk and sat in his high-backed leather desk chair. He opened the file, picked up a sheet of paper then put it down and closed the folder. He leaned his elbows on the desk and tented his fingers, resting his chin on them.

"Your mother came to me a few months ago to discuss her estate. She said she'd discovered certain irregularities in her tax returns. I asked her if she needed help from our legal investigators, but she declined. I assumed from the way she acted it was perhaps a family matter. Of course, now I wish I'd pressed the matter, but I suppose that's water under the bridge.

"Your mother asked me to make certain to her will that I'd hoped we wouldn't be addressing this soon." He picked up the folder again and pulled out the top sheet. "I've prepared a summary for you, I'll read now, and then I've got a complete copy of all the documents I'll give you when we finish probating the will."

He cleared his throat and began to read. It might have been a summary, but it was still filled with legal language.

Prior to the change, the bulk of Avanell's estate would have been divided among her brother and children, with a generous additional bequest going to her scholarship fund. Under the new plan, Bertrand would receive nothing. Scholarship trust funds were set up for all the grandchildren, with Avanell's community scholarship plan manager administering the payout. Marcel was to receive a fishing camp on the Toutle River and a rental property in Olympia.

"You probably understand the next bequest better than I do," Nathan said. "Your sister Michelle will receive her inheritance in the form of an annuity that will pay out a modest fixed income and will be administered by an investment management firm. It's an unusual arrangement for a competent adult heir."

"Well, Michelle, as you may have noticed, is not your typical adult heir," Aiden said. The muscle in his jaw twitched. If Nathan Bohne didn't hurry up, Harriet thought, he was going to have another death on his hands.

"Now the part that involves you." Bohne folded the summary paper and put it back in the folder. "Everything else goes to you," he said.

Utter silence filled the room. Harriet squirmed in her seat and finally broke the silence.

"What, exactly, does that mean?"

The lawyer cleared his throat. "It means everything Avanell owned that I haven't yet mentioned—her house and its contents, vacation properties with the exception of the fish camp, several investment properties and a number of financial instruments. Oh, and of course, her financial interest in the Vitamin Factory. When we've completed the probate process, I'll have a list of your new holdings. We also have a listing of her insurance policies and can help you with exercising them."

Aiden leaned back in his chair. "I don't know what to say."

"I know this is a difficult time for you and your family, and I don't want to make it more so by what I'm going to tell you next, but I can't in good conscience let you leave without having a clear understanding of what's going on.

"The contents of your mother's house, as well as her cars, boats and any other vehicles are yours. Your sister has no right to sell, trade, distribute to other relatives or even touch anything in that house. Any conversation she might have had with your mother regarding individual objects was rendered invalid by your mother's latest will. She made her intentions very clear regarding your sister. You don't have to let her stay in the house; and frankly, now that your mother's funeral is over, you would be well served by showing her the door as soon as you return to the house."

"That sounds a little harsh," Aiden said.

"I don't wish to make trouble between you and your sister, but she is not as innocent as she might appear."

Harriet didn't think she appeared innocent at all but was pretty sure Aiden was still trying to give her the benefit of the doubt. Apparently, the lawyer was going to make sure that didn't happen.

"I'm embarrassed to tell you that one of my clerks is an old college friend of Michelle's. Your sister coerced our employee into revealing certain facts about your mother's will without my permission. When she overheard your call a short while ago, she broke down and confessed that Michelle had called in an estate agent and planned to sell everything, including the cars and house. Michelle knew you would find out eventually but figured she would get as much as she could and apply it to her debts, and she assumed she could convince you that it was her due."

Aiden stood up.

"I'm sure you'll want to process everything," Nathan Bohne said. He stood and held his hand out. "If I can be of further help, let me know." He adjusted his gold silk tie. "I'll be down the hall in the library if you have questions. Take as long as you need. I know this is probably a bit of a shock."

He left, and Aiden sat back down. He propped his elbows on his knees and held his head in his hands.

"I can't believe Michelle was trying to sell Mom's house out from under me. She's my sister, for God's sake."

Harriet didn't know what to tell him. Money did crazy things to people.

"I'm sure she must have been desperate to try to scam you at a time like this."

"I don't think *desperate* is the word I'd use." He stood again. "I better get you home. Then, I need to go talk to my sister."

"Are you sure that's a good idea? Maybe you should let things cool down a little."

"I have to talk to her. She's my sister. Besides, I need to make sure that estate witch has cleared out."

Chapter Thirty

Aiden pulled in behind the blue Town Car in front of Mavis's cottage and let Harriet out.

"I'll come back later on foot and pick up the rental car. I guess I can get rid of it now that I own four."

"Maybe you could call Mavis when you're leaving home so you don't scare us to death when you get here."

He agreed, and she got out of the car and stood on the porch while he drove away. She turned to open the door but stopped when she heard a rustle in the rhododendrons to the left of the porch.

"Who's there?" she called. She listened. "Is anyone there?" she called again.

A figure in a baggy black jacket came around the bush.

"Carla?" she said.

"Hi, Harriet," the young woman replied and looked at the ground.

"What are you doing here? Did you come to see Mavis? I'll get her for you."

"No," she said. "I'm not here to see Mavis."

"I don't understand," Harriet said and stepped off onto the grass.

"You want to help Misty, right?" Carla asked, her voice stronger.

"Yes, but what does that have to do with anything. What are you doing here?"

"Shhh," she said and held her forefinger to her lips. "I found Misty. She's in a potting shed in the woods. She's not good. I took her to the shelter and we talked to the counselor, but she took off again. The counselor is getting her prescription filled, and she was hiding at my apartment till it was ready, but she was afraid to stay there. She was going to take off again, so I convinced her to come to the shed. I remembered it from when we used to play in these woods when we was little. It's not great, but at least it's dry and she feels safe. At least, I think she feels safe. I don't want to leave her, but I have to get her some food and water. And I have to work."

"Can I talk to her?"

Carla looked up at her. "Yeah," she said. "I think that might help."

She led the way around Mavis's cottage, across the yard and through a hole in the fence and into the woods. The shed was probably no more than five hundred feet beyond the wooden fence. Harriet could hear Misty before the two women went through the door.

"Hush, little baby, don't say a word," she chanted in her monotone.

"Misty," Harriet said. "How are you? Do you remember me? We spoke at Mrs. Jalbert's funeral."

Misty started rocking, her arms wrapped across her middle, her left hand picking at her right elbow. Harriet's heart went out to the girl. When you were different, no matter how, people were cruel. Misty was lucky to have a friend like Carla to look out for her.

"Misty, this is important," she continued. "Can you tell me who shot Mrs. Jalbert?"

Misty's eyes got real big. She started humming the Van Morrison song again.

"Misty? Did a brown-eyed woman shoot Avanell?"

With the woman rocking and picking and humming, Harriet couldn't be sure if she'd seen her shake her head or not.

"Misty, do you know who shot her?"

"Man oh man oh man oh man oh man." Misty's rocking kept time with her chant.

"Misty, what are you telling me?" Harriet asked, but it was no use. Misty was in her own world. "Carla, do you know what she was trying to tell me?"

"Sorry," Carla said. "She don't make much sense most of the time. Every once in a while she'll come out with somethin' and sound just like she used to, but now I'm not sure them spells is any more real than when she's singin' and rockin'."

"Can I do anything to help?"

"No, I think she'll stay put here. She seems to do okay when she's hidin'— I think she feels safe out here. The counselor at the church shelter gave me some vouchers to use at the Foggy Point Market. I'll get her some food and water. If you could go to Myca's House Counseling Center tomorrow and pick up her perscription, it would help. I can call and tell 'em you'll come by."

"Yeah, sure. I can do that. Is there anything else? Do you want a ride to the market or anything?"

"Seems to me you got your own troubles to worry about, but thanks for offerin'. If you get the medicine and give her a dose as soon as you can, that should do it."

"I better go back to the house. Mavis might come looking if I don't come in soon."

It turned out she needn't have worried—Mavis was stretched out in the recliner sound asleep when she came in the door. She woke up when Harriet touched the remote control dangling from her hand, and pulled the lever that brought the chair jolting upright.

"I was about to call the emergency room again," she said.

"I can see that." Harriet smiled.

"That must have been some walk."

Harriet explained the events of the afternoon over a cup of fragrant orange-spice tea.

"I can't believe Michelle was trying to steal her brother's inheritance," Mavis said when she had finished. "Avanell had been worried about her. She told me Michelle and her husband were living way beyond their means. She tried to work with them, but she said she was tired of throwing good money after bad. I'm not surprised she changed her will."

"Unfortunately, her new will only confuses things. On the one hand, if Michelle didn't know it had been changed, she would have a motive to kill her mother, but it sounds like she did know. On the other, if Aiden knew about the change, it would give him one."

"I just have a hard time believing he could do something like that. And besides, that doesn't explain your part of all this. If it was simply the family trying to get Avanell out of the way, why would they be coming after you?"

"The killer must think I pose some kind of threat to them."

"What possible threat could you pose to anyone in Foggy Point? You've hardly been back a month."

"If we could figure that out, I think we'd know who killed Avanell."

Mavis got up, poured more water into their cups and pulled a box of mixed teabags from the cupboard over the stove. She held the box out; Harriet chose green tea this time, and Mavis put the box back. They were staring into their cups when the phone rang.

Mavis got up and answered it and had a short conversation that consisted of uh-hm's and yeses, and finished with "I think that's a fine idea. I expect we'll pick it up when the show closes on Saturday."

She came back to the table and sat down.

"That was Bertrand. He said he'd like to hang Avanell's last show quilt in the lobby of the Vitamin Factory. He says it will be a permanent tribute to Avanell's two loves."

"I'm guessing he either doesn't know about the new will or he thinks no one else does."

"There is another possibility. He's either already talked to Aiden, or it hasn't occurred to him that he needs to."

"I suppose. And it *would* be a nice tribute."

"Since you're the quilt depot, I thought maybe we could go to Tacoma on Saturday morning, have a good look at the exhibits and see who won, then have lunch and check out All About Quilting over on Thirty-first Street, then come back and pick up the quilts when the show closes at four. What do you think?"

"As long as you let me do the driving, I think that would be fine. I'm worried that you're getting worn out being my bodyguard and waiting on me hand and foot."

"Your aunt Beth would do the very same thing if one of my boys were in trouble. And just because I'm not as young as I once was doesn't mean I'm weak."

"I know. This is just so hard. I know Aunt Beth is trying to give me a kick-start in getting on with my life. I was mad at first, but maybe she's right. Maybe I do need to make some changes. And I was, for a couple of days. And I liked it. Now things are even worse than they were before I left Oakland. There, at least, my limits were of my own making. I'm very comfortable here, and I truly appreciate how much you're putting yourself out to protect me; but I'm not free to come and go, much less work, and the worst part is, I don't even know why or, more important, when this will all be over?"

"How about I make us ham and cheese omelets and toast and then we put aside our troubles, just for the night. I rented a couple of movies from DeAnn the other day and they're due tomorrow. Maybe we could watch one of them before they go back."

"That sounds so good. I could use a break. And I'm starving."

Chapter Thirty-one

Harriet woke early the next morning; between her walk with Aiden and watching the romantic comedy with Mavis, she'd gotten a good night's sleep.

Mavis was already in the kitchen and had the kettle on when she came out of the bathroom.

"How are you feeling this morning?" Mavis asked.

"I slept really well. I'm getting a little tired of pink and purple, though." She held out the hem of her pink shirt. "Is there any chance we could go by my house and pick up some clothes?"

"Oh, honey, I don't think that's a very good idea. You've only been out of the hospital for two days. Until the police have some idea what's going on, I think you need to stay away from there. We could ask Darcy if that skinny blond woman who drives the patrol at night could go over and pick up some clothes for you."

"I don't want some stranger going through my clothes. I don't care if it is a woman."

"We could go by the thrift store on Second Street if you want, or if you feel up for a drive, we could go to the Wal-Mart."

"The thrift store is fine. Surely, they'll have something I can wear—I really only need a couple of shirts and maybe another pair of jeans."

"I usually go to my hand-piecing group on Friday mornings at Pins and Needles," Mavis offered hopefully.

"That sounds like fun," Harriet said without much enthusiasm.

"We can stay here if you're not up to it."

She needed to go into town. She had to get Misty's medicine and give it to her. The girl might not have seen Avanell's murder, but Harriet was sure she knew something.

"I think a trip to town would be great. I can stop by the thrift store and then maybe I can find a hand project I can do at Pins and Needles."

"Do you do hand piecing or do you prefer redwork?" Mavis asked and started a conversation that lasted through breakfast.

Harriet was surprised at Mavis's defense of the controversial trend of painting on art quilts. There were a few artists painting images on fabric then stitching around the image and entering them in competition. Harriet understood that the predecessors of pieced quilts were bedcovers made by doing intricate stitching on a single large piece of fabric, but in that case the *stitches* were the art. She definitely was on the side that felt sewing a backing onto a painting didn't make a quilt.

In the end, though, she had to concede that images painted in dye and combined with art stitching were, in fact, art quilts.

They moved on to discuss various hand-piecing styles, and by the time they got into the car, Harriet was pretty sure she was going to try doing some Grandmother's Flower Garden blocks using English paper piecing style, where hexagonal images were cut out of paper, a circle of fabric hand-stitched around the paper piece and then the edges of the hexagons whip-stitched together, removing the paper from the back when all the stitching was done.

Mavis had shown her a picture of a Civil War-era quilt using the technique that was made in navy blue and tan with just a touch of red. Harriet decided if she could find the right fabric she'd give it a try.

Wisps of fog swirled close to the pavement as Mavis parked at the curb across the street and halfway between Pins and Needles and the thrift store.

"I really think I could go to the bank and the thrift store without an escort," Harriet said. "I promise I'll come right back to Pins and Needles when I'm done."

She could tell Mavis was having a debate with herself. Harold emerged from the bank before she'd decided.

"Good morning, ladies," he said. "What brings you to this fair city?"

"Mavis has a stitching group this morning, and I was just trying to convince her I could go to the bank and the thrift store without her. She doesn't need to babysit me in downtown Foggy Point in the middle of the morning."

"I'm sure she's trying to look out for your best interests, but might I suggest an alternative?"

They both looked expectantly at him.

"What if I follow along while you do your errands and then we go to Annie's

Coffee Shop for some hot cocoa?"

"Okay," Harriet said immediately.

Mavis looked skeptical but agreed. Harold held the door for Harriet.

He was gracious enough to stay outside the thrift store and make phone calls he probably hadn't needed to make so she could shop in peace. She found a serviceable pair of flannel pajamas, three long-sleeved T-shirts in neutral colors, a black long-sleeved Flax shirt-jacket, a pair of Calvin Klein khaki pants and a dark-green lightweight jacket. She got the whole collection for twenty-five dollars, which seemed like a pretty good deal. She came out of the store in just over fifteen minutes.

"That was quick," Harold said. He put his hand on her elbow and guided her to the left. "Annie's is around the corner on Ship Street."

They discussed the fog and whether it was expected to lift later or not until they were seated at a dark wooden table with matching chairs that had calico fabric seat cushions. A young woman with a blond braid that brushed her waist brought them steaming cups of cocoa.

"I don't remember this place," Harriet said and looked around the small book-lined room.

"I think it's been here about three years or so." He nodded toward a middle-aged woman on the other side of an antique library table that served as a counter in the small shop, "According to Bertie, Annie used to be the head librarian at the Foggy Point branch of the Calallam County Library. He says she got tired of busting people for sneaking food and drink into the library. She decided folks wanted a place to do both, so here we are." He spread his arms to indicate their surroundings. "She has a swap party a couple of times a year, so her stock of books gets freshened."

"It seems like a good idea." Harriet looked around at the half-filled space. "It looks like she does okay."

"We're between crowds right now. The working crowd has left and the stay-at-home moms and senior citizens haven't arrived yet."

"Speaking of Bertie, what's he like?" she asked. "I knew Avanell when I was young, since she and my aunt were friends, but I didn't know the rest of her family."

"What do you want to know?" Harold countered.

"I don't know. It seems like Avanell was such a big part of this community, I guess I wonder if Bertie will be able to fill that role."

Aiden clearly didn't think so, but she wondered how much of that opinion had to do with his father's death and the aftermath.

"It's true Bertie prefers to stay in the background. I'm sure he'll do whatever's necessary."

Clearly, he wasn't going to give up any information. She wondered if he didn't like to gossip or if his evasion was more purposeful. What would he have to hide?

"Would you mind walking over to Myca's House on our way back? One of the young women in the Thursday night group needs me to pick something up for her."

Harold agreed, and they sipped their cocoa.

"I assume the fact you're still living with Mavis and she's not letting you out of her sight means the police haven't caught whoever attacked you."

"They haven't said a word, so I interpret their silence as meaning they aren't getting anywhere."

"You can't keep living with Mavis forever, can you? I mean, if it were me, I'd be going crazy living with anyone else under those conditions. And what about your business?"

"You've pretty well summarized my life. I have to go back to work. Mavis is nice, but I'm not used to living with anyone, and Aunt Beth isn't due home for two more weeks. And that's no guarantee of my continued safety. The whole thing makes no sense. I haven't done anything to anyone, I don't have anything anyone would want, I don't know any big secrets. There is absolutely no reason for someone to break into my house, destroy my clients' work or hit me in the head."

"Maybe you know something but don't know that you know it."

"This just goes in a big circle, Harold. If I know something, then whoever it is didn't need to trash my aunt's place. If they're looking for something, they didn't need to hit me on the head down by the docks." She covered her face in her hands. "Could we just not talk about this for a while?"

"Of course. How did the show go? Did Foggy Point represent itself well?"

"Actually, with all that's been going on, I don't know who won what. Everyone's assuming Avanell won the best of show, but other than that it's anyone's guess. I suppose Lauren's quilt wasn't up long enough to have been judged. But I wouldn't be surprised if there were a few prize winners in the group."

"When is it over?"

"Tomorrow's the last day. Mavis and I are going to Tacoma to bring them all home."

"What happens to the quilts after that? Do they go on to other shows or do they retire to the linen closet and a life of service?"

She smiled. "Some of both, I suppose. A few people enter their work in other shows, but I think most of the women in our group will just take them home and either put them on a bed or give them to the grandson, niece, sister or friend they were intended for.

"That brings up a good point. They're supposed to collect them from my house on Monday. The people in the group I go to know about my relocation, but some of the ones I took were from other people. I need to call them so they don't show up at my aunt's house. I hate to ask Mavis to let me have people collect them at her house. I feel like I've been such an intrusion on her life as it is."

"Could you deliver them to people? If there aren't that many and since Foggy Point isn't that big?" Harold suggested. "At least, I assume there aren't that many," he corrected. "I could help you on Sunday if you want. You will be home Saturday night with them, won't you?"

"Hmmm." You know, I think that could work. But you don't need to spend your Sunday driving around with me."

"I hate to point out an unpleasant reality of your life, but in fact, no one is going to let you go anywhere by yourself. And I don't mind—really."

Harriet was silent. She tried to think of an alternative but nothing came to mind. She sighed.

"You're right. I just hate this."

Harold picked up his cup as if to drink but found only thick chocolate sludge in the bottom. He set it back down. "If you're ready, maybe we should go pick up your package at Myca's House and get you back to Mavis before she sends out a search party."

He pulled two dollars out of his thin lizard-skin wallet and laid them on the table. He picked up Harriet's bags from the thrift store and helped slide her chair out.

"Follow me," he said as they reached the sidewalk. "I know a shortcut."

He led her to a narrow cement-paved alley between two buildings. It widened into an asphalt courtyard of sorts. He crossed the open area diagonally and entered another dark alley between buildings that faced on the next block. Once they reached the sidewalk there, Myca's House was two doors down.

"I'm impressed," Harriet said. She wondered how a guy who wore pressed slacks and a bow tie everywhere he went learned about back-alley shortcuts.

"Would you like me to wait out here?" he asked.

"No, it's fine. I'm just picking up something for a friend."

She opened the door and stepped into a tired-looking lobby. Three scratched plastic chairs sat against the wall. Two six-foot-long folding tables topped with peeling plastic laminate separated the sitting area from the rest of the office. Cardboard boxes overflowed with papers. A grey-haired man with a short curled ponytail and sparse salt-and-pepper beard came into the office and asked if he could help her.

She explained why she was there. He asked to see her driver's license, but then looked up at Harold.

"I'll vouch for her identity," Harold said. "Harriet, this is Joseph. He's the office manager here at Myca's House. Joseph, meet Harriet Truman. She's Beth's niece. Harriet here has just taken over Beth's business. Maybe once she gets settled, she'll join us at Rotary."

Harriet was a little annoyed with two men discussing her as if she were a small child incapable of speaking for herself.

"Oh, yeah, I heard you've had a little trouble up at your aunt's place."

She wondered if there was anyone in Foggy Point who didn't know her business. She didn't say anything, and the silence became awkward. Joseph picked up a white paper bag and handed it to her.

"Dr. Mason said to tell you there are three doses. He said that should be enough to get the patient stable enough to come in by herself. He said to make sure she gets in before the third dose wears off."

"Thanks," Harriet said.

"See you next week," Harold said to Joseph and followed her onto the sidewalk.

"I guess we better get you back to the quilt store," he said. He led her around the block this time, and didn't speak until they'd turned the corner.

"I don't mean to pry, but it sounds like your young friend might be unbalanced."

"I couldn't say. She's more like a friend of a friend." She held up the white bag. "This should help."

"Would you like me to go with you when you deliver the medicine? I mean, it's possible this person was involved in your attack, isn't it?"

"I doubt it. I don't think she's got her act together enough to do something like that. Besides, like I said, this is a friend of a friend kind of thing. It doesn't have anything to do with me. But thanks for offering."

She wasn't about to bring anyone, much less a man, to see Misty. Harold's sudden helpfulness was bothering her, too. He'd been quick to leave the first few times she'd seen him, and now suddenly he wanted to be her constant companion. It could be his awareness of Aiden's interest, but she wasn't sure.

"If you change your mind, call me. I'll be at the factory all day."

"Things must be strange there with Avanell gone."

"She will be missed. She was the spirit of the company, that's for sure."

"Well, here we are," Harriet said and stopped one door away from Pins and Needles. She held her hand out for her bags.

"I'll call you Saturday night, and we can talk about our delivery plan," Harold said. He turned and walked away before she could thank him for the hot cocoa.

She watched as he strode briskly down the block and wished she felt something—anything. Instead, images of another man came unbidden to her mind, and the butterflies awakened. She told herself Harold was the man she should be thinking about. He was the right age. He was considerate, and punctual, and he planned ahead.

Aiden was exciting.

Harold wasn't fat, but he had a soft, rounded look.

Aiden was lean and long, and had washboard abs.

She had to stop thinking about Aiden. She had to remember he was the one who had everything to gain when his mother died.

"Are you coming in or are you going to stand out here on the sidewalk all morning?" Mavis said from the door of Pins and Needles. "Marjory pulled a few bolts of fabric for you to look at for your Grandmother's Flower Garden. She has templates of various sorts and pre-cut papers for English paper piecing, too, if you want to go that route."

"Sounds great," Harriet said and entered the shop. She put her bags by a chair at the table in the big classroom, where the group was meeting. She greeted the women and assured everyone she was feeling better and that the police still had no idea who had it in for her. As quickly as she could gracefully escape, she went to the back of the store and found Marjory.

"Bet you're getting tired of talking about your problems," Marjory said.

"That's the truth."

"Looks like you got a little break this morning, though."

"Yeah, Harold Minter went with me to the thrift store and took me to the coffee shop."

"So, how was that?" Marjory asked.

"It was fine. He's a nice man. I mean, I don't know him that well, but he seems nice. Do you know him?"

"I've seen him around town." She hesitated. "He participates in community events."

"So, what are you not telling me?"

"Nothing," Marjory said. "He's always been polite when I've spoken to him."

"But? Come on, Marjory, don't hold out on me."

Marjory leaned across the cutting table and lowered her voice. "It's nothing I can put my finger on, but there's just something about the guy that leaves me cold. I don't know. It seems like he's a little too perfect, too polite. Every move he makes seems planned."

"Planning can be a good thing," Harriet said.

"It can be boring, if you ask me. A person needs a little spontaneity. And a person needs to laugh. I can't imagine Harold laughing."

"He offered to help me deliver quilts from the show on Sunday."

"You wouldn't catch me being locked in a car with that man for hours on end. So, tell me about this Grandmother's Flower Garden project," she said, effectively ending the discussion of Harold.

Harriet chose several dark blues, a cream-colored tone-on-tone print and a red print. She decided to make things easy for herself and bought a bag of pre-cut hexagonal papers. In only a few minutes, she was seated at the big table cutting pieces of her new fabric among a group of middle-aged women she'd never met before today. Mavis made the appropriate introductions, and Harriet was grateful when the women went back to their stitching without asking her any more about the recent events in her life.

She had just stitched her first complete flower when Mavis stood up and rubbed her back.

"I don't know about you, honey, but I'm starving. What do you say we go find us some lunch?"

"Sounds great." Aunt Beth would have a cow if she saw how often Harriet was eating out in her absence. She was trying to make good choices, but she knew it didn't compare to the "all salad all the time" diet Aunt Beth had put her on when she arrived.

"I been feeling like Mexican food," Mavis said. "What do you think?"

Harriet's heart skipped a beat. She reminded herself there was probably more than one Mexican restaurant in Foggy Point.

"I like Mexican food," she said, her voice sounding strange in her ears.

"Anyone else want to join us?" Mavis asked. She was thanked for her offer, but Harriet was relieved when, one by one, they declined.

"Shall we walk over to Tico's Tacos?"

"Can we stop by the car first and drop off my new wardrobe?"

"That can be arranged." Mavis looked out the shop window and pulled a plastic rain hat from her pocket. "Looks like it's going to be a wet walk. Did you buy anything waterproof?"

Harriet was already pulling the green jacket from her bag. "I hope I don't run into the person who donated this to the thrift store," she said with a smile.

"The same people own another store in Port Angeles. I'm pretty sure they swap the stuff between the stores for that very reason."

A light mist filled the air as Harriet and Mavis said their goodbyes and stepped out onto the sidewalk. Harriet's new jacket didn't have a hood, and by the time they had walked to the car to deposit her bags and then on to Tico's her hair was damp.

A young woman with thick black hair pulled back into a neat braid showed them to a booth by the window. Harriet got up immediately and went to the restroom to use the hand dryer on her hair. When she returned, Mavis was dipping a blue corn chip into a stone bowl overflowing with guacamole. Harriet grabbed a chip and had just dipped it into the bowl when a pair of hands covered her eyes.

"Guess who?" Aiden said.

It was all she could do to not scream. She pried his hands off her eyes and turned around.

"What happened to your eyes?" she asked, and felt the color drain from her face.

"What do you mean?" he asked. "Oh, these?"

He pointed to his eye then cupped his hand in front of his face and pinched his eye surface with his thumb and forefinger. A brown sliver of plastic fell into his hand. He held it out for her to see. His eye was now its normal pale color. The other one remained dark brown.

"Mom got me dark contacts the first time we traveled out of the country. When I was in Africa, I had to wear them all the time—my eye color freaked out the locals. I still have a bunch of them, and frankly, it's easier sometimes to blend in."

"It's amazing how different they make you look," she said.

"They look natural," Mavis said. "Sarah wears colored lenses that make her eyes a color of green never before seen in nature."

"I'd be happy to have normal brown or blue eyes like everyone else," he confessed.

"Don't try and tell me you didn't use your looks to your advantage with the girls when you were in high school," Mavis said. "I was here, remember."

He had the grace to blush. "Are you ladies having lunch?"

"Would you care to join us?" Mavis invited him.

"I thought you'd never ask," he said and sat next to Harriet, his leg pressed against hers.

Harriet was distracted during lunch in spite of the delicious tomatillo enchiladas and Spanish rice she ate. Aiden was at his charming best, making Mavis smile throughout the meal, but there was something about this brown-eyed Aiden that bothered her.

"Are you about done?" Mavis asked her.

"So soon?" Aiden protested.

"Almost," Mavis said. "I'm going to powder my nose, then I think I need to get Harriet home for some rest. We've had a busy morning, and she's looking a bit peaky."

"I wish people wouldn't talk about me as if I weren't here." She found this one of the less charming aspects of life in Foggy Point. Perhaps it was inevitable when most of your friends were old enough to be your mother.

Mavis patted her arm, got up and went to the restroom.

"So, what's wrong? And don't tell me you're just tired," Aiden demanded.

"I am tired, but not like Mavis means. I'm tired of being in limbo." She looked at the sleeve of her green coat. "I can't even wear my own clothes."

He put his arm around her and pulled her to his chest. "This is bound to be over soon."

"Have you heard something? Do they know who killed your mother?" She looked into his brown eyes.

He slumped. "No. I stopped by the police station on my way here. They have no idea. They're still going on the belief that she came back to work after dinner and startled a thief in the process of robbing the factory."

"You still don't believe it?"

"No, and don't try to tell me you do, either. I don't know who did it, but I'll bet it's not some stranger. It's going to be someone we know."

Mavis cleared her throat as she approached the table. Harriet straightened up, buttoned her coat and slid out of the booth.

"Can I come by and see you later?" Aiden asked.

She hesitated.

"We'll take a rain check," Mavis answered for her. "We're going to Tacoma tomorrow and need to rest up."

"Thank you," Harriet said when they were outside again.

"I may be old, but I can catch a hint with the best of them."

"I can't deal with Aiden and Harold right now on top of everything else. They're both trying to be so helpful, but I'm not sure I completely trust either one of them."

"We can agree to disagree about Aiden, and I don't know Harold well enough to have an opinion, but you don't need any more pressure right now."

"That we *can* agree about."

Chapter Thirty-two

Harriet waited until Mavis had fallen asleep in her chair before she went out to the potting shed in the woods.

"Misty," she called quietly. "Misty."

"Hush, little baby, don't say a word..."

Harriet opened the door slowly. "Misty? It's Harriet. I have your medicine."

It took a moment for her eyes to adjust to the dark room. She couldn't see Misty at first, but finally spotted her cowering in the corner on what looked like a pile of rags. She stepped closer and could see the woman was methodically tearing a baby quilt into small strips.

"I brought you your medicine," she said, and held out a pill and a bottle of water—she wasn't sure Misty had heard her.

The young woman started humming again. "Hmmm, my brown-eyed girl... hm hm hm hm hm hm, ohhh my brown-eyed girl."

"Misty?" She thought the woman was going to continue ignoring her, but suddenly Misty leaped at her and grabbed the pill. Harriet held out the bottle of water. She wasn't sure what she'd do if Misty threw the pill into the rag pile but was pretty sure she was going to find out.

They stood looking at each other for a long minute. Misty opened her mouth, tossed the pill in and tilted her head back, dry swallowing it. She sank onto the rag pile, picked up the tattered remains and began picking.

Harriet set the bottle of water on the floor and backed outside. She hoped one pill would cause enough of a difference to make the next easier to administer.

She stood for a moment outside the shed but realized there wasn't anything else she could do until the medicine had a chance to work.

Mavis was still in her chair asleep when she returned. Fred came out from behind the sofa and climbed on her lap when she sat down.

"So, what does it all mean, Fred?" She scratched his ears, and he started purring. "Is it just a coincidence that Misty is out there shredding her quilt? Could she have killed Avanell?" She looked at the cat. "If Misty is the killer, what motive would she have for trashing Aunt Beth's house or Lauren's quilt?"

Fred didn't have any answers. Harriet pulled a throw pillow down from the back of the sofa and propped it on the arm. She and Fred were both asleep a moment after her head hit it.

WHEN SHE WOKE UP, IT WAS DARK OUTSIDE; AND FRED WAS LICKING HER FACE.

"Stop," she said and sat up. She set the cat on the floor and went into the kitchen. The tea kettle was still warm. She pulled an English Breakfast teabag from the cabinet and poured water over it. Mavis came in as she was stirring sugar into her tea.

"Do you feel better?" Mavis asked.

"Yeah, I guess. My head doesn't hurt anymore, but my stitches are starting to itch, so I guess that's a good sign."

"I'm glad you're head is better, but I'm thinking that's not what was bothering you this afternoon."

"You're right. It wasn't my head. It was the two men I was with. First, Harold, who seems perfectly nice. He's very kind, but..."

"He doesn't light your fire," Mavis supplied.

"I guess you could say that. But what was bothering me today was what Marjory said about him."

"What did she say?"

"Nothing specific. It's just a feeling she has, I guess. I know you don't know him, but did Avanell ever say anything?"

"Not much. I know he hasn't lived here that long. Bertrand hired him when their longtime finance guy left suddenly. Avanell was happy Bertie found someone so quickly. He's been active in various community groups. I guess I don't know any more than that."

"Do you know if he's seen any women since he's been here?"

"Avanell didn't say anything about it."

Harriet looked into her tea. "And then there's Aiden. I know you don't think he'd hurt his mother but now that we know what her will says, he does have the most to gain from her death. And apart from that, he's made it very clear he's ready to jump into a relationship. I'm not sure I'm ready for a relationship with anyone, much less a man ten years younger than me."

"Just hold on a minute. Are you sure you're looking at this situation right? I raised five boys and I don't mean to be indelicate, but I don't think it's a relationship that boy is hoping to jump into. Specially after three years in Africa. Maybe you're the one who's got relationships on her mind."

Harriet started to speak, but her protest died on her lips.

Mavis went to the sink, dumped the cold remains out of her cup, put a fresh tea bag in and poured hot water over it.

"Age doesn't matter one whit when it comes down to it. My dear Thomas was six years younger than me, and it didn't make a lick of difference. If you've got designs on that boy, you need to figure out whether you can get past his age, but if it were me, I wouldn't be counting my chickens before they were hatched."

A soft warmth crept up Harriet's neck and spread onto her cheeks. "I don't have 'designs on that boy.'"

"He is a cute little thing, though, isn't he?" Mavis said and smiled.

"He's attractive, he's intelligent, and he has good energy."

"But?" Mavis asked.

"It's just all so much so quick. I haven't spent time with any man for five years, and now suddenly I've got two men calling me up and taking me out to dinners and wanting to go on drives and hikes and out to coffee."

"I imagine it's a little overwhelming. But you know you don't have to take things any faster than you want to, honey. Any man worth having will be willing to take things however slow you need to go. If he isn't willing to put on the brakes, well, then that tells you something right there."

"That's easier said than done. I had a counselor tell me once that my problems stem from an unwillingness to set boundaries. She'd probably think my willingness to let Aunt Beth give me her business without a moment's notice is a prime example of that. And I suppose it's true."

"There has to be a difference between setting boundaries and just rejecting everything out of hand."

"There is. In the case of Aunt Beth's gift, she felt that I needed to make a change and I wasn't going to make it without a boot in the rear end. It happens it might have been the right thing to do. I didn't think so at first, and I'd like to think that if I truly believed coming to Foggy Point is the wrong thing to do I'd leave. But frankly, other than at the hospital, I haven't considered anything but staying here and making a new life for myself."

"I'm glad to hear you say that, 'specially given what's been happening lately. How about I heat up a couple of frozen dinners and we put on a movie and escape for a while?"

"Sounds good to me," Harriet said. She was beginning to have a real appreciation for Mavis's well-developed ability to avoid reality.

Chapter Thirty-three

HARRIET WOKE EARLY THE NEXT MORNING BUT WAITED UNTIL SHE HEARD MAVIS TURN on the shower to pull on her jeans and sweatshirt and slip out the back door into the woods. Carla was already in the potting shed when she pulled the door open.

"How's she doing?" she asked.

"I'm here, too," Misty said. "Don't act like I'm not."

"She didn't mean anything, Misty. Harriet here is a friend. She got your medicine for you."

"She doesn't care about me," Misty said. "She just wants what she wants."

"I'm sorry, Misty. I really do want to help you. I just think you can help me, too."

Carla must have arrived just a few minutes earlier; she had a fast food bag in her hand. She dug two white Styrofoam boxes from the bag and handed one to Misty.

"Here, I brought you some breakfast. You might feel better if you eat. It's time to take another pill, too." She opened her own box and started wolfing the contents.

"I don't want to talk about Miz Jalbert and her family." Misty wrapped her arms around herself and started to rock. "That family is bad, bad, bad."

Carla opened the top of Misty's box, revealing two pancakes, a pale yellow clump of scrambled eggs and two strips of bacon. A ball of whipped butter slid from the pancakes to the side of the box. She stabbed a white plastic fork into them.

"Try to eat something, okay? I gotta go to work, but I'll come back when I get off." She pulled a paper-wrapped bundle from the bag and set it on the wooden box that served as a table. "They don't make nothing but breakfast food in the morning, but I got you an egg sandwich you can have for lunch." She took the pill bottle from the windowsill where Harriet had left it and shook one out into her palm. "Here," she said and handed the pill to Misty.

She picked up the bottle of water from the floor and held it out. Misty didn't say anything, but she took the pill and swallowed it. This time she did follow up with a long drink of water.

Carla put her empty container in the fast food bag and took it with her as she went to the door. She held the door open, and Harriet realized she was waiting for her to leave, too.

"She should be better by tonight. She'll be more normal when she's been on her medicine for a while, but that don't mean she'll remember everything that happened when she was off it. I mean, she remembers, but she can't tell what was real and what wasn't."

"I have to try to talk to her. I think it's very possible she saw Avanell's murder."

"I liked Miz Jalbert. I hope they catch whoever killed her, but if it depends on Misty, don't get your hopes up too high."

Harriet followed her out of the shed. Carla disappeared down a path, and Harriet went back to the house. She came in just as Mavis emerged from the bathroom.

"My turn?" she asked.

Mavis looked at her. "It's all yours."

Harriet was thankful she didn't ask more.

After her shower, she dressed in her jeans and one of her thrift shop shirts. Mavis was in the kitchen. Harriet watched as she loaded a thermos, two bottles of water and several plastic baggies filled with carrot and celery sticks into a padded carry bag. She started toward Harriet then turned back and grabbed a box of crackers.

"We can't be too good," she said with a sheepish grin.

The drive to Tacoma seemed shorter this time, but Harriet supposed that was the result of having made it so many times it was becoming familiar. Mavis looked at her watch as they pulled into the show grounds.

"We're early," she announced. "What do you say we go find a cup of coffee or tea and some kind of pastry? That should give them time to open."

Harriet agreed, and Mavis directed her back out on the highway and off again at the next exit.

"Any exit that has more than two gas stations has to have a coffee shop," she announced.

She was right.

The show was open when they pulled into the parking lot the second time. They bought their tickets and proceeded to spend the next three hours looking at all the exhibits in great detail. It always amazed Harriet to see the infinite number of ways people could combine color and fabric and thread and stitching to create truly unique works of art.

They saved the Loose Threads display until the end and were not disappointed. There was a small sign where Avanell's quilt had hung. Viewers were directed to the display of prize winners in an alcove at the front of the building.

"This can only mean one thing," Mavis said. "Avanell must have won the overall."

"Look," Harriet said. She pointed at Robin's blue-and-yellow log cabin. It had a red rosette pinned to its corner.

"Looks like Jenny did all right, too," Mavis said. The pink rosette pinned to Jenny's quilt was a perfect complement to its berry-and-sea-foam-green color scheme.

"Let's go to the quilt store and get some lunch, then we can come back and start taking these down and bagging them for the trip home."

Mavis drove them across Tacoma, first to the quilt store then to an Italian restaurant called Tremonte's. Frank Tremonte had been a friend of her husband Thomas when they were in the Air Force together. She told Harriet she and Thomas had been among the first customers when Frank and his wife Rosalie opened the place and continued to eat there a few times a year ever after. Tremonte's specialized in the hearty dishes of southern Italy. It was located in a two-story bungalow-style house painted the same green that made up the end stripe of the Italian flag.

Harriet breathed deep as they walked into the warm room. The smell of garlic and oregano permeated the air. A narrow shelf rimmed walls with a display of colorful patterned plates she recognized as Sicilian. A slim young woman in a green apron led them to a corner booth.

"Where are your parents off to now?" Mavis asked the dark-haired man who brought a basket of crusty French bread to their table moments later. "Harriet, meet Tommy Tremonte. His parents turned the restaurant over to his capable hands when they retired. Seems like they've been traveling ever since."

Harriet made the appropriate small talk, and the two women placed their orders. Her fettuccine Gamberi featured shrimp and basil in a cream sauce. Mavis chose the hearty Tuscan chicken and vegetables, and Harriet could quickly see this was one of those places where everything on the menu was worthy of selection.

"I guess this will be dinner, huh?" She asked.

"This might be all we need until next week," Mavis said and groaned. "I guess we better go back and get our work done. Moving around a little will do us some good."

Harriet was folding Avanell's quilt when Jeri approached her. The long-limbed blond woman was dressed in navy-blue wool flannel pants and a white oxford-cloth shirt. Her sleeves were rolled up to the elbows. She held out a manila mailing envelope.

"Could you take this to your group?" she asked. "The individual prize premiums are in sealed envelopes inside. Since all the winners were within your group entry, you might as well save us the postage."

Harriet reached for the envelope. The woman pulled it back a little.

"You'll need to sign the receipt indicating you're taking responsibility for the funds." She held a slip of paper and a pen in her other hand. "We weren't really sure where to send Avanell Jalbert's prize money." She lowered her voice. "I understand her daughter put her house on the market right after the funeral."

"Things have changed," Harriet said. "But I'll take it anyway."

She wasn't sure if Michelle had actually left Foggy Point or not, but if she'd been Aiden, she'd have changed the locks the minute his sister walked out the door. She could imagine Michelle waiting until he left in the morning then going in and taking the prize money and anything else she thought she could get away with. With him having been out of the country for three years, anything Avanell had acquired while he was gone could be fair game.

She finished folding Avanell's quilt. She looked in the tote bag she'd used to carry the quilt sacks in, but it was empty. She knew the quilt had arrived in a pillow slip, but it was nowhere to be found.

She carefully slid the quilt into the tote bag. She'd have to look in her car when they got back to Foggy Point.

Thinking about her Honda made Harriet want to cry. It wasn't just one more freedom she'd lost in the last week. Her Honda was the first major purchase she'd made after Steve died. It was the first step toward her new independent life, and now it was sitting unused in her driveway while she hid away at Mavis's house.

That was going to change, she decided. When Monday came, she was going back home. She'd call an alarm company, change the locks and turn Aunt

Beth's house into Fort Knox if she needed to, but she was going home.

She carried the bags of quilts to the front of the display room. Mavis had a stack of others on a pushcart.

"One of the janitors loaned me this cart to help us get out to the car." She stopped. "What's got into you? You look like you just won the lottery or something."

Harriet knew she was smiling. "I'm going home," she said.

Mavis looked at her over the top of her glasses. "What do you mean, home?" she asked.

"I'm going back to Aunt Beth's on Monday. I'll do whatever I need to do to be sure I'm safe, but I'm going home."

"All right, then," Mavis said. "You tell me what I can do to help and I'll do it."

They spent much of the ride home discussing the various safety measures that could be taken to prevent another break-in.

"We should talk to Darcy," Mavis said. "Unfortunately, her job has schooled her well in what doesn't work, safety-wise."

"Thank you for not trying to talk me out of this," Harriet said and felt tears forming in her eyes. "I'm not sure Aunt Beth would be so supportive if she were here."

"Even your aunt Beth can't believe you would be well served by hiding out for who knows how long, waiting to start living again."

"Well, I appreciate your support."

"By the way," Mavis said. "Did you ever find that girl Misty?"

"I did, but she hasn't been much help so far."

"How's that? Won't she talk to you?"

"I think she will when her medicine takes effect. It turns out she's bipolar. As long as she takes her medicine she's fine, but when she was let go from the Vitamin Factory, she left her pills at her work station. She went back on Wednesday to try to sneak in and get them. At least, I think that's what happened. I think she may have seen what happened to Avanell, but her friend Carla says she goes downhill pretty fast without her pills. Without a job, she doesn't have insurance, and with no insurance, she can't get medicine. Carla is helping her get set up with the free clinic, but she has to become stable enough to go in for evaluation. In the meantime, she's too out of it to say what, if anything, she saw. She seems really scared, too, but it's hard to tell if that's real or her condition."

"If she did see who killed Avanell, we should tell the police. She could be in danger."

"She's in no shape to talk to anyone about it. I don't even know if she saw anything, and if she did, I don't know if the killer knows they've been seen. All I know is when I try to ask her about Avanell, she gets real agitated."

"I don't guess she's said anything about Avanell's or Lauren's quilts."

"She's way too out of it for that. I did see her ripping up the baby quilt she was making, but that might not mean anything."

Chapter Thirty-four

IT WAS FULLY DARK WHEN MAVIS GUIDED THE TOWN CAR DOWN THE WOODED LANE TO the cottage. She'd let Harriet drive to Tacoma but had insisted on taking the wheel for the rest of the trip.

Harriet yawned.

"We need to get you inside and into your jammies," Mavis said.

"I don't know why riding in a car makes me so tired."

"I think your tiredness has more to do with what's happened to you in the last few days. You need more than a few good days of doing nothing to recover your strength."

"I don't think I'm going to be able to rest until I figure out who attacked me and why."

"I hope you do find out, but the way things are going, that doesn't seem likely. I don't mean to be negative, but I watch those crime shows, and they say if they don't have a strong lead in the first forty-eight hours, they aren't likely to solve the case. And face it—robbery isn't a high priority, even in Foggy Point, and especially when nothing was really taken."

"Oh, God, you mean this will never really be over? I'll just go back to Aunt Beth's, triple-lock my doors and set my new alarm and jump out of my skin every time the tree branch scrapes the window?"

"I'm afraid that's more likely than not."

Harriet got out of the car and went into the house. "I need to drown my sorrows in a cup of Earl Grey," she said, "Care to join me?"

Mavis nodded and walked over to the phone. The red message light was blinking, indicating there were three messages. The first was her middle son, asking if she could babysit the following morning. He said he'd just been asked to sing a solo at the eight o'clock church service. The next message was Harold saying he would come by at ten to help Harriet distribute the quilts. He said she should only call if that wasn't okay.

"That will be perfect," she said. "You can go babysit and I'll be with Harold, so you won't have to worry."

"You mean except for the two-hour difference from when I leave until Harold arrives."

"I really don't think I'm in danger here. When I was attacked it was because I was in the way. Someone wanted to destroy Lauren's quilt. The first time, I was admittedly in the wrong part of town. Besides, I promise I will lock the door."

"There is some truth to what you say. There hasn't been any indication anyone has come looking for you here."

"No strangers, anyway," Harriet said. She turned to the stove and put the kettle on the burner.

Mavis pushed the button to listen to the final message. Aiden was calling to ask if he could stop by. Michelle had left town, and he was feeling lonely. Mavis called him back and invited him to join them for tea.

Harriet poured their tea, and put their mugs and the sugar bowl on the table.

"I think I'll stay in my room and read when Aiden gets here," she said and sat down. "It sounded like he really was looking for a maternal shoulder to cry on."

"*I* think he wants to see you and I'm a convenient excuse." Mavis joined her at the table.

"Yesterday you said Aiden wasn't interested in me and I was the one imagining things."

"You misunderstand. I said he wasn't looking for a serious relationship right now. That doesn't mean he isn't interested."

"Well, I'm not interested in just being 'friends with benefits.' This town is too small."

"Is there no middle ground? Can't you try dating and see where it leads? And please, don't try to tell me Harold is a serious contender for your affection."

A knock on the door prevented Harriet from having to answer. Mavis got up and let Aiden in. His eyes were back to their icy blue-white color. They were also swollen and rimmed in red, as if he'd been crying. Mavis poured hot water over a peppermint teabag in a mug and handed it to him. He pulled out the chair next to Harriet's and sat down.

"My sister and I had it out today," he said and looked down at his tea. "She'd been hiding at Uncle Bertie's, but she came back. I found her rifling through Mom's jewelry box."

"Oh, honey, I'm sorry," Mavis said and put her hand over his.

"It got worse." His eyes filled with tears, and he blinked rapidly and took a deep breath. "She says if I don't pay her debts off, and help Uncle Bertie, she'll cut me off. She'll never speak to me and she won't let me see my nieces. And she says Uncle Bertie feels the same way."

"She's just upset," Mavis protested. "She can't mean it."

"Oh, I think she means every word of it. You didn't see her."

"I'm sure she'll think differently when she gets past her grief about your mother."

Harriet was with Aiden. She hadn't known Michelle as long as Mavis had, but what little contact she'd had made her believe Michelle was a self-centered, spoiled brat. She hadn't once seen the woman express any emotion about Avanell. It was all about the money.

"Maybe I should give her the money," Aiden said. "I don't need it. I could sell the house. That should pay off her bills."

"Would that really solve anything?" Harriet asked. "I mean, it's none of my business, but it seems like your mom went to pretty great lengths to *not* rescue your sister."

"That was my other thought. Mom did make pretty elaborate arrangements to have an allowance established for Michelle. Who am I to second-guess her?" He covered his face with his hands. "It's all such a mess. I had a lot of time in Africa to think about my family. I had such big plans for my return. I thought I had everything all worked out. None of this is how I planned it."

Mavis reached over and rubbed his back. "You don't have to decide this tonight, honey. Why don't you give it some time? When Michelle knows she isn't going to get any money from you, she'll have to do something else. Once she's figured her life out, then you can try again. She'll see things differently then."

"I'm not sure she'll ever figure things out," he said. "She's a lawyer, for God's sake. She and her husband both make good salaries, but somehow it's not enough. Nothing is ever enough for Michelle."

"I've got an idea," Mavis said. She pulled a worn metal box from a kitchen drawer and set it on the table. "Maybe you..." She looked at Aiden. "...can forget about Michelle, and you..." She looked at Harriet. "You can forget about whoever it is who trashed your studio and drugged you."

"I don't know," Aiden said. "That's a tall order." He started to smile. He clearly recognized the metal box.

Mavis opened the lid of the box, revealing a very old-looking set of dominos. "Nothing relaxes the mind like a rousing game of dominos."

Harriet looked skeptical, but two hours later, she had to admit she hadn't thought about her problems since the game began. Mavis was both skilled and cutthroat. It took every bit of her concentration to avoid being totally skunked. She looked over at Aiden. He seemed to have been distracted, too.

Mavis stood up. "I don't know about you kids, but I need my beauty rest." She arranged the dominos in the tin box and put the lid back on. "I trust you won't stay up too late," she said and looked over her reading glasses at Aiden.

He stood up. "Yeah, I need to be going, too." He picked up their mugs and carried them to the sink, and generally loitered in the kitchen until Mavis was in her room with the door shut.

Harriet followed him to the door. "Can I see you tomorrow?" he asked her.

"I have to return the quilts from the show tomorrow morning. Harold is going to drive me."

Before Aiden had come over, she had decided she wasn't going to see either him or Harold after tomorrow morning until she was moved back home and her life had returned to some semblance of normalcy. Now, in response to her news, Aiden looked like he'd lost his last friend—which in a way he had, at least, as far as his family was concerned.

"Why don't you come over in the afternoon?" she relented. "Call first to make sure I'm back."

He put his hands on either side of her face. "Thank you," he said, and brushed his lips over hers. She felt a tingle all the way to her toes. He turned and went out the door.

Chapter Thirty-five

MAVIS WAS UP EARLY THE NEXT MORNING.

"You stay inside until Harold comes to the door. And you look through the peephole before you open the door," she instructed. "I mean it. I don't want any repeat performances."

"Yes, ma'am," Harriet said. She wished Mavis would leave. She loved the older woman, but she was so looking forward to having two whole hours alone, with no one but Fred for company.

"You'll be returning quilts to people who aren't in Loose Threads," Mavis continued. "Don't go into those houses without Harold. You understand? No risk-taking of any sort. I'll be home by lunchtime. Don't let Harold leave until I'm here."

"Don't worry," Harriet said with a smile. "I don't want to spend any more time in the hospital. But I think we both agree that I'm not really the target. I just happened to be in the wrong place at the wrong time. No one is going to kidnap me as I deliver textiles, but I will stick like glue to Harold's side."

"You keep your cell phone with you and turned on, Miss Smarty."

"Unfortunately, I don't know where my cell phone is at the moment. I'm hoping it's in the studio somewhere."

"Well, I suppose if you stick with Harold, you shouldn't need it."

"I'll be fine. If you don't leave, your son is going to miss his performance, though."

"Okay, you just be careful, and I'll see you in a couple of hours."

"Bye, Mavis. Don't worry," Harriet said as she followed her to the door and locked it behind her. "Fred," she called. "Here, kitty."

Fred ran out from her bedroom.

"Fred." She picked him up. "We have the whole place to ourselves. What should we do?"

She knew what she wanted to do—she wanted to go see Misty. Unfortunately, she didn't know where Mavis kept her spare key and decided it probably wasn't a good idea to leave the house open and unattended. She didn't really think anything would happen, but then again, everything that had happened since she'd come to Foggy Point was pretty unbelievable.

"I think I'm going to take a bath in that big tub," she announced to Fred, as if he cared.

She went into the bathroom and searched in the cabinet for bubble bath of some sort.

"Look here, Fred. Mavis has quite a collection of bath potions." Three cut-glass jars held bath crystals in tints of pink, blue and lavender; two cork-stoppered bottles held pale liquids. She knew Mavis wouldn't mind if she helped herself.

She picked a bottle labeled *Muguet de Bois.*

"Perfect," she said.

She went into the bedroom and looked at the paperbacks. Mavis had every book Carolyn Hart had ever written, or so it seemed. She picked one from the bookstore series and took it to the bathroom with a clean towel and her fresh change of clothes.

She added hot water to her bath twice, but after an hour her fingers were so wrinkled it was getting hard to turn the pages. Fred was meowing by the front door when she finally came out of the bathroom.

"What is it?" she asked. She peered out the peephole, but no one was standing on the porch. She went to the window, but she didn't see anything. She turned back to the cat.

"No one's out there," she told him. She held him up to the window so he could see for himself. She walked into the kitchen and put a piece of bread in the toaster. While it was toasting, she decided to organize the quilts piled in the corner of her bedroom.

She brought them out to the living room, got the stack of registration receipts and did her best to organize them into a logical delivery order.

Her toast was cold and burned when she returned to the kitchen, so she threw it out and put a fresh slice in the toaster and pushed the lever down again. Fred wove through her legs as she paced the kitchen.

She jumped when the toaster popped.

"Get a grip," she said out loud. "It's not like you've never been alone before."

She buttered her toast and ate it with a glass of orange juice then carefully washed her hands before she returned to her organization project.

She and Mavis must have been getting tired at the end, she decided. They had done a careful job of folding on some of the quilts, but a few were sticking out of the ends of their bags. She stacked the bags according to neighborhood and looked at her watch. She still had an hour before Harold was due.

She looked at the door again. She really wanted to go check on Misty.

"What are we going to do, Fred?" she asked the cat. "Mavis will kill me if I go outside alone, but we have a lot of time."

Fred meowed.

"Okay, maybe we'll have a closer look at the winning quilts."

She spread Jenny's quilt over the recliner. Every corner was perfect. She ran her fingers over the surface. All the join areas were completely flat. She wondered if she would ever reach that level of skill.

"Oh, Fred," she said. "There's so much to aspire to."

She put the quilt back in its tote bag and pulled out Avanell's. As her hand closed over the center fold her fingers felt something hard; something that definitely didn't belong.

She laid the quilt over the recliner then spread her fingers and systematically ran her hand over the surface.

Like Jenny, Avanell made flat, smooth seams and joins. Harriet turned her attention to the trapunto areas, which were filled with more cotton batting than the rest of the quilt. She hoped she hadn't been imagining things. She placed her left hand underneath and right hand on top and squeezed each section carefully.

When she reached the third square she felt the lumps. She manipulated the area again. It felt like small pebbles were inside the batting. Was it possible gravel had gotten into the quilt when Aiden used it to carry the injured dog? She had repaired a rip, but she could have sworn it was in the pieced, hand-dyed area.

She went into the bedroom, found Mavis's sewing kit and located the seam ripper and a needle and thread. She picked up a tissue in the bathroom and came back to the quilt. She sat in the chair and pulled the lumpy section into her lap.

She wanted to leave the least evidence of her work, so she turned the quilt over and located the back seam nearest the area in question. Carefully, one by one, she picked out a row of stitches. When she had an opening about four inches long, she reached inside with her fingers then, with the other hand on the outside, worked the objects over to where she could reach them and pulled out the first three pieces.

"Oh, my God!"

In the palm of her hand were three perfect diamonds. She laid them on the tissue and dug into the slit again and again. By the time she could feel no more lumps, she was looking at twelve diamonds. The smallest had to be nearly a carat in weight. The largest might be twice that.

Harriet didn't know whose diamonds she was looking at, but it suddenly became clear why someone wanted a quilt so badly.

Fred meowed, and she jumped at a knock on the cottage door.

"Who's there," she called.

She looked through the peephole as Bertrand called out, "It's Bertie, Avanell's brother. I've come to pick up her quilt."

She opened the door.

"Harold told me he was going to help you deliver the exhibits from the show," Bertrand continued, "and I thought since I was going right by here I would come by and pick ours up. You know, save you a trip."

"It's really no problem for me to deliver it," she said, and realized how stupid she sounded as soon as the words were out of her mouth. "Let me lock my cat in the bedroom," she said and shut the door. She hurried across the room and scooped the diamonds into her pocket.

"I'll take those if you don't mind," Bertie said. He'd opened the door and followed her in.

"What are you talking about?"

"Don't play dumb with me—it's not becoming. We both know if you were, in fact, dumb, you would have left well enough alone and I would have picked up the quilt and no one would have been the wiser."

Harriet was going to protest again but could see it was no use. She also saw for the first time the shiny gun in Bertrand's hand.

"Give me the diamonds."

"I don't know what you're talking about."

"Don't play coy with me, Miss Truman." He motioned with the gun. "Turn out your pockets."

Harriet stalled, feigning trouble getting her hand into her jeans pocket. She was so focused on the gun she didn't see Misty come in through the open door.

"It was him," she cried. "He's the one that killed her."

Bertrand turned his attention briefly away from Harriet to the girl. In that split second, Harriet grabbed Avanell's quilt and threw it over his head.

The gun went off.

"Run," she yelled as she dashed to the door and pushed Misty through it. She ran around the side of the house, passing her, then pulled her through the fence and down the trail. She heard the front door bang but didn't look back to see how close Bertrand was.

Misty started for the potting shed, but Harriet signaled her past and through the woods beyond the yard to the trail she and Aiden had taken to his mother's house. She felt a burning pain in her shoulder before she heard the second gunshot. She knew she couldn't think about it. She kept running, Misty close on her heels.

She imagined she heard Bertrand wheezing then realized it was Misty. She couldn't take much more. Harriet tried to remember how the trail went.

The gun sounded again, but not as loud this time. She left the trail and went into the woods, again pulling Misty after her. The underbrush pulled at their clothes and blackberry bushes scratched their hands and faces, but she kept them moving. She couldn't hear Bertrand anymore.

Ahead, she saw a tunnel some animal had made into a large brushy mound. She dropped to her knees and pushed into the bush. Misty followed her, gasping for breath. She had to be careful; the forest didn't go on forever. It was dense, but she wasn't sure how wide the greenspace was, and whether Bertrand would be able to take the road and get ahead of them.

The tunnel widened into a low den-like area. They squatted in the narrow space. Harriet listened but didn't hear anything. Her shoulder hurt.

"He killed her," Misty repeated. "I saw him kill her. She was yelling at him. He said give me the bottle." Tears ran down her cheeks and dripped off her chin. "She pulled a bottle out of her pocket, and he killed her."

"I'm sorry you had to see that, but right now we need to worry about ourselves. He's out there somewhere with a gun."

"The police will come," Misty said. She was calmer than Harriet had ever seen her, but she wasn't sure if this was the real Misty, or if the drugs were giving her serenity she shouldn't feel in this situation.

"We have to be as quiet as we can. Harold should be arriving to pick me up soon. Hopefully, he'll see something's wrong and either come looking or call the police."

"Harold and Bertrand are friends," Misty said. "They eat lunch together every day."

"That doesn't mean Harold won't get us some help." Harriet wasn't sure, but she didn't want to upset Misty any more than she already was.

She couldn't tell how much time had passed before Misty pulled a watch with a broken strap from her pocket.

"What time is it?"

"Ten-fifteen," Misty said. "Carla should be to town by now."

"What are you talking about?" She prayed there was a rational answer.

"Carla and I were coming to talk to you. We saw Mister Bertrand go into the cottage, and I told Carla she should go call the police. I had already told her he killed Miz Jalbert. She doesn't have a car, so she had to walk to town."

Harriet thought she heard a siren in the distance but couldn't tell if it was coming their way or not.

"Let's go back to the potting shed. You can stay there, and I'll get closer to the cottage and see if I can tell what's going on.

She crept back out of the tunnel of brush and retraced her steps to the path.

"If we meet Bertrand before we get to the house, I'll keep him busy, and you run," she told Misty when they were both on the trail again.

Misty nodded and followed her closely as she crept back toward the house. They reached the potting shed, and Harriet had to argue to get Misty to stay there.

"Think of your baby," she said, and Misty finally agreed.

Harriet paused to survey the cottage before she went through the hole in the fence. Nothing seemed out of order. She crept around the side of the house, staying close to the camellia bushes that crowded the windows.

When she could finally see the driveway, a dark Mercedes was parked there. She rounded the corner and could see the front door was shut. She was considering her next move when a voice spoke from behind her.

"Looking for someone?" Bertrand asked. He pointed the gun at her again. "Now, I believe you have something of mine. And don't bother waiting for Harold. I sent him on his way. He believes I came by as we had prearranged so I could pick up the quilt, and that I arrived and found you already gone."

Harriet knew that going in the house would be a death sentence.

"I think we both know you're going to kill me no matter what, so can I at least know why you killed Avanell?"

"If you're thinking you can keep me talking long enough for someone to come rescue you, you can think again. We are going inside—now."

She was trying to decide which direction would give her the greatest chance if she made a break for it when Aiden came out of the woods.

"What's going on here? I was walking Randy in the woods, and I heard gunshots." He kept walking toward Bertrand.

"Stop. Don't come any closer. I've got a gun," Bertrand said, as if Aiden couldn't see the weapon in his hands.

"What? Are you going to shoot me? You can't kill us both. If you shoot me, she'll run, and if you shoot her, I'll kill you."

Bertrand spluttered but couldn't come up with a response. His gun hand started to shake.

"It's over, Uncle Bertie. Whatever it is that's going on here. You can't kill everybody."

Aiden moved surely toward his uncle and grabbed the gun. The two men struggled for a moment, but three years of hard living in Africa had toughened Aiden in ways his uncle couldn't compete with. He pulled the gun away and quickly dumped the bullets out onto the ground.

Bertie started to cry. "You don't understand. They will kill me. They said if I didn't get the diamonds back they would kill me. I'm a dead man."

"Don't worry, Uncle Bertie. You're going to be in protective custody," Aiden said.

"If you don't get the death penalty," Harriet added. "I'm going to call the police."

AFTER THE POLICE ARRIVED AND COLLECTED BERTRAND, HARRIET TOOK AN AMBULANCE ride to the Jefferson County Hospital for the third time that week. This time Misty was her roommate for the drive. It turned out the bullet had streaked across the flat of her shoulder blade without penetrating anything important. She had a painful groove, but was eventually able to leave after promising to return to the clinic the next day to have her bandage changed.

The doctors decided that, all things considered, Misty needed to stay until she was properly hydrated, fed and stabilized on her medication. After a week and a half on the lam, she was ready to sleep on clean sheets and eat three squares a day, even if it was in a hospital.

Mavis had arrived while the doctor was dressing Harriet's wound and refused to stay in the waiting room.

"Oh, honey, does it hurt?" she asked. "Are you okay? I mean, obviously, you're not okay, but can I do anything?"

"You can get me out of here before they decide to try and keep me."

"This is my fault. I never should have left you alone."

"As soon as you sign the paperwork, and I write your prescriptions, you can get out of here," the doctor said as he came back into the emergency cubicle. He was holding an x-ray up to the ceiling light. "Looks like no bones were broken. We didn't think there were, but we have to check. Don't forget to come in to the clinic tomorrow so they can clean your wound. One of your prescriptions is for a fairly strong antibiotic, but you still need to keep it clean."

"I will do whatever you say as long as I can go home."

Mavis tried to talk Harriet into staying at the cottage one more night.

"I really appreciate everything you've done for me, but I need to be in my own bed in my own bedroom."

In the end, the only way Mavis would agree is if Harriet let her come along.

"I know Bertie is in custody and the danger is over, but I don't think you should be alone after all you've been through. Beth would kill me if I just sent you home on your own."

"Could we pick up something to eat on the way?" Harriet asked. "I'm starving."

Mavis's face turned pink. "I think we need to go to Beth's first and see what we have there."

"I can tell you what's there. A bunch of rotting vegetables and some canned goods."

A nurse wheeled Harriet to the door. Mavis had parked in the emergency lot, and after a brief negotiation, the nurse agreed to push her all the way to the car.

"It makes no sense for me to have to go around the block while you sit outside in the cold, just so I can pull the car up to that other doorway."

"So," Harriet said after she was settled in the front seat. "Exactly why is it that we don't need to pick up some food?"

"Well, it's entirely possible that the Loose Threads have taken care of that."

"How could they possibly know I'd be coming home today?" Her shoulder twinged as she turned toward Mavis.

"I called Jenny to ask her to call people and tell them their quilt delivery would be delayed. She offered to go to my house and pick them up and make the deliveries herself. Well, as you can imagine, I had to tell her something. I couldn't let her go to my house and find the police."

"Keep talking."

"Jenny figured you could use some comfort food. She said she could make some macaroni and cheese. She offered to call Robin and see if she had a pie she could bring by. Robin is our group pie maker," Mavis said this last as an aside, as if it explained why Robin would have a pie baked and waiting to be delivered on a moment's notice. "I'm sure Robin called DeAnn, because they do everything together." She shrugged her shoulders. "Things just sort of took off from there."

Harriet unlocked the studio door and was immediately greeted by Fred.

"How did you get here?" she asked.

Aiden came in from the kitchen.

"I brought him here after I finished giving the police my statement," he said. "I hope it's okay—I brought Randy, too."

"Don't make her stand out here," Mavis told him. "Let the girl sit down."

She ushered Harriet into the kitchen. Jenny, Robin and DeAnn sat around the kitchen table. Sarah stood by the sink, taking the lid off a casserole dish. Mavis pulled out a chair and guided Harriet into it. Robin got up, filled a bowl with macaroni and cheese and sat it in front of her.

"Eat," she said. "Then we want to hear everything."

"Don't start yet," Marjory said as she came through the door from the studio. "Have all of you met Carla?" she asked and indicated the young woman who had followed her into the room. "She works for me at the shop."

Carla's face turned a shade of red that bordered on purple.

"I'm not sure I know any more than most of you have already heard," Harriet protested.

"Well, I don't know anything, so why don't you start at the beginning?" Marjory said.

"You all know about the break-in here," she started.

"Did she mention the part where she clubbed me in the head?" Aiden asked.

Six pairs of eyes glared at him.

"Sorry," he said.

"It turns out that someone was looking for Avanell's quilt. And by the way, the attack on Lauren's was a case of mistaken identity. Avanell had sewn her binding on in her office. She had bound and backed her quilt in the same red fabric Lauren used.

"What the thief didn't know is that Avanell's quilt had a slight misadventure when Aiden was delivering it to me. He had to take it to the dry cleaners. When the break-in happened, it was gone. It was at the show when the thief tried again, but the organizers had taken it off display because of Avanell's death. Lauren's quilt was in the spot where Avanell's had been. The show organizers hadn't switched the name cards yet, and the thief thought he knew what the quilt looked like.

"His third attempt was when I came home to repair Lauren's quilt. Again the thief had the two confused. Since I now know he was looking for diamonds Avanell had hidden in one of the sections of her quilt, the shredding of Lauren's makes more sense." She stopped to take a bite of macaroni.

"Avanell hid diamonds in her quilt?" Jenny asked.

"Where did Avanell get diamonds?" DeAnn wondered.

"Why on earth would she think a quilt was a good place to hide diamonds?"

"Give the girl a chance to speak," Mavis scolded.

"I only discovered the diamonds this morning. I was looking at the show quilts, and when I picked hers up I felt a bumpy spot. I thought it was gravel from the misadventure it had been through. I opened the seam and found a small handful of diamonds.

"I have no idea why Avanell hid the diamonds there, but Bertrand showed up and demanded I hand them over."

"I think I can help out with that," Aiden put in. "Once the police took my uncle into custody, he started talking. They suggested he call a lawyer, but he insisted on telling them everything.

"Apparently, the reason money has been so tight at the Vitamin Factory these last couple of years is that Uncle Bertie had developed a bit of a gambling problem. He borrowed from some shady characters who saw an opportunity to use the Vitamin Factory to launder money. When they found out the factory imported a lot of herbs and supplements from China and Vietnam, they saw an opportunity to smuggle gems into the country as well.

"Unfortunately, Mom intercepted one of the bottles of gems. She must have hidden them to give herself time to deal with Uncle Bertie.

"According to him, she broke a mirror and put glass in the bottle. He confronted her and demanded the gems. She handed him the bottle but told him she would not keep quiet.

"Mom never could see Uncle Bertie's flaws. I guess she didn't believe he would resort to violence."

Carla cleared her throat. "My friend Misty got fired that day. She left her medicine in her toolbox and went back to get it that night. She was going to see if she could sneak in and get it without anyone seeing her.

"She knew the back warehouse door had a broken lock. She jiggled the door open, but discovered Miz Jalbert was back there packing vitamins. She hid between the stacks of boxes. Mister Bertrand showed up and he and Miz

Jalbert had a big fight. Misty said he demanded the diamonds, and Miz Jalbert handed over a vitamin bottle. Mister Betrand pulled a gun out of his pocket and shot her in the head. Misty said Miz Jalbert fell to the floor, and he stood over her and told her it was her fault." Carla looked down.

"I can't believe there have been organized criminals operating out of Foggy Point," Robin said. "Have they caught the other people involved?"

"Uncle Bertie is a mess, but hopefully when he gets a lawyer and understands how much trouble he's in, he'll give up some names. He was still blubbering about how 'they' were going to kill him. He doesn't yet understand that he could get the death penalty. The police detective said it would be up to the DA to decide whether Mom's murder qualified as happening during the commission of another crime, in which case it would be death-eligible."

"This certainly hasn't been the welcome back to our community we'd intended to give you," Marjory told Harriet.

"This has taught me something important," Harriet said. "I had pretty mixed feelings about staying here when I first read Aunt Beth's letter. Having someone try to take the choice away from me has brought my feelings into focus. I want to stay here and make Aunt Beth's business my own."

She paused and took a sip of the tea Mavis had set on the table in front of her.

"I've learned something else out of all this." She paused a moment. "I lived in my last apartment in Oakland for five years. I had a nodding acquaintance with two neighbors, but I realized while I was at Mavis's that no one I knew in Oakland would have taken me in on a moment's notice like she did, or welcome me into an established group like the Loose Threads did. Look at this," she said, and spread her good arm wide to indicate the feast in front of her. "I don't even know anyone in Oakland who can boil water. You guys made macaroni and cheese and pie from scratch. I know you did it because of Aunt Beth, because I'm her niece, but that's part of it, too. I have a root here, and I need to quit running away from it. I just hope I can repay the love and support you've already given me so freely."

"Oh, honey," Mavis said, "you already have."

The food hadn't even been dented by the time the Loose Threads left. Mavis cleaned the kitchen while Aiden carried her bag upstairs to Aunt Beth's room.

Mavis hung her damp dishtowel on the oven door handle.

"If you're doing okay, honey, I think I'll go upstairs and put my feet up."

She crossed the kitchen to the staircase and waited as Aiden came down. She patted him on the back as he passed her then ascended the stairs.

Aiden joined Harriet at the table.

"So, you're going to stick around, huh?" A grin creased his tanned face. "Does this mean we can go on a real date?"

END

ABOUT THE AUTHOR

Attempted murder, theft, drug rings, battered women, death threats, and more sordid affairs than she could count were the more exciting experiences from ARLENE SACHITANO'S nearly thirty years in the high tech industry.

Prior to writing her first novel, *Chip and Die*, Zumaya Publications Oct 2003, Arlene wrote the story half of the popular Block of the Month quilting patterns "Seams Like Murder" and "Seams Like Halloween" for Storyquilts.com, Inc. She also has written a scintillating proprietary tome on the subject of the electronics assembly.

ABOUT THE ARTIST

APRIL MARTINEZ was born in the Philippines and raised in San Diego, California, daughter to a US Navy chef and a US postal worker, sibling to one younger sister. From as far back as she can remember, she has always doodled and loved art, but her parents never encouraged her to consider it as a career path, suggesting instead that she work for the county. So, she attended the University of California in San Diego, earned a cum laude bachelor's degree in literature/writing and entered the workplace as a regular office worker.

For years, she went from job to job, dissatisfied that she couldn't make use of her creative tendencies, until she started working as an imaging specialist for a big book and magazine publishing house in Irvine and began learning the trade of graphic design. From that point on, she worked as a graphic designer and webmaster at subsequent day jobs while doing freelance art and illustration at night.

In 2003, April discovered the e-publishing industry. She responded to an ad looking for e-book cover artists and was soon in the business of cover art and art direction. Since then, she has created hundreds of book covers, both electronic and print, for several publishing houses, earning awards and recognition in the process. Two years into it, she was able to give up the day job and work from home. April Martinez now lives with her cat in Orange County, California, as a full-time freelance artist/illustrator and graphic designer.

CPSIA information can be obtained at www.ICGtesting.com
Printed in the USA
LVOW06s1200170713

343296LV00002B/183/A